# RIGHT TEXT WRONG NUMBER

### OFFSIDES BOOK ONE

## AUTHOR OF THE RIVAL LOVE SERIES
## NATALIE DECKER

This book is a work of fiction. Names, characters, places, and incidents are either products of the author's imagination or are used fictitiously. Any resemblance to actual persons, living or dead, business establishments, events, or locales is entirely coincidental. The author makes no claims to, but instead acknowledges the trademarked status and trademark owners of the word marks mentioned in this work of fiction.

Copyright © 2017 by Natalie Decker

RIGHT TEXT, WRONG NUMBER by Natalie Decker
All rights reserved. Published in the United States of America by Swoon Romance. Swoon Romance and its related logo are registered trademarks of Georgia McBride Media Group, LLC. No part of this book may be used or reproduced in any manner whatsoever without written permission of the publisher, except in the case of brief quotations embodied in critical articles and reviews.

Epub ISBN: 978-1-946700-18-6
Mobipocket ISBN: 978-1-946700-19-3
Paperback ISBN: 978-1-946700-76-6

Published by Swoon Romance, Raleigh, NC 27609
Cover design by Danielle Doolittle

*Sometimes a wrong number is just what you may need to brighten your day. Ethan and Leeah you're the best parts of me.*

# Right Text Wrong Number

## Offsides Book One

# Chapter One

*Layla*

Beep! Beeeeeeeeep! "Stop screwing with your phone and pay attention to the road!" I blow my horn some more. The light is green, has been for a good forty seconds. I glance over at my best friend for some support for my general crabbiness this morning. She's not giving it though, she's too busy tapping away on her own cellphone.

"You believe this guy? Same to you, Buddy!" I yell as I catch his middle finger pop up in front of his rearview mirror.

Rachel doesn't say anything. She's still engrossed in messages from whomever is texting her. Possibly the latest gossip, or party happening. Who knows?

I'm usually a perky, non-violent person. All of this has seemed to change recently. I saw an episode on the news about how much society is turning into walking mutants because they're so absorbed in their phones. You won't catch me searching for the perfect snap shot of yourself, only to be mauled by a huge mountain lion ready to pounce from behind. I don't want to be mauled by some crazy animal in a park. I mean how awful would that be, death-by-selfie. So, I gave up on taking poses in the cute outfits I wear and selfies altogether.

And don't get me started on texting. I loathe it. I know what you're thinking. What kind of weirdo hates texting? The kind who's dyslexic. And when everything looks like absolute gibberish anyway, and now I have to read words on a small screen just to find out who made out with whom; no thanks. If it weren't for my text-to-voice app, I'd be screwed. People would think I'm a complete airhead because I couldn't decipher a silly text.

"Sorry; what were you having a beyotch fit about?" Rachel asks drawing my eyes from the road and landing on her. "Austin was telling me what happened to Jared during football practice yesterday. Plus, I guess there is this monster party after the game Friday. You in or out?" She looks up from her phone.

"In," I answer reverting my attention to the line of cars turning into the school's parking lot. I know my boyfriend Adam will want to go hang out with his team so it's a given that I'll be tagging along. Although I really would rather it just be him and me this weekend. Lately we're either in group functions, at parties, on double dates at the movies, or hanging out with his friends. I just want some me-time with him. No disgusting belching contests happening in the background or listening to other couples make out next to me. Gross.

"Austin wants to know if your sister's coming?"

This question shakes me from my miserable funk, and I

snort laugh. My twin sister at a party? HA-HA-HA. OMG; I think I peed my pants a little. "That's not happening. Unless the words 'book,' 'ComicCon,' or 'mud' were in front of the word 'party.' Then she'd probably go. But yeah; no. Why's does he want to know? Is he crushing on my sister?" That could be news I could get down with.

"He said one of the guys was asking."

Raising a brow, I inquire, "Which one?" It's probably Chase, but that would be weird considering he's her best friend and knows her daily schedule.

She's tapping away again as I pull up to the school parking lot. "He won't say."

"Why not?"

"Do you really care or are you just morbidly interested that someone might actually like your super wacked out sister?"

"She's not ... wacked out."

Rachel is my best friend, but she's not a fan of my sister, Juliet. In fact, she pretty much despises her. My twin isn't mean or anything, she's just ... super smart. And sometimes tends to let her geekiness fly. She can recite the first five chapters of each Harry Potter book. She knows all the lines word-for-word in every Star Wars movie. Every stinkin' one.

Speaking of my awesome twin, she pulls up next to me and slams her Jeep door. "You did it again! You know you only have one simple chore. One. And every time I get stuck with it."

I roll my eyes at her. "Calm down, sis. I'll get it next time."

She smiles wickedly at me. It's like looking in a mirror

since our physical features are almost exactly the same. The only one small difference isn't something most people notice just from looking at our faces: she has a small birthmark on her neck just below her ear, shaped like a heart, whereas I do not. Everything else is definitely the same, from the dark, rich brown hair to the mossy-green eyes, right down to the height of a whopping 5'6". I've thought about cutting my waist-length hair to my shoulders just so people can tell us apart.

"You say that every time! I'm done helping you out Layla. Maybe next time instead of rushing off to get Starbucks, see Adam, or pick up your BFF you'll do your chores and stop putting them on me. I have a life too you know."

Rachel cuts in. "You have a life, since when?"

"Butt out Rach." I shift my attention back to my sister who is currently glaring at my bestie. "Juliet, I'm sorry," I say.

Her eyes cut to me. She shakes her head and walks away. I call out, "Juliet." She doesn't look back. Instead, she flips me off—and okay this time —I rightly deserve it.

I totally thought she'd take out the recycling for me again. "Dang it. Mom's going to kill me."

"This is why your sister is a freak," Rachel says as we head into the school. Once we're inside, she ditches me for Austin and I head to my destination, Adam.

"Why are you going to be in trouble? Juliet didn't take out the trash." Adam complains.

"No. It's my job. She's been covering for me. She has every right to be mad at me."

Adam scowls. He's not even looking at me. He's staring at his phone and texting someone. "Well, at least you'll be at Mitch's after practice."

"Most likely I'll be grounded."

I slap my locker closed, and we head to first period. After, we have lunch and sixth period together. I watch him stare idly at his phone while we walk to class. He occasionally pushes his strawberry blond hair out of his eyes. Yes, those Prince Harry types gets me every time. It also helps that he has a small spatter of freckles just across his nose and shoulders. Oh, and he has honey-brown eyes and thick lashes. And wow, does football pay off, because my boyfriend has muscles like you wouldn't believe.

"Who are you texting?" I ask.

He doesn't answer, just laughs as soon as an audible ping comes from his cell. I wait impatiently for his answer but he just keeps typing away.

We're almost to class and he says, "What did you say?"

"I asked who you were texting?"

He nods, but I'm certain he hasn't heard a word I said. He continues to text. I swear sometimes I want to break his stupid phone. I'm not a cray-cray girlfriend though. That's the kind of thing those types do. But seriously, I'm having a freaking conversation with him, and he doesn't seem like he can be bothered. Why do I even try anymore?

We arrive to First Period just before the tardy bell rings.

Ms. Batistel would have a fit if I were late again. She's the head of the junior Elites club; the only club Juliet and I both belong to. My mom thought it would look good on our college applications. Juliet was, of course, all for that. Me on the other hand, I'm not considering getting into Yale or Harvard. I'll be happy if I can get into Coastal Carolina University.

"Miss Valentine. Mr. Kent. So, glad you two could join us in a timely manner. Mr. Kent, put the cell away, or consider it mine for the rest of the day."

Adam shoves his phone into the front zipper pocket of his backpack. Seconds later it's buzzing. *Texting his buddies my ass.*

# Chapter Two

*Layla*

I drag myself through the front door of our house. My legs feel like lead; Coach Mallard was a real tyrant today. My voice is a little sore from yelling but that's the sacrifice of being a cheerleader.

The last thing I want to deal with is my mom's glowering expression as soon as her attention lands on me. Her work phone rings. "Be my Valentine; how may I help you?" my mom says cheerily into her phone. I should mention it's fake cheer, because there is a deep scowl on her face at the time. Her finger motions downward, indicating that I should sit.

I slump into her office chair and sigh. "Well, Dolores, did you read the pamphlet I gave you on how to strike up a meaningful conversation, dear?" she asks.

My mom is a matchmaker. Julie hates what our mom does for a living. She calls it poison to the soul. I think Mom's job is pretty cool; she's finding people love. Mom claims it's her calling. After our dad died a few years ago, Mom needed to get a job. She started working at this matchmaker service, and got really into it. They got a kick out of her last name being Valentine. Of course, once she started pulling in dough out the wazoo for that place, she realized she could make more on her own. Enter the creation of "Be My Valentine, where your perfect person is just a click or phone call away."

Mom hangs up the phone a few seconds later and then narrows her eyes at me. "What were you supposed to do today?"

"Take out the recycling and the trash."

"So why is the recycling and trash canister still against the garage?"

I huff. "I forgot. I had to get to school. Coach Mallard is breathing down the whole cheer squad's neck about the state competition."

"And what does that have to do with the one chore you have around here?"

"Mom, I'm really sorry. I won't forget again."

"I know you won't, because you're grounded. Don't think I haven't noticed your sister covering for you the last few times."

I clamp my mouth shut. Dang it. "I'm really sorry."

She shakes her head. "Don't apologize to me. Apologize to your sister, who's been picking up the slack for you. In fact, as a tradeoff, I think you will have to do her chores and your own for the next two weeks."

"W-what? But I have homework and cheer practice!"

"We all have things we have to do, Layla. This is about meeting your responsibilities, not slacking off and expecting someone else to take care of it for you. Or if you prefer, I can ground you for three weeks. What will it be?"

I grumble. "Extra chores."

"Good. Go start on your homework."

A knock prods my door open a smidge. Juliet peeks in, and I want to launch a pillow at her face. "What do you want?"

"Um ... can I talk to you about something?"

"No. Especially not if you've come to gloat about me getting all your chores."

She flinches. "I'm sorry ... I was mad. I'll talk to mom. It's cool. I know you have way more going on than me. You don't have to do my chores."

"I'm going to. I don't need a reminder of all the things you do better than me."

"Ugh. It's not like that, and you know it. I get crap all the time for not being more active in school and more social."

It's true she does. Sometimes I think our mom likes to pit us against each other so we both try as hard as the other. Juliet is book smart and great at soccer. Me. Well, I'm the more flexible one and good with people. I cheer and do gymnastics, and I've got over ten thousand followers on Facebook, Instagram and Twitter. Juliet has no social accounts. Even our 80-year-old grandma has Facebook. But Juliet thinks sites like that are just a waste and eats brain cells like crack kills a person. My twin is very unique.

I frown. "I'm tired. Can we talk later?"

"Yeah, sure."

She closes the door, and I glare at my algebra. The numbers are so jumbled; I have to calm myself and focus. Numbers always look wonky to me. Sevens and ones look the same. Fours and Nines look the same. Threes tend to look like Eights.

Adam sometimes laughs at me when I try texting without using my voice app because it looks like a drunk person typed it. But the wonderful app on my phone can't help me pass Algebra. It certainly can't help me muddle my way through English.

A lot of people, especially in our family, believe Juliet got all the brains. Maybe they're right. Heck, I didn't even start talking until I was four. By the time I was in first grade, I was just learning to read my own name. I've been to tutors and specialists, and not much helps. There is no cure for Dyslexia. I just have to take longer breaks than normal students.

Maybe that's why I focus better at sports. No one is asking me to find x while flipping in the air. No one is asking me to read when I'm working on the balancing beam.

My phone pings, and I sigh. Great, a text message. I turn on my app and it sounds off in a generic voice. Message from Adam:

```
Hey U. R U grounded?
```

I use the microphone and say:

```
Not exactly. Have to do extra chores.
```

```
Adam: That Sucks. No party Friday?
Me: Not sure. Can we do something else?
Adam: Babe. Srsly? I want 2 prty.
Me: I get that. Trying to get Homework done. TTYL
Adam: Can't I g2g2 zzz.
```

That's bullcrap. He doesn't go to bed until at least twelve. It's only seven. At least I think it is. I chew on my lower lip.

```
Me: Yeah Ok.
Adam: Heart U.
```

Heart? No love? What the heck?

I don't bother to acknowledge him. I push my phone aside. He'll get the hint his lack of typing out "I love you" really ticked me off.

My phone pings again. I don't look at it immediately. After about four more pings, I can't ignore it anymore and look. He sends me a pic of him making a kissy face at me. My resolve wanes a little. The next picture is a selfie; with his left-hand he makes the universal sign for "I love you." I melt a bit but still refuse to answer.

```
Adam: Sry.
Adam: Luv u.
Me: I'm sorry too. Just stressed.
Adam: We could correct that  :-).
```

I hate when he hints at sex. He'll put on a whole pouty

act because I refuse to go all the way. Why does waiting for a right moment have to feel like a ticking time bomb? What's with it with guys thinking they're only awesome if they go all the way with their girlfriends?

> Me: I told u. I'm not ready.
> Adam: I know. When u r I'm here.

I want to say 'really, then why keep mentioning every chance you get?' But this will lead to a fight so I simply take the cowardly way out.

> Me: I have to finish this homework. Love you.
> Adam: Luv ya too. Sweet dreams.

I set my phone aside and stare at my math. The whole sex thing has me in a way worse mood. We've been together for almost a year. I don't want to be that corny girl who gives it up on prom night. I don't want to wait until I'm married either, I just … I'm scared.

All my friends who've done it said it was super painful the first time and you can't even enjoy it. They also claim every time afterwards is amazing. Still pain before doesn't make me want to try it any time soon. If I'm being completely truthful though, pain isn't the only thing holding me back. What I'm really terrified of is losing Adam afterwards. I already feel like our relationship is on its last thread with his constant pressure. Then with him being so distracted, he can't even hold a conversation with me anymore. I'd be completely mortified if I did share that experience with him and he just dropped me as easily as the snap of a finger.

Every single one of my friends who gave up the v-card to a guy they were dating said it was like that's all the guy was after—nailing the virgin—because they broke up quickly after. Some waited a week, some a couple days, others less than twenty-four hours. That is what I'm terrified of: that Adam will go from this wonderful, amazing person to a grade-A douche. And I'll forever remember him as that guy who took my virginity and left me.

I stare mindlessly at my homework. I'm never going to get this done if I keep letting myself get distracted with texts and worrying about sex. Around nine, I finally finish my homework and then I turn in.

# Chapter Three

*Layla*

He's amazing. Adam taped a rose to my locker with a note that asked, "Dinner, Saturday?" Awww!

As Rachel and I are gushing over it, my sister stops by. My sister never comes by my locker, FYI; so this is major.

"You lost?" Rachel sneers.

Juliet glares at her. "Do I look lost?" Then she turns to me. "I need your help."

"With what?" I ask.

Juliet twirls a piece of hair around her finger. "Um. So, if you saw something. Maybe you weren't really sure what you saw. But it looked like something. Anyway, if this thing could hurt someone would you tell if you weren't a hundred percent sure? Or would you just let it go?"

"What do you think you saw?" I ask.

Rachel elbows me. "She probably saw her favorite nerdball friend smoking pot or something."

"It wasn't ... just never mind." Juliet storms off mumbling

curses at Rachel.

I face my friend with a glare. "Why do you do that? This was obviously really bugging her."

Rachel flips her auburn hair off her shoulder as Mark, Jared, Tyler, and Austin stroll past us. Rachel waves, "Hey, boys."

Austin nods. "S'up, Rach. We on for tomorrow?"

"Sure are, sexy."

I roll my eyes. I love my friend, but she's a total nympho. Really, she is. I think her goal is to hook up with all the hot football players in the senior and junior class.

I grab my things from my locker and shut the door. Rachel turns to me. "I like messing with your sister; it's funny. Besides, she knows I don't mean it."

"Whatever. Next time could you keep it zipped? She was really upset."

"Fine," she says, followed by a noise of disgust.

I know it's a lost cause to ask for some peace between them. Whatever, I can't worry about this now. I continue down the hall and suddenly something slams into my side. I can't catch my balance before my butt hits the floor. A tall guy with brown hair topples into me, and is now using my body to break his fall.

"What the hell?" I roar as I smack the guy on the top of his head.

Out of the corner of my eye I notice Austin laughing. Jared helps the guy off me. The guy looks back at me with a smirk. "Ah, thanks for breaking my fall, Layla. But we should probably keep our love for each other to ourselves." Then Tyler Richardson winks and extends a hand to me. "What would Adam think?"

I smack his hand away and push myself up onto my feet. "You're such a jackhole, Tyler!"

He shrugs. "You love it."

"Keep telling yourself that." I brush some dust off my shorts.

"I will, Princess." Ugh! I hate when he calls me that. He then proceeds to bow.

I give him one last hot glare then march off down the hall.

Aside from my sister's meltdown and being used as a safety pillow to break someone's fall, my day was pretty much a bore. I went to all my classes. Got assigned homework in some of them. Saw the same people causing trouble in the cafeteria and the same girls ditch Gym using the same weird excuses. This week it was a sprained foot. Mind you, Kat the girl claiming her foot was injured, hasn't done any physical activity in or out of class to cause this. She was perfectly fine before class. I should know because she sits next to me in history. This meant our teams were uneven for volleyball again.

Instead of my day ending and me going home, I have cheer. Unlike most schools, our field is not located on our high school grounds. It's actually near our middle school.

Since I'm grounded, Adam and I devised a plan for me to catch a ride to the field with him to and back. Instead of actual alone time and possibly talking about our day so far, he cranked up the radio so loud I could barely think.

When we pull into the parking lot, he shoots out of his seat then says, "Babe, come on. I got to lock up my car."

I feel my brows gravitating toward the middle of my face as I grab my gear and get out of his stupid car. *Your car is a total POS; no one would ever dream of stealing it.* No kiss, hug, just get out of my car. "I'm sorry for getting grounded," I grit out.

He starts tapping away on his phone. "Back at ya babe."

"What?"

He looks over at me. "Didn't you say you loved me?"

Oh, my God! I can't right now. I storm off to my practice.

Usually I'm excited to cheer, today however, is a different story. My boyfriend is being a total jackass and now, my coach is yelling at all of us. We aren't getting the routine down because she keeps changing it up and adding more stuff in. We haven't even had a chance to perfect what she had us do yesterday or the day before. Our first meet is in a few weeks. I don't want to be the one to remind her we lose every year because our squad isn't prepared. And we always end up with two girls who can only do back-handsprings but can't do an aerial to save their lives. All the other squads can do multiple tricks, flips, and twists. They kick our butts because they actually function well as a team and don't fumble around.

After practice is over with Rachel growls, "Water breaks. That's all I'm saying."

I nod as she waves and hops in Austin's truck. My joints

and muscles protest in agony as I search the parking lot for Adam after practice. He's my way back to school since he insisted we ride to the field together.

I can't seem to spot him anywhere though, and I have to return to school for my weekly Junior Elite's meeting.

I make my way to the fieldhouse, where the football team's locker room is located. As I reach the door Jared Black plows out of it. "Oh, hey, Layla ... "

"Hey. Is Adam in there?"

He runs his hand through his wet, dark locks. "Um ... I think he bounced."

"What? He was supposed to give me lift back to school."

He shrugs and walks toward the lot, and I follow. "His car doesn't seem to be here," Jared says then looks over at me. "If you need a lift back to the school ... um ... Tyler probably has room. That's where we're heading. If you can wait around for two more minutes."

Great. My man leaves, and my only option for a ride back to the school is the class clown. Fan-freaking-tastic. I frown. Everyone else I know has already cleared out. "If you two don't mind."

He smiles. "Yeah, Ty drives an SUV; there's plenty of room."

I snort at his comment about plenty of room. Has he seen Tyler who's well over 6'3 and has a massive ego?

Jared makes his way over to Tyler, and I stay back observing. Tyler peers around Jared with a smirk then nods. I should run away. Catch a bus. Grab an Uber. Something else. If that smirk was any indication of what this ride back to the school will be like, I should leave right now. I'd really hate to wind up in a vehicle when Tyler has bad gas or something. I think guys can handle bad farts, but I can't.

Tyler and Jared head toward me after a moment, beaming like he's just won the lottery. "Adam left? What did you do tell him, you two have to start wearing matching pink shirts? Or that you're secretly in love with me?"

My veins pulse with annoyance. I shoot Tyler a glare. He is such a jackhole. This boy thinks everything in the world is one big fat joke.

"No. You know what? I think I'll go catch a bus instead." I know I'll be late for my meeting but I'd rather be late than deal with this jerk for the next ten minutes on the ride back to school.

"I'm kidding, Valentine. Damn; learn how to take a joke." He smiles at me, and it looks almost wicked. A shiver spirals down my spine. He walks over to a silver Jeep Grand Cherokee.

"Need help getting in, Princess? Or do you think you can figure it out?"

God, I want to punch him in the mouth.

"Tone it down, Ty," Jared warns.

"Yeah, all right." He climbs in on the driver's side.

Jared smiles at me. "Front or back?"

"Back." I'm not sitting next to Tyler. Ugh. I'd rather chew my own hand off.

After I climb into the back, Jared shuts my door and gets into the passenger seat. I notice the plush leather seats in Tyler's Jeep. I also notice it's surprisingly clean.

"What's up, Princess?" Tyler asks as he eyes me in his mirror.

I hold back my groan at the stupid nickname. "Your Jeep is pretty spotless. I'm shocked."

He laughs. "Duh. No girl wants to get down and dirty in a trash can, Honey."

And with those words I feel my stomach turn. What a pig! This is why I can't stand hanging out at his house or going to his parties. He has to turn every conversation into a dirty one. I'd stick my earbuds in if they were in my gym bag, but they are at home on my nightstand where I left them this morning. Note to self: *never leave home without them ever again*.

Jared glares at him then turns back to me. "Um … how's Juliet been?"

"Uh … she's fine." This is strange. No one ever asks me about my sister.

"Cool. Does she plan on going to the game on Friday?"

I laugh. "Juliet doesn't do games."

"Oh. I thought she did."

I shake my head. "Nope. She's not into it. Now if you asked me if she was going to get that Jeep of hers covered with mud this Friday, I would say that's a high possibility."

"No way, your sister takes her Jeep mudding? What trails does she usually take?" Tyler asks.

"Um, yeah. Don't know what trails she takes. I don't go with her."

"Well, I think it's cool as hell." He elbows Jared. "At least someone doesn't have a stick wedged up their ass."

What? I don't … ugh! This ride cannot end fast enough. "She also dresses like characters from whatever books she reads to the kids at the library. I personally think she could read the books without the whole dress-up bit, but what do I know?" I say.

I catch Jared smiling. "I think that's cool." Yeah, sure he does. He's probably saying that to be nice because Jared is genuinely super sweet. And he's not going to call my sister a weirdo to my face like most people do.

Tyler shakes his head. "Nah, man. I think that's strange, but to each their own."

We pull into the school a few seconds later, and I hop out. "Thanks for the ride." I hurry off into the school and down the hall to the art room where the Junior Elite meetings are held. I skid into the table where Rachel sits, plop down beside her, and huff. "Oh, my God, my everything aches."

Rachel gives me a funny look. "Did you and Adam, like, *do it* in the parking lot after practice or something?"

"What? Ew! No! I'm not a skeeza." Then I bite my tongue because I remember Rachel telling me a month ago that she and Harris, a senior at our school, did it in the parking lot. I shudder at the memory. Yes, my best friend loves to overshare. She will tell you every detail about the deed and how it was performed, and rate boys from one to ten. I lower my lashes and say, "He totally left me at the field."

"Shut up! What a prick. How did you get here then? I would have had Jenna totally come back for you."

I rub my temples. "It's fine. He probably has a lot on his mind. Anyway. I caught a ride with Tyler and Jared."

"Ugh. Did it smell like sweaty balls? Did Tyler give you a shit ton of one liners?"

I wrinkle my nose. "Nooo. It smelled like … " Hmmm, what *did* it smell like? Not sweat. Or even anything disgusting. "Rain storms. And Tyler was kind of a jerk but it was whatever." I don't mention Jared had asked about my sister. Rachel flipped out because she has a major crush on Jared. Plus, he was probably being nice and there is no need to get Rachel all riled up over nothing.

She nods. "Interesting." Then she throws an elbow into my side.

I look over at the door. Instead of Ms. Batistel, the advisor who's in charge of overseeing everything we do, it's my sister, dressed like a wizard or something. *Omigod, why didn't she change?* I shrink in my chair. I love her but sometimes I can't believe we're related.

"Is that a wand in her pocket?" Rachel snickers.

"Shut up!" I'm not in the mood for Rachel's snide remarks about my twin. Even though I am pretty sure that is a wand in her pocket. She really has no shame in showing people how truly nerdy she is.

"Geez, you need to chill or something," Rachel snaps.

"I'm fine." I fold my arms over my chest. Truth is I'm still ticked Adam left me. He's never done that before. There are a lot of things he's been doing lately that he's never done before though. Maybe it's a phase or something. Couples go through that. Right?

Still, it bothers me. What if this isn't a phase? What if … crap. I turn to Rachel and whisper, "Do you think he's going to break up with me?"

"Um … I'm not sure. Did you all make a date when you'll do the big deed yet?"

I shake my head. I don't know why it's so important. Big deal, I have no interest in having sex yet. I shouldn't have to set a darn date for it. Shouldn't it be when the moment's right? Ditching me and texting 'heart you' instead of saying I love you on the phone is not helping him get what he wants. More like helping me decide he shouldn't be my first at all.

"Well, you might want to do that if you don't want to lose him."

I glance over at my sister. Maybe dressing up like a dork and not caring about the consequences is the way to go. At least then you can see who really cares and who doesn't. Right now, I'm starting to question who is actually in my corner.

# Chapter Four

*Layla*

"Hey babe. Sorry about bailing on you earlier. My dad has been on my case about helping him organize the garage," Adam voicemail says. "Call me later."

Um. No. I'm not going to just call him later. He could have texted me before bailing. He could have made an effort.

I shut my phone off, and hook it up to the charger. There's a knock on my door. When I say, "Come in," my sister enters my room dressed in a shirt that says, "*Call someone who cares*."

I raise a brow. "What's up with the shirt?" She glances down and then shrugs. "Well, that's a good way to not make friends."

"This doesn't apply to real friends. Only fakes." She takes a seat at my desk. Juliet looks like she's about to hurl chunks all over my floor.

"Please tell me you're not drunk and going to get sick all over my carpet."

She glares at me. "I'm not sick. I'm just … I don't know

how to say this. I can't ask Mom this either; you know how she is."

"What do you need to ask?"

She chews on her lower lip then sighs. "How did you know Adam liked you?"

"What?"

"Never mind." She starts to get up.

"Whoa. Don't leave. What did you want to know? Are you into someone?"

She plops back down and shrugs. "I'm not sure. I mean he seems nice. But he also seems like he's nice to everyone with a pulse. You know?"

I roll my eyes. "Um, yeah. Most of the guys there are like that. Who's the guy?"

"Mark Whalan. I'm crazy, right? He wouldn't like someone like me. He's like a hot Greek god or something, and I'm, well … I'm a nerdy peasant."

"Nerdy, yes. But so what? I hear that's a totally awesome thing to be right now. And yes, Mark is very nice. He's nice and he doesn't have a rep for being a player. And he'd be stupid as hell if he wasn't into you. Just … " I grab the hem of her shirt and give her a look. "Maybe put on a nice shirt, and do your hair. I can braid it tonight and when you take it out in the morning your hair will look like soft beach waves."

She frowns. "I don't know. I mean, aren't you supposed to be yourself to find the right guy for you? I don't want to be one of those puppets at school. They're all flipping their hair, caking on makeup, and dressing like future thots to get guys to notice them. But what are they really seeing? Just a girl showing off all her goods and not making the boys work for it." She huffs and takes a seat on my bed. "I want a guy to work for my affection."

"Boys don't work for it though." I say this like I'm some kind of expert.

"I know. Doesn't really matter anyway. Addy says she fully believes Mark is the devil. I don't know why. She also says he's going to do nothing but break my heart into a million pieces. That's his specialty."

"No offense to your friend but she has a tendency to be a miserable biznach. Might be a reason why Mark doesn't hang out with her."

"I guess. He said he liked my shirt the other day. You know that one that says, '*I'm too awesome for a #hashtag*?'"

I laugh because I got her that shirt. "Yeah. It's a great shirt."

"He never talked to me before. His friend Jared always says hi to me. I just … I thought he was playing a joke on me or something."

"I don't think Mark is a jerk like that." He better not be. I'll kick his butt. Okay, I'll get someone to beat him down because he's at least twice my body weight.

Juliet sighs. "I just wish it was simple. Like grade school. People used to write notes to one another. *Do you like me? Check yes or no.* Not the most difficult thing in the world."

"Yeah." I slap her knee. "But that's what makes it fun. Because there will come a moment when you'll know if he's into you or if it's only you who's into him."

"And if that person feels nothing for you and you feel everything for him, you're left with a broken heart and no glue."

I shake my head. "Way to make it depressing. But yes.

You're right. It could happen. Then you need to remember what Mom always says: 'Don't regret trying. Regret never asking and wondering.'"

"That's stupid."

"Well, some of it sounds a little dumb."

She smiles and then starts to make her way off my bed and out of my room. "Thanks for listening."

"You know Adam does play football with Mark, and I am a cheerleader. We have the same practice schedule, and I can always magically bump into Mark. Put in a good word for you."

She shakes her head. "That's okay. If he really likes me, he'll find a way to tell me."

I give her a thumbs up. "Atta girl."

As soon as she leaves my room I let her words repeat in my head. Jeez, even for a girl who's never had a boyfriend before, she's smarter in that department than I am. At least she gives better advice than my best friend did. I'm not going to just forgive Adam like usual. If he's truly sorry, he's going to have to do more than send me text messages. He's going to have to really work for it.

Adam races up to me in the morning before first bell. "Babe. Babe. Babe. I'm so-so-so sorry. I'm the biggest asshole in the whole wide world."

Instead of staying strong and making him really work for my forgiveness, I cave like a house of cards. I'm such a loser.

My own sister wrinkles her nose at Adam as he presses his lips to my cheek. She walks past us, and I feel slightly pathetic.

"Aw. I knew you'd make up," Rachel coos from behind us.

Before she can gush anymore, Jared and Mark walk past. Rachel instantly turns her attention to Jared. "Hey Jared. There's a party at Melanie's tonight. You coming?"

"Probably not. Got curfew."

"Oh, that's too bad. You could have seen my new bikini. It's red."

He shrugs and keeps walking while Mark elbows him. I turn to Adam. "Are you going to Melanie's?"

"Not sure. Hey, uh … you want to go out to dinner this Saturday?"

"Dinner? Really? You still want to do that?"

He nods. "Yeah. I was thinking dinner and a movie."

I kiss him. "I'd love that."

"Great. We'll talk about what to see at lunch."

"Okay."

Maybe I had it all wrong. Adam really could be awesome when he wanted to.

# Chapter Five

*Layla*

Adam is running late for our date. I look back at my phone, trying desperately not to worry. Maybe something bad happened. He would have called, right? What if he couldn't call though? Oh, my God, I can't stop freaking out!

I start to pace the living room when my doorbell rings. I rush to the door and frown as soon as I see Chase.

"Hey Layla. Is Juliet up in her room?"

I nod and step aside so he can enter the house. He smiles at me. "You look nice. Date night?"

"Something like that. Did you see Adam out there?"

He raises a brow. "Like out on the street or parked in the driveway?" I must look crazy cause he takes a step back and says, "Nope." He goes towards the stairs and hitches a thumb in that direction. "I'm going to go hang out with Juliet now."

"Okay."

It doesn't take him long to bolt up the steps. I glance down at my phone again. Thirty minutes late. Adam is officially thirty freaking minutes late. I'm starting to panic and become upset.

I hope he's not in an accident somewhere. Then again, I hope he is because then I can't be mad at him for being this late. Because if he's not physically unable to call me and tell me why the hell he's late then I have every reason in the world to be so mad at him.

The doorbell rings again. I open the door to Adam. Instead of flashing the smile I had intended to give him, I'm ticked off. "Where were you?"

"I had to do something. It took me longer to take care of than I thought it would. But I'm here now. Why are you mad?"

"You're late."

"By a couple of minutes. Don't stress out. Are you ready?"

I glare at him. "Yeah. Whatever."

"Jesus, Layla. Don't be all pissy with me."

Right? Cause I should be happy he's here. Well, I'm not. He basically said he could have called but chose not to. Any other time that damn phone of his is attached to his hand. He has no problem texting everyone and their mother about stupid, pointless shit twenty-four seven. Yet one phone call to tell me he's running late and the boy all of a sudden doesn't know how to operate a phone.

I slam myself into the front passenger seat of his car and strap in.

"Damn it, Layla. I'm sorry, okay? Jesus. Next time I'll be twenty minutes early."

I shift in my seat. "It's not about being early or on time. It's about respecting me enough to at least tell me you're running late. I was worried. I thought something horrible happened to you. But it's like lately … " I start to sniffle, "it's like lately I don't even matter anymore. And I don't want to be *that* girlfriend. I don't. It's hard though, because you used to be this responsive guy. You used to hold my hand and do sweet things for me. You used to tell me you couldn't take me home but then found me a ride. You used to show me you gave a damn about me."

"And I still do. I just got distracted. I'm sorry."

I nod, still pissed.

♥

At our table, I'm growing more and more frustrated with him. He hasn't set his phone down once. Not one freaking time. He texted someone while he ordered his drink and his food.

This is supposed to be a date. He supposedly cares about me but he's proving just the opposite. He drops his phone into his lap and smiles at me. "What?"

"Who are you talking to?"

"Just the guys. Why?"

"We're on a date. Why can't you talk to them after you drop me off?"

He shrugs. "I didn't think it was a big deal."

"It is."

"All right. No cell phone. I'm going to the bathroom."

He fiddles with the buttons on his phone and sets it down on the table. I grab a breadstick from the basket, and his phone vibrates.

That's it! I'm about to give someone a piece of my mind. I pick up his phone and open the text.

```
Diane: Baby. I miss u. Come over 2nite.
I'll b waiting 4 U just like this.
```

The phone buzzes in my hand again, and there on the screen is a naked girl with a mask on her face. What the hell?

I scroll through the messages, and my heart shatters. What in the hell? There are lots of sex messages between them and pictures. Lots of naked pics with masks and downright dirty poses.

I blink a few times hoping the images will change or delete themselves. They don't. The phone trembles in my hand. My boyfriend of almost a year is cheating on me. How could ... I need more proof. That seems absurd, I know, but I need to know how long this has been going on. And if there are one thing movies have taught me about this crap, don't jump into conclusions. Heck for all I know she could be some loser stalker who is really into him and he doesn't have the heart to shut it down. Maybe it's a joke---like a really stupid joke one of his idiot friends is playing on him and he's trying to catch them red handed. Whatever it is I need this girl to tell me how long this crap has been going on, but I won't do it using his phone.

I pull out my cell and save her number. I put his phone back in the same spot and swipe away the stray tears from my eyes. As soon as Adam returns I say, "I don't feel so good. Can we go home?"

"Um … yeah. I hope you're not coming down with a bug or something, and I catch it. We've got our game against Maysville this week."

"Yeah. Me too." Jackwad. I hope I don't catch anything from your newfound thot!

We get our food to go, and he pays for the meal and then drives me home. I don't kiss him goodnight. Hell, I don't even say I love you. I just walk up to my room and begin texting the girl named Diane.

I sniffle a lot so my microphone only catches bits and pieces of what I'm saying. I take a chance and start using my thumbs to type out my warning.

> Me: You should know Adam is a two-timing jerk and you should probably stop sending him naked pics of yourself.

The mysterious Diane doesn't respond right away. So, I set my phone aside and lie on my bed until I hear the soft buzzing sound.

# Chapter Six

*Tyler*

Kelly, one of the four hottest cheerleaders on the squad, takes a seat in my lap. Austin is next to me with his hands full of Rachel. She's what I like to call a "cheer-bunny." Not only is she a hot cheerleader, but she only dates football players. There are seven players on the team who haven't yet tapped that.

Well, make that six, because it looks like Austin is about to head upstairs with her. Kelly's hand skims down my chest, drawing my gaze back to her. She giggles at something funny.

She sways a bit and I roll my eyes. "Babe. You're gorgeous and all, but I think you should go lie down in the spare room."

She licks her lips but it looks overly exaggerated. I pick her up and carry her up the stairs. She giggles as the hoots and hollers reach us. Freaking rosebuds. I deposit her in the guestroom and say, "Don't open this door for anyone. Got me?"

Kelly looks confused, and I sigh. "I'm locking you in here so no one tries messing with you. You're too drunk. I won't put it past some of these guys to take advantage of you. Sleep it off."

"But … "

Yeah, I don't sleep with girls so wasted they're practically comatose. I turn away from her after she starts peeling off her clothes. I open the door and flip the lock then shut her in the room.

This party is a bust. I don't feel like returning to the drunks downstairs, so I head to my room. As I take a seat in my gaming chair in front of my 70" flat screen, my phone vibrates in my pocket. I'm half tempted to ignore it since it's probably one of the dipshits downstairs.

With a sigh, I pull out my phone and read a text message from some random number.

```
Random number: u sboulo knaw Adam is
o 5 tinimg jerk & o should probobiy stop
sendlng him naked pLcs ot ursit.
```

Um, what the flying hell? Drunk people should not be allowed around phones. I stare at the message then start laughing like a toddler at the word "naked." So, the gist of the message is Adam, the jerk, should stop sending naked pics of himself to himself. Maybe. Wait; that makes no sense. Of course, drunk people rarely make sense. Let's try this again. I read it a few more times. We have a few Adams on our football team. Maybe it was meant for one of those guys?

Me, Larken, and Kent have done a lot of dumb shit for

laughs, but sending junk pics to people on my team isn't one of them. Whoever's doing this must be one dumb son of a bitch.

I could be nice and say, "Hey, you've got the wrong person." But I'm dying to get a rise out of someone tonight. Sure, it's an asshole move on my part. But at this point, I really don't care.

> Me: Can't help if ur man wants to see all these goods.
> Random number: Did u knaw he has a GF?
> Me: Not sure wtf that was but if you're asking if I knew he was with someone I did. And I don't really give a shit.
> Random number: You sound like a real bitch! You better hope I never see you in person.
> Me: Whoa! I'm just having fun here. No need for all that. Let's keep it classy.
> Random Number: Classy? You're the 1 sending naked pics to someone else's man.

Oh shit, this is just too freaking funny.

> Me: Well it's been fun. Gonna go find someone to hookup with, and btw I'm a guy, and your boyfriend sounds like a real prick.
> Random number: Wait, what?
> Me: Not a chick.

> Random number: But you have girl parts. I saw the pics.

I laugh so hard my abs ache. I haven't had a laugh like this in ages.

> Me: Wrong number.
> Random number: Y didn't u say something sooner?

I really can't argue. But hell, whoever this is, totally entertained me.

> Me: Just having a little fun.

Part of me felt like I knew her, or at least wanted to. Hell, if she's looking for revenge sex to get back at Adam, I'm down. Teach that prick a lesson. Greater good and all. But I'll draw the line if it could cause a shit ton of problems on our football team.

> Me: Sorry. Hope u find whoever u were looking for ...
> Random Number: I'm Faye btw
> Me: Cool. Maybe try again when ur sober tho.
> Faye: I'm not drunk!!!
> Me: Yeah. OK. Well. Ur texts are a little drunk sounding.
> Faye: F U! I'm dyslexic

Ah shit! Way to step in it, Tyler.

>Me: Sorry.
>Faye: Whatever. I hope my misery is making ur night.
>Me: I really am sorry. For what it's worth the guy seems like a total tool.
>Faye: He's been cheating on me.
>Me: Sucks. How did u find out?

Why the hell am I asking this Faye chick this? I should stop texting her and go back to the party. I don't need to get involved in someone else's drama. For all I know she's probably crazy.

>Faye: They were texting each other while we were supposed 2 b on a date.

Aw. Jeez what an idiot. Okay, even if this Faye chick is possibly batshit crazy, he's a dumbass. I'm not the cheating type. But if I were, I'd be smart enough not to text the other girl while on a date with my girlfriend.

>Me: Yeah, he's a moron. Ur better off.
>Faye: Thanks.
>Me: I have 5% battery left. I hope u tell that bitch off. And kick ur ex in the sack. He deserves it.
>Faye: Thanks. Gonna hang out with my sis & eat chocolate.

```
Me: Chocolate and hanging with fam is
always a good choice.
    Faye: G'Nite.
    Me: U 2.
```

♥

"What's up, Ty? You're not even making the easy shots," Jared says as he smacks me on the back.

This is by far the worst game of pool I've ever played in my entire life. I keep thinking about Faye. I woke up this morning and reread her texts. Then I went searching for her in the yearbook. But she wasn't in there. She must be new, or maybe she goes to Blackhawk, our rival school.

"Dude. What's wrong with you?" Jared asks breaking my concentration.

"I got a weird text last night. Anyway, I decided to mess with the person. Turns out the girl's boyfriend cheated on her. She texted me by accident, thinking I was the girl he was cheating with."

"Let me guess. You made her cry by pretending to be screwing her boyfriend or something."

"Kind of. I feel bad about it."

Jared shakes his head. "Did you apologize?"

"Yes. I just feel bad still. I mean I hope she finds the person she needs to."

Jared gives me a look. "Wait. Do you know the person

who texted you?"

I shrug. "She said her name's Faye. But I didn't find anyone named Faye in the yearbook."

He wrinkles his nose. "Dude. You're joking, right?"

"Nope. Why?"

"Uh you probably didn't find a Faye because you're probably talking to some thirty-year-old."

No way! "Ah shit," I say. He could be right. It shouldn't matter since we're never going to talk again. But she didn't seem like she was older than me.

We shoot a few more balls in, and Mark enters my game room. Jared shoots him a glare then huffs, "I, uh … gotta get back home."

Mark swaps glances at both of us then he settles on Jared. "I just got here. Are you serious, bro?"

Jared drops his stare to the floor. "Yeah, sorry. You know how my dad is with the training and stuff. Gotta bounce." He steps past Mark and throws out a closed fist to me. I tap it with my own.

"See ya," I say.

As soon as Jared leaves, Mark snaps, "You believe him? He's still pissed at me."

"Well, he didn't tell me about it. Trouble in paradise?" I joke.

Mark shoves me. "Stop saying shit like that."

I chuckle. "Fine."

Mark grabs a pool stick and starts hitting balls into the pockets. "I think it had to do with me telling Austin I was going to ask Juliet Valentine out."

I stop smirking at him. "Dude. That's not cool. You

know Jared has been wanting her since elementary school. Seriously?" What in the hell is wrong with him? No wonder why Jared went all Dr. Freeze as soon as Mark showed up.

Mark shrugs. "What? I like her. He's had plenty of chances to make his move. Are we all supposed to sit back and not ask out certain people because Mr. All-American might like them? Everyone kisses his ass. I'm freaking fed up with it."

Part of me gets his point. Jared has had plenty of time to grow a pair and ask Juliet out. At the same time, there are rules, and this is definitely a bro-code violation. "Dude, you're a jackass." I pull out my phone, scroll through random messages, and land on my conversation with Faye. Okay, yes, I saved her name in my phone. Don't ask me why but I want an unbiased opinion on breaking total bro-code.

> Me: Hey you. I hope you're doing better. Also I wanted to apologize again for being a jerk.
>
> Faye: Hi. It's ok. Thx 4 the apology again tho.
>
> Me: Few questions. U'r not 30 r u?
>
> Faye: Nope. 16. U?
>
> Me: Same. Hey, if 1 of ur friends had a crush on some1 would u ask them out?
>
> Faye: That's really random. But no. That's wrong. It's simple friend code policy. You know ...
>
> Me: Exactly. You can call me R.
>
> Faye: Really? R. That doesn't sound totally disturbing at all.

> Me: Hey, U could be one of my crazy fans. I need to keep some of this protected.

I look up from my phone. "Faye says you're in the wrong, dude."

"Who the hell is Faye?"

I shrug. "Some girl. But she says you're in the wrong, man."

Mark drops his pool stick. "You know what, I thought you were going to be on my side on this. But you and your girl can kiss my ass. I'm out."

As soon as he leaves, I glance down at my phone.

> Me: So ... My friend left. Know what that means?
> Faye: ...
> Me: U have 2 entertain me. Did u kick ur ex in the balls?
> Faye: LOL. No. I have to break up with him still.
> Me: Hold up! U caught the dude cheating and u'r still 2gether? That's all kinds of messed up Faye.
> Faye: Kind of. I mean I never said Hey you're a dillhole and we're done. I'm doing it today.
> Me: U should have done it last night.

Why am I getting worked up over this? It's not like we're about to get into a relationship or anything. But I hate when girls do this. They purposely drag out the breakup for dumb reasons.

Before I can express my opinion, she tells me she has to go do chores. Which leaves me bored, so I head upstairs. One look around, and I groan. The whole house looks like a bomb went off. Shit. I need to clean this up before the 'rents come home.

Usually for this kind of cleaning, I call Mary Ella, our housekeeper, but she's on vacation with the 'rents. This leaves me with two choices: call a maid service or just do it myself. I've got nothing better to do, so I head to the pantry, grab a box of trash bags, and get to work.

I start at the very top; it's not as trashed as the other floors, but that's because I keep these areas off limits. Once I'm there though I immediately return downstairs for some extra supplies, one of them would be gloves. There are a few used items in the bedrooms that there is no way in hell I'm touching them with my bare hands. Trash cans, people! We have trash cans all over this monstrous house. Yet some jackass has to leave crap on the floor or on my parents' bed. Yeah, that would have been a great lecture.

I strip beds, wash everything, and make my way downstairs. Five trash bags later, I've got the whole house cleared of trash and vacuumed, and the floors mopped. It all gleams and I almost can't believe I'm the one who did this.

Snatching up the trash bags, I head outside to dispose of them. Before I even make it to the cans, I grumble. The front lawn is completely jacked up. Seriously, I want to know what dipshit thinks, "Hey, here's a buttload of toilet paper, let's go cover the trees and lawn with it." Then think this is super cool. It's not. In fact, it's pretty stupid. Now, thanks to that brilliant jackass, I'm going to spend the rest of the afternoon cleaning up the lawn. Freaking awesome!

# Chapter Seven

*Layla*

Rachel is sitting on my bed, and we're discussing penises. Well, she's talking about the sizes and stuff, and I'm stuck listening.

"Austin was fantastic. I can't believe I waited this long to be with him. Even if he's small." She motions to the downstairs area.

"Um … Rachel, I don't want to hear this."

She pulls a blue sucker out of her mouth and points it at me. "You're my best friend. I have to listen to all your dull Adam stories. You're going to listen to my exciting Austin ones"

My sister has a word for Rachel's sex life. Well, she has a lot of them, actually. Slutty is usually her top choice, followed by dirty, and degrading. Normally, I stick up for Rachel and tell Juliet to mind her own business. At least Rachel is putting herself out there unlike my sister, who would rather hole up in her room with books. Sorry, but those Mr. Darcy characters aren't going to pull themselves from the pages and magically appear. But today I'm starting to see Juliet's point. It's not putting yourself out there if almost every guy in school has had a piece of the pie.

"Oh my God, his tongue definitely made up for the lack of length."

I stick my fingers in my ears and sing, "LALALALALALA."

She pulls one out and says, "Seriously; grow up. I'm telling you this so when you do give it up to Adam for the first time, you'll know how to rate it." She gives me a square look. "If you've got nothing to compare him to and no expectations, how will you know if it was really good or not?"

I shoot her a look that is half self-doubt and half embarrassment. "I'm not ever giving him anything!"

"What? Why? Oh, does his kisses not set you in that kind of mood?"

If my eyes could shoot laser beams, I'd blast her. "No! I don't know, anymore. He's cheating on me."

"Wait, what? With who? Tell me you went postal on him and the bitch."

I shrug. "Her name is Diane. I don't know her. I didn't exactly see a face shot of her.

"Oh, hon. I'm sorry. When the hell did this happen?"

"Last night."

She shoves my shoulder. "And you didn't tell me until now? We could have already slashed all his tires and painted *I have crabs* on his hood."

I laugh. "Yeah. No. I'm not going to do anything crazy."

"We totally should. That's not even the craziest part of what would be the most epic revenge ever."

I shrug. "What would be the point? I won't feel any better. I keep thinking this is somehow my fault."

Rachel stands and starts walking to the door. "Where are you going?"

"I'll be back." She leaves my room and moments later I hear, "What the hell, Rachel? Get your hands off me!"

"Shut up. Your sister needs you."

Juliet enters my room looking super pissed. "You needed to send her to my door? Uck. I better not get the clap or something 'cause she touched me."

Rachel sneers at Juliet. "I'm perfectly clean; thank you, miss bitter prude."

"Ladies! Seriously, knock it off. Rachel, why did you get my sister?"

"Because even though her future is probably a house with a thousand cats and her books, she can talk some sense into you." She turns to Juliet. "Layla thinks because she didn't sleep with Adam, she's to blame for him sexting some other girl."

Juliet wrinkles her nose and glares at me. "Did she really drag me out of my room for this conversation?"

"Yes. Now tell her!" Rachel says.

"There is nothing to tell. She already knows it's not her fault." She sighs as she looks at me. "If you weren't ready, you weren't ready. If he was a prick and couldn't wait, that's not your fault. And he doesn't deserve the honor, as Mom puts it."

I smile at Juliet. "Thanks."

She nods. "Can I leave now? I was in the middle of Recon."

Rachel glares at her. "Ugh, you're a disgrace."

"Hey. No, she's not. Yes, Juliet, you can go."

Juliet rolls her eyes at Rachel then exits my room. Rachel shakes her head at my door. "You have to admit she's never going to get a date."

"That's her thing. Video games, books, cosplaying her favorite characters, and mudding in her Jeep. So what? At least some jackhole won't rip her heart out."

Rachel sits back down on the bed. "Well, you need to quit moping and get yourself another man."

"I can't. I'm kind of … I still haven't … "

She scrunches up her nose. "Damn it, Layla! Please tell me you dumped his sorry ass as soon as you found out he was parking his car in someone else's garage."

I have no idea where she comes up with these phrases. My face heats with shame and embarrassment. "Not yet. I'm going to tell him we're done."

"Please tell me you aren't going to go all drama queen on his butt at school on Monday. That shit never ends good, Lay."

"I know. I'm not. I'm going to do it tonight when he comes over. He texted me." I swing my phone to show her, and she shakes her head.

"'My face misses yours. Coming by tonight. Cool, baby?' Is this how he always texts you?"

I pull my phone back. "Pretty much."

She purses her lips together. "Yeah, no wonder you haven't been giving it to him. Why didn't you dump him sooner?"

I narrow my eyes. "I don't know. I thought … I thought we were good together and he loved me. And I guess I thought his texts were sweet."

"They're not sweet. This is sweet." She pulls up something on her phone and reads, "'Hey gorgeous, I can't wait to spend a day with you. The air is sweeter when you're around me. I need to get lose in those baby blues. Counting the minutes.'" She smiles. "That is sweet and hot, right?"

"He sounds like a fifty-year-old stalker. Who wrote that?"

"You can refer to him as Sexy Butt."

"What? Why are we calling him that?" I cringe after the question leaves my mouth because in all honesty I don't want to know.

"Duh. He has one amazingly sexy butt. He's our age and into poetry."

"Oooohkay. Why not call him by his real name?"

Rachel rolls her eyes. "Hello, my phone's password must be knowledgeable to all. Mom's new 'We don't have secrets in this house' crap. That means the little monster from hell, loves to get into my phone. And if Patina doesn't know their real names she can't find them or tell on me either."

I raise a brow. "You do know Patina could call them."

"Right and when a deep hot throb voice answers what's she going to say, 'Hey ya sexy butt' The guy will laugh and hang up on her. Besides my mom thinks she should quit snooping around so much anyway."

"So, you labeling them this ensures Patina won't tell on you?"

"Pretty much because she'll get grounded. Last week I purposely named one rocking hard on and she told mom. You should have been there. My mom made her stay in her room with no electronics. She also told Patina if she ever used potty mouth language again she won't leave the house until she's fifty." Rachel laughs.

I frown a bit. Poor Patina. But I can also feel for Rachel. Patina does love to stir trouble. She's a freshman at our school and has already crashed a few parties, tried to get pictures of Rachel drinking in order to show their mom. But the best was when she wore one of Rachel's outfits to school and tried hitting on one of Rachel's ex's Perry Porter. Everyone in elementary school used to call him P.P. and then giggle. Okay, I still giggle and some people still call him that.

Rachel glances at her phone. "Hey ... I have to run. I got to take the monster to the mall to get a dress for this dinner thing she has."

"Okay."

"Text me later with the deets of you punching Adam in his throat."

I smile at the thought. He'd come to my door and I'd slam my fist right into his neck. Then he would croak, "What did I do?" I'd say, "Ask Diane." Then I would slam the door in his face.

She hugs me. "Good idea, huh? I can actually see your brain working it out. Thinking something evil is actually putting a smile back on your face. Yay. I did my job. Remember; text me." She pulls back and heads out the door.

# Chapter Eight

*Tyler*

I pull into the school parking lot and step out of my ride when a car almost takes me out as it whips into the spot next to mine. I glare at the driver, and then shake my head. Of course, it would be *her*. Princess Layla can't drive for shit.

"You almost ran me over."

She looks me up and down then shrugs. "You look fine to me."

God. I've never hit a girl in my life and never will, but she's really pushing it. "What the hell is *your* problem?"

Rachel steps between us and then smiles at me. "Tyler, be a dear and walk me inside."

I untangle myself from her grip and head into the school. There is no way in hell I'm going to be seen strolling up to the front door with Rachel Little on my arm. Especially since Austin hooked up with her the other night. That's a pot I'm not about to stir.

As I head to my locker, I can't help but notice the odd

stares. I pass by a group of sophomores on the cheer squad. "I guess he gave her something down there so she dumped him," one of them says.

"No. I heard she was cheating on him with the Blackhawk's new quarterback and they both dumped her," the other girl says.

"You're both wrong. I heard Adam asked her for a three-way, and she blew up."

I glance back and notice Layla following me with her eyes glued to the floor. Rachel keeps glaring at the different sets of people they walk past. I turn back around. Whatever is going on is none of my damn ... "Hey man! Did you hear?" Mark says as I stop at my locker.

"Um ... that Ridgeville's right guard is out for the whole year? Yep."

"What? No. Really?"

"It was in the paper."

"Shut the hell up. You read the paper?"

I glare at him. "Only the Sports section." What's wrong with reading the paper anyway?

Mark looks puzzled for a second. Then he shakes his head right as Jared pops open the locker on the other side of me. "Hey. Did you guys hear that Layla kicked Adam in the nuts yesterday? That's what Rachel told Austin. And check this shit out." Mark pulls up Instagram on his cell and there is a whole shit ton of dirty pics of some masked chick on Adam's page with a caption: gettin' down with this hottie tonight.

I can't really tell who the masked chick is, but I think it's low to post private pics of your girl on any form of social media.

Some random sophomore yells to Layla, "Nice boobs!"

Layla flushes and screams, "It's not me, you stupid pervert!"

"Whoa." Mark says. "He was nailing some other chick. No wonder why she nailed him in the coconuts."

"Dude, come on," I say with a cringe. Getting a shot to the balls is painful to think about, let alone talk about. Although between the social accounts, and Austin's big mouth who loves to spread drama it doesn't surprise me the school is buzzing about Layla and Adam's break-up.

Mark throws an elbow into my ribs. "Oh shit. Look, look."

I turn and watch as Adam approaches Layla in the hall. He tries grabbing her hands but she backs up and slaps him right across the face. They're about five yards away from us but the sound of her hand hitting his jaw echoed loud enough to make me flinch.

I don't condone cheating, but I feel bad for Adam's jaw right now. Please do not mistake this for sympathy for Princess Layla. I don't give a crap about her. If you think I'm an asshole for saying this, you don't know Layla Valentine like I do. From day one, that girl has found ways to treat me like scum. She told people to call me "Dick-son" because some people named Richard like to use the nickname "Dick". Whatever. My last name is Richardson end of story. She farted in class and it smelled rancid. I know it was her, she sat in front of me in third grade. It was loud and the smell hit me instantly. That little brat shouted, "Tyler that's gross." Everyone thought it was me. Anytime Adam would attend one of my parties she would come get him seconds later. She loathes me for no freaking reason, so I don't care for her back.

My thoughts halt when Jared growls next to me as Mark says, "Hey, Juliet. Do you mind if I walk you to class?"

She agrees and they walk off together. I glance over at Jared, who slams a fist into his locker. "Dude. Calm down," I whisper.

"He's just going to mess with her. He doesn't even know her," Jared snaps.

"Neither do you, man. You never even talk to her," I say.

"I know her."

I shake my head. "Really? What's her favorite color then?"

"Red."

"Yeah? Okay, we'll see." I spot her friend Adaline. "Hey Addy."

"What are you doing?" Jared warns.

"Relax." I run up to Addy. She gives me a "go burn in hell" glare. "Hey, quick question. Is Juliet's favorite color red?"

"What?" she asks as her hands ball up at her sides.

I smile at her. "Jared and Mark were having an argument about it. Jared said red. Mark said it was pink," I lie.

She curls her upper lip. "You guys are pathetic. Tell Mark to leave Juliet alone."

"Okay. But which one was right?"

"Jared." She continues to stalk down the hall right as Jared glares at me.

"What did you do that for?"

I shrug. "I wanted to see if you were full of shit or pissed off for a reason."

"And what is your conclusion?"

I smack his chest with my hand. "You should be pissed at

yourself for not growing a pair and asking her out."

Jared starts to grumble some shit about timing not being right as Austin grips my left shoulder. "Did you hear?"

I roll my eyes. "What you told Mark yesterday. Yes. Pretty sure the whole school knows. Kudos. You really should think about becoming a news reporter."

Austin laughs. "I'd probably be excellent at that. But that's not what was I going to say. Rachel and I are hooking up again this weekend."

"You do realize she's been with almost the entire football team?" Jared points out.

Austin shrugs like it makes no difference. I personally don't want to be with someone most of my teammates have done things with. I don't want to think about getting someone's sloppy thirds, or in her case, thirtieths.

Layla shoulders into me as we start to move closer to the whole Adam-and-Layla scene. I glare at her and snap, "'Excuse me,' is what you're supposed to say."

She glances up at me with red-rimmed eyes and flips me off. And this is why I call her Princess Layla. She expects everyone in school to bow down and kiss her feet. Well, I kiss absolutely no one's freaking feet. My dad owns the most powerful law firm in the country. My mom runs a bunch of charities. My uncle is mayor of our town. My sister is a bestselling author. My brother-in law owns a huge construction company in the Capes.

She's not better than me. Not at all. Big whoop, her mom owns a dating service. Maybe she should run some etiquette classes and enroll her daughter in them.

Restraining myself and the rest of the remarks I want

to unleash on her, I turn away and continue down the hall. Austin, being the dipshit he is, says, "Hey Adam. Rough day?" Then he starts chuckling.

Jared and I exchange looks. "Dude, why do you always have to start?" Jared asks.

Austin smirks. "Because, he's a prick and he knows it."

"Yeah. But now he's going to be a shithead at practice today," I state the obvious.

Austin is my boy and all, but he really doesn't think. He shrugs like it's no big deal, but that punk doesn't have to deal with Adam in the huddle.

As we're about to break away for our classes Jared mutters, "Screw me." I glance over at him then down the hall at the large man coming toward us like a freight train.

Austin gives our coach, AKA Jared's dad, a nod. "'Sup, Coach?"

"You three, in my office. Now. Where are Whalen and Kent?"

I glance back at Adam looking like a deer caught in headlights. "Kent is back there and Mark is probably in class," I say.

"Can't this wait, Dad?" Jared mumbles.

"No. Now. I'll call Whalen into my office." He marches past us and heads toward Adam. He says something to him then veers off to the main office.

I raise a brow at Jared. "What the heck was that about?"

He groans. "There are going to be big scouts at our games. He wants to make an impression now so they come back and try recruiting us next year."

"Dude, I'm not interested in playing college ball," Austin

says. "My meal ticket is basketball. So why do I have to go?"

Jared shrugs.

Austin darts ahead of us. I glance over at Jared. He seems to slow his pace. I feel sorry for him. Jare is cool, smarter than all of us combined, and extremely talented on the football field. But my boy literally has no life. He probably won't admit it but that's probably one of the reasons he doesn't ask Juliet out. He's probably scared as shit his dad will blow gasket or something.

We slip into Coach's office and all try cramming onto the faux leather couch. Adam strolls into the room. One side of his face has the makings of an angry handprint. "Dude, so what's the real story with you and Layla?" Austin asks.

Adam gives him a fake laugh then says, "Mind your business."

"I kind of can't. You just got bitch slapped in the hall by one of the hottest, most popular cheerleaders in school. Who also happens to be your girlfriend. Wait, I mean ex-girlfriend. Seriously man, what did you do? Cause' there's a lot of rumors flying and one of her friends said you were messing around on her. So what story is true? Did you knock her up?"

Adam grits his teeth and holds white-knuckled fists at his sides. "Shut the hell up, Reed!"

Austin stands up and takes a step toward Adam. I throw myself between them before a fight breaks out. "Sit down," I snap at Austin, and shove him.

"I did something stupid," Adam admits.

"Aw shit. You got her knocked up?" Austin chimes.

"No, dickwad! I was seeing someone behind her back."

Austin shakes his head and takes a seat. "You didn't just do something stupid; you *are* stupid."

"F you!" Adam yells as the office door flies open. Jared's dad steps in with Mark trailing behind him.

Coach looks at us then takes a seat at his desk. "I called you all in here to discuss something important."

# Chapter Nine

*Layla*

Everyone knows.

Well, they know Adam and I are no longer together. As for why. that's completely muddled.

Some people say he posted naked selfies of me on the Internet. Girls have begun calling me "Easy Lay." The guys make lewd comments like "nice rack" or "juicy booty." Some ask if I want to see them after school.

My favorite rumor flying around, though, is Adam got me pregnant.

I'm so embarrassed and disgusted by it all. How could I have dated such a creep?

As I sit in my usual spot at lunch, I notice the stares and the hushed whispers, and it's almost too much. I'm half-tempted to leave when Rachel plops down in the seat beside me. "So … how are you holding up?"

"I think I'm going to puke. Why do all these people keep talking about me?"

Rachel smiles. "Because they need gossip to fuel their boring lives. It's what they look forward to. Don't worry; it will blow over eventually."

I glance around the room and spot my twin sitting with her one friend, looking out of place but doesn't seem to mind. I pull out my phone and for some reason I have the urge to be someone else for a change. I shoot a text off to R. And since I also don't want anyone else up in my current business, I take a stab at typing instead of using my voice app.

> Me: Hey. How's your Monday morning?
>
> R: Hey u. I c we might have started erly in the mornin day is Eh. The usual. Drama queen with no manners acting like every1 owes her the world. Dude on my team can't handle being told he got demoted to 2nd string. U?
>
> Me: you play football? I wish this day would be over already.
>
> R: Yep. Sry to hear that. Do u like football?
>
> Me: It's okay. I don't really care for it when it's cold.
>
> R: That's a crime. Looks like we can't be friends now.

I giggle.

"What so funny? Is it one of those dog videos?" Rach asks.

I pull my phone close to my chest. "Um, no."

"Oh. Well, are you going to tell me?"

I shake my head as my lips pull at the corners.

She sticks her tongue out. "Fine be that way."

```
Me: That's a shame. I thought we were going to prom together. Way to crush my dreams.
    R: Oh dancing and I r a no go babe.
    Me: Babe? That sounds a little deep. And u won't take me to prom?
    R: Nope won't do it.  :-)
    R: Quick? What's the last name of the dude u were with?
```

Shit! What if this R person knows Adam? Knows me? If he puts two and two together he'll figure out it's me. Then he'll probably think I'm sad and pathetic like everyone else in this school. I chew on my lower lip and then I turn to Rachel.

"What's a sexy last name?"

"Sexy, huh? Are you creating a list of potential name changes in case this whole Adam-the-cheating-douche mess doesn't blow over?" she waggles her eyebrows and I just laugh.

My reply is taking too long. I know this. He'll know it's me. Shit.

"I don't know. I don't really find last names sexy. But if I were going to pick a good one to change to it would probably be DiAngelo or McLaugan."

```
Me: DiAngelo. Sorry my friend was telling me a story. You know how they get
```

when you half listen.

Hopefully he buys that bag of BS.

> R: Sorry what?
> R: Kidding. Yeah. I get that. So ... I take it you don't go to Blackhawk. 'cause I know all those fools and none of them have that last name.
> Me: Nope.

Oh shit. Maybe the mysterious R goes to Blackhawk. Hmm. I wonder.

> R: If u would have said Kent I would have told u, u weren't the only 1 he screwed over. Dude probly had a different girl from each HS.
> Me: Really? Do guys normally do that. Take on as many girls as they can from different schools?

In my mind, I'm freaking out. Thank God, I didn't give him Adam's real last name. Crap, this person knows me if they play football with Adam. Definitely never forking over my real name. From here on, I've got to be extremely careful what I say to this mysterious R.

> R: Only assholes do that.
> Me: Are you one of the good ones?

```
R: Getting a little personal there
aren't we. We haven't even held hands
yet. I can't reveal all my secrets so
soon. You might be a stalker.
Me: I am not a stalker!
R: That's what they all say. Right?
```

I snort. And Rachel glances at me with a raised brow. "What?" I ask.

"You've been super into your phone for most of lunch. Seriously, who are you talking to?"

"No one."

"Um … Okay. Don't tell your best friend. I see how it is. Hopefully it's a guy," she says with a wink.

I'm about to tell her it is when my phone pings.

```
R: What class r u in now?
Me: Lunch. You?
R: Same. Do u have crappy food too?
Me: Oh yeah.
Adam: Babe I miss you. Please talk to
me. I'm sorry.
```

I scrunch up my nose and growl.

```
Me: The ahole just texted me.
R: Tell him to F'off and you found
something better.
Me (to Adam): I found something better.
Adam: Who?
```

> Me (to R): He's asking who?
> R: Tell him none of his damn business. He lost the privilege as soon as he screwed around on you to know who, what, where, or why when it comes to you.

I repeated the message to Adam because honestly, that was a good response.

> Adam: We need to talk after practice.
> Me: I'm busy.
> Adam: Bullshit!
> Me: Leave me alone!
> R: What did he say?
> Me: He wants to talk to me. I told him no.
> R: Good for you.

I don't say anything for a minute. Then my phone buzzes softly against my palm.

> R: Save me?
> Me: From?
> R: Remember the friend I told u bout?
> Me: Vaguely. Yeah.
> R: Max drama. He f'd up n knows it. She's comin 2 our game fri 2 cheer on my bro-code breakin friend. Tryin 2 think of things 2 do 2 get my buddy's mind off his f'up.

> Me: Set him up w some1 else.
>
> R: Yeah. That's on the list. So is throwing a party. Get him wasted.
>
> Me: Honestly he should probably tell her how he feels. She might like him more than the other guy n has been waiting around 4 him 2 make a move.
>
> R: Girls. Y do u all go 4 the jealous move?
>
> Me: Not all of us do. Most. Not all. Gotta go bell rang.
>
> R: Same here. Have a good rest of the day Faye.
>
> Me: You too R.

As I am walking out of lunch someone bumps into me from behind. I hear, "Sorry about … never mind." I turn and face Tyler. Ugh! Asshole!

"Walk much, Tyler?" People cannot walk and text at the same time. So sick of these jerks with their phones out not paying attention all the damn time.

"Just mind your own business, Princess."

I glare at him and smack his phone from his hand, which sends it flying. "What the hell, you crazy bitch?"

"That's what you get for walking and texting. It's dangerous to those around you, you insensitive jackass!"

He's on the ground searching for his phone while most of the student body is filing out of the cafeteria.

"Wow. You need help, Valentine!"

I give him the universal sign for suck it, right as Rachel

swoops in and starts dragging me away. "Are you trying for social suicide? That wasn't cool, Lay. Didn't he give you a ride the other day when Adam ditched you?"

I take a deep breath and let the shame of my actions wash over me. "I ... just ... I don't know what came over me. He brings out the worst in me. You know that."

"Yeah, well, you need to apologize or go help him find his phone before it gets smashed into a million pieces."

I turn toward the chaos behind me. Tyler is still searching for his phone, and I spot off to the left by the cafeteria doors which is in the area he isn't even looking. I groan, pick it up, walk toward him and hand it over. "I'm sorry. I was ... out of line. I'm having—"

"I don't care!" He snatches his phone from me and storms off.

Rachel shakes her head. "Let's get to class."

Yep, let's go to all the classes I dread going to: Algebra, followed by English. So much fun.

♥

I'd love to say my day got better. It didn't. Not one darn bit. In Algebra, my teacher, Mr. Williams, called me up to the front of class to complete a problem on the board.

To Mr. Williams credit, he did ask me in low voice so only I could hear him if he needed me to read it. Which okay, I did, but I'm tired of people seeing me as a helpless idiot.

I was determined to do this by myself. My stubbornness obviously bit me in the butt because instead of writing the correct answer, I ended up showing everyone how stupid I am.

The whole class snickered. Then Mr. Williams ended up reading the problem but the damage was done. This only made the giggles turn into snide remarks.

I was utterly humiliated. Screaming and crying wouldn't help but I really wanted to do both. I wanted to smack the girl up front who whispered loudly, "No wonder Adam broke it off with her. She's a complete airhead."

She and her sophomore friend didn't make the cheering squad this year, and to say both of them were nasty to me is an understatement. They called me names and told me to dye my hair blond. Usually, I just ignore them. I can't help it they're mad at me for not making the team. It wasn't my decision, but even it was they would have been cut.

They didn't know the routine. That was obvious. They thought because they were on the freshman squad last year they were shoe-ins. But varsity squad requires tryouts. They fumbled the routine and shrugged it off like it was okay. Coach Mallard doesn't tolerate fumbling, especially if you had four days to perfect a routine.

It's funny how fake people can be. Towards the end of last year, they were sweet, smiled at me, and always complimented me. After tryouts this summer, they showed their true colors. Every class I have with them they insult me, laugh at me, and make me so mad I want to rip their hair out.

I somehow rein back my tears and pretend not to hear them. Not one word.

When the bell rings, I rush to my last class of the day, gritting my teeth. The two witches are following me, recapping how stupid I am. They're making a scene, making me feel so much worse. I try to pick up the pace without making it noticeable that I'm running away when I slam right into my twin.

She hits the ground, and her friend Chase gives me a dirty look. I glance down at my sister. I feel my lower lip wobbling. "Hey. Layla, what's ... " Juliet starts as she pulls herself up from the ground.

The witches giggle loudly, then reenact my screw up from class.

I squeeze my eyes shut and suddenly I'm pulled down a hall. "Layla, listen to me. Those girls are nothing. Don't worry about it. Do you hear me?"

"I had to ... it was so embarrassing. Everyone saw how ... stupid ... " I can't even get the last bit out because I'm choking on my sobs.

"Layla, you are not stupid! You're really smart. You just struggle more than others, yes, but you don't let those challenges rule you. You overcome them, and that makes you brighter and stronger than anyone else I know. Got me?"

I nod as I wipe away a few tears. Then I spot Jared, Tyler, Austin, and Mark coming toward us. I quickly hug my sister then shove off to class. I do not need anyone seeing me cry, especially Tyler.

# Chapter Ten

*Tyler*

I'm heading to Weight Lifting with my friends when I spot the twins. I'm just about to nudge Jared when Layla looks up with red-rimmed eyes, and then she hugs her sister quickly and takes off. Wow, who knew the Ice Queen actually had emotions?

I don't feel one single ounce of sorry for her since she went all crazy and knocked my phone out of my hand. She's lucky it's still intact and the screen isn't smashed to hell.

I glance over at Jared. He's staring at something with a confused look on his face. I follow the direction of his gaze and notice Juliet talking to Chase. He's on the team with us and in all the AP classes with Jared and Juliet. Like Jared, he's cool for a nerdy type, he just hardly comes to any of our parties after the games. We invite him, but I think his dad's super strict and doesn't want him out late or whatever.

"What's up with her and Chase?" Jared whispers.

"I think they're best friends."

"Yeah, right! He can't just want to be friends with a girl like her," he snaps.

"If she's anything like her sister, I'd wonder why he'd want to be friends with her in the first place."

Jared glares at me. "Layla is actually nice. Not to you, because you're an ass. But she is nice."

"That's bullshit. She just went all psycho and threw my phone because I bumped into her. And yes, I said sorry."

Jared raises a brow. "All right, well, that's a little extreme."

"You think? I mean, shit; I gave her a ride when Adam bailed on her. Then she acts like I'm a jackass. Throwing my phone. Slamming into me without so much as an I'm sorry. She's a straight-up royal bitch. I'm happy if she's suffering. She deserves it."

"Really, man?"

I shrug. "Yeah. I call them like I see them."

I walk into the locker room and quickly change into my workout clothes then head to the weight room. It's the only class besides lunch that we all have together. As Jared takes a bench, I go and grab some weights. Adam's next in line. "Hey man," he says.

"Hey."

He steps up and grabs two 45's from the tree, as I like to call it, then asks, "Hey, do you think Coach put me on second string because of Layla?"

I raise a brow. "Um ... no. I think he put you on second string because you've been weakening the left side for weeks now."

"I've been distracted."

Mark comes over and laughs. "Well, that happens when

you can't keep track of your dick, bro. One woman at a time."

Adam sets the weights down beside his bench. "Screw off, Mark. You don't know what the hell you're talking about!"

"Dude, you did confess this morning that you were screwing around on her," I point out. "But I get it. She's a total bitch, if you ask me."

He nods and looks over at Mark, who is walking to the bench in the far corner of the room. "Well I've got needs, and she wanted to save herself for marriage or something," Adam says.

"Wait. You're telling me she's saving herself until marriage? I thought after a year you guys were already, you know." Why am I asking him about this? Why the hell do I even care? Something is seriously wrong with me. But I could have sworn those two hooked up at one of the parties I was at.

Adam shakes his head. "Don't tell the others though. I don't want it spreading that I couldn't go around all the bases with her."

I nod, grab the weights I need, and head back toward Jared.

"Dude. You know Adam never even hooked up with Layla?"

Jared rolls his eyes. "Why do you care?"

"I don't. I'm just saying that's probably why she's a super prude."

"Bro, shut up. You're starting to sound like an asshole."

I laugh. "Just calling it like it is."

"Yeah, well. I'm ready to lift whenever you're done *calling it like it is*."

He places weights on one side of the bar and I set mine on the other. He settles on the bench and we take turns doing reps. We have to do three sets of ten. Then we switch and head to the next station, which is called Peck Deck.

Mark and Austin pass us with a nod. I don't know how Jared can keep his cool the way he does. He's a better person than me, that's for sure. Because if Mark was going after someone I liked, you better believe his ass would've been thrown into a wall.

"Maysville is getting a beat down this Friday," I say.

Jared takes a deep breath and says, "Yep."

"Dude, you better focus or your dad is going to be riding you like a cowboy does a bull."

He stops shooting glares at Mark while clenching his teeth together. "I want to hit him in the face. What he's doing is straight-up bullshit!"

"I agree. But dude, come on. In all fairness, you did have a billion chances to make a move."

"No, I really didn't. And you know it."

I shake my head. "Look man, all I'm saying is you need to put it behind you for now. Find a distraction."

"I'm not using a girl to forget about Juliet."

"Well, you should probably think about it."

He stops and gets off of the machine. "Maybe."

We switch positions and I start my reps. This continues until it's time to change and head to the football field for practice.

A whistle blows loudly. "Again!" Coach Black screams.

Sweat is dripping off me and running into my eyes. I want to rip off my helmet and wipe it away but there isn't time. I get into my spot and glance over at Jared as he settles behind the center. He signals off the count. When Dan, our center, snaps the ball, I take off down the right-hand side of the field. I continue full speed on my route and then dart over to the left when I reach the twenty-yard marker. I'm almost lined with the center of the goal post when the ball is fired at me. I catch the ball with ease and sprint into the end zone.

Coach is not thrilled though; he throws down his clipboard and screams, "No!" He sets off across the field, heading directly to Jared. "You practically waited until he stopped! He's supposed to get the ball right as he gets there. That means you fire before, not after!"

I don't hear Jared's response but I bet it's nothing but, "Yes, sir." Jared has never mouthed back. Not like the rest of us. And yeah, we had to run like you wouldn't believe. Then after the running were the push-ups because Coach Black doesn't tolerate backtalk. If you talk back and don't do the punishment he dishes out then you can take a walk off the field.

One time some cocky kid named Garth tested Coach, said something ridiculous like he was going to sue the school for abuse. Coach is still here, but Garth had to transfer. He plays for Anchor Shore, a fancy prep school we play at the end of the season.

As Jared is getting laid into by his old man, I take this moment to wipe the sweat from my face. The team's water boy sprints out to us, and a few of the defensive guys take some waters.

Mark walks over to me and says, "Juliet said she's coming to the game."

"Fantastic. Is she coming dressed as a wizard?"

"What? Why would she dress like a wizard?"

I place my helmet back on my head. "Because her bitchy sister said she likes to dress up like one." I look over at Jared then back at Mark. "Why are you even doing this shit man?"

"I told you; I like her."

"Really? What do you even know about her?"

"She's hot. Drives a Jeep. So that's cool. She's like in all the smart classes. She's best friends with Chase Bromwell and Adaline Frost."

I shake my head. "Real freaking deep, man. I could have told you that shit. What did you talk about with her? For real, because I'm trying to wrap my head around this."

"What is your problem, Tyler? I know she likes to read, and she likes art, and she's really cool. Why does it matter?"

I shove him. "Jared knows more things about her than that. I bet if you asked him what kind of books she reads he could tell you. Jared's right; you're just trying to get with her to piss him off. You don't *really* like her. Just lay off, man."

"You're wrong. I do like her." He shoves me back. "We talk mostly about the things I like, not what she does. She likes it. She'd tell me if she didn't." He shoves me harder. "Mind your business."

Someone grips my arm then yanks me back. I turn and see Coach breathing hard, ready to lay into me. "What the hell are you two doing?"

"I was just … "

"Not a damn thing. Now run the route again. No stopping this time, Richardson!"

"Yes, Coach."

He quickly releases me, and I hurry back to my position. Jared waits until Mark is on his side then he counts it down. As the ball is snapped, I take off and this time, there is no stopping. I get there right as the ball does. I reach out, catch it, and hurry into the end zone.

Coach starts clapping. "That's what I want to see. Do it again."

We ran the play three more times before we were finally dismissed to the showers.

# Chapter Eleven

*Layla*

After practice, I drive around for a bit. I should probably get back to the house so I can start homework. God, knows it's going to take me practically all night to get it done. But I also need to think.

I pull into a parking space and get out of the car. Walking over to the nearest park bench facing the lake, I sigh and take a seat. The sun is low in the sky. It'll be dark soon.

I take out my phone and stare at the screen. I don't know why, but I'm curious about how R's day went.

```
Me: Hey
R: sup
Me: I was just wondering how your day went?
R: Oh, u've been thinkin bout me? It went ok. Practice was a bitch. Almost punched my friend.
```

```
Me: Wow. Why?
R: I just don't like what he's doin'.
I mean he knew our other friend wanted
this grl yet he's being a total shit
stain n sayin he likes her now 2. So,
he's making a move.
Me: Ok. Why did you want to hit him
tho? Do you like the girl?
```

I don't know why but this makes me uncomfortable. I'm not sure I really want him to answer this question.

```
R: Nope. I think if she's like her sis
well, hell will freeze over be4 I would
ever b in2 that.
Me: Whoa. That's way harsh. Is her
sister not pretty or something?
R: She's gorgeous but she's also a
total bitch.
Me: Oh. That's not good.
R: Yep. Well, I gotta get this homework
done. I'll talk 2 u 18r.
Me: Okay. Night.
R: Night.
```

I head back to my car and drive home.

As I enter the house about ten minutes later I notice my mom being all cheery in the kitchen. "Um. Hey."

"Hi honey. How was practice?"

"It was good. What's got you in this little mood?"

"Oh," she leans in and whispers, "a cute boy showed up for your sister. He's out in the living room. I think she might get her first boyfriend. Isn't that great?"

I raise a brow then walk into the living room. On the couch are my sister and Mark Whalen. Whoa. What the hell is happening? I snatch my phone and immediately call Rachel, right as Mark says to my sister, "Yeah, sometimes we have to run the same routes like ten times before Coach lets us shower."

"Oh," Juliet says, and then she reaches into a bowl on the table and brings some chips to her mouth.

"What up, Girl?" a voice booms, pulling my attention away from my sister and to my phone.

"Rach. You will not believe this. Mark Whalen is sitting on my couch with my sister."

"No way! Take a pic and send 'cause I don't believe you."

I snap a pic and send.

"Holy crap! I thought you were messing with me. Did he ram his head into the goal post recently?"

"Rachel," I groan. "That's my sister."

"Your very nerdy sister, I might add," she says. "Is he using her for tutoring or something?"

"I don't know. My mom was all weirdly happy about it."

"Of course, isn't that part of her job. Match making? She's probably planning out their whole future together."

"Rach, that's silly. She ..." I am about to say, 'she would not,' but my mom was way too chipper when I walked into the house. She didn't even grill me about where I was.

"I'm right, huh?"

I frown. "Maybe. I gotta get off and tackle this homework."

She sighs. "Ugh. Yeah, same here."
"Okay. Talk tomorrow."
"Yep."
We hang up, and I head to my room.

The next day, I hurry to my locker and start collecting my books. Right as I shut my locker and turn around, Adam pops into my path.

"We really need to talk."

"Why?"

He smiles and that dimple dents his one cheek, the same that caused my heart to flutter when we first met. A week ago, I would have been a puddle. Today, it just irritates me.

"Babe, look. Me and you, we're good together, right? We're like ... peas and carrots."

"Did you just quote *Forrest Gump* at me? Seriously, Adam; I can't do this right now."

"Because you found someone else?" He drops to his knees and hands me a rose he had been hiding behind his back. "Please."

"Adam, get up. You're embarrassing me."

He looks around at the people staring. Some have literally stopped what they were doing to gawk at us. I can feel my cheeks burning. What is wrong with him? There are plenty of girls to choose from, girls dying to be with him. Why doesn't he bother one of them? Or all of them?

Adam rises and tries to give me the rose again. I step back. "You need to leave me alone."

"I love you, babe."

"No, you don't. If you loved me, you wouldn't have cheated on me. If you loved me so much, you would have just respected me enough to wait for me to be ready."

"Stop being like this. You know you want me, Layla."

My phone buzzes in my back pocket. Adam keeps trying to close the space between us. My hands are clammy, and I just want him to leave me alone. I take a deep breath, grab my phone, and walk away while texting R back.

Adam follows. "Who are you talking to?"

> R: mornin u.
> Me: Mornin life saver.
> R: Is that so? I don't think I've been called 1 of those b4. I like it Y am I a life saver tho?
> Me: Currently being stalked.
> R: I don't EVER say this but boot him in the balls. He'll leave u alone. Most guys will.
> Me: I'm in school.
> R: So? He's making u uncomfortable. He'll get the point loud n clear.

"Who the hell are you talking to, Layla?" Adam says in a loud enough voice that everyone hears.

I turn around, and as soon as he starts to reach for my

phone, I blast him in the junk with my foot. "I told you to leave me alone, you lying, cheating asshat!"

He groans and drops to the floor, curling into a ball. "Llllaylaaaaa."

I whip around and spot Tyler coming up the hall, his phone in hand with his buddies surrounding him. Someone shouts, "Man down!"

I glance at my phone and smile as I walk past the group. Tyler, says nothing, which is a first. He always has some wise crack ready to spill from his lips. He glances down at his phone then back up at me.

I roll my eyes and head down the hall to class while texting R.

>     Me: I really don't get some ppl.
>     R: Me either.
>     Me: :-) What's your first class?
>     R: American Lit.
>     Me: Uck. I hate English.
>     R: It's pretty boring.
>     Me: That's not why I hate it.
>     R: I know. It still sucks even without the learning disorder to mess u all up.
>     Me: My sister doesn't think so.
>     R: ur sister sounds just like my friend.
>     Me: She's pretty awesome. I gotta put my phone away.
>     R: K have a good day.
>     Me: u 2.

I don't know why but I'm grinning and can't seem to stop. I slip my phone into my backpack and then pull out my books. Rachel throws an elbow into my side while we wait for our Biology 2 teacher.

"Someone put you in a good mood," she giggles.

I feel my smile widening and my cheeks flush. "It's nothing, really."

"Is it the mystery man?"

I laugh. "Is that what you're calling him?"

"Yep."

"Well, in that case, maybe."

"Why won't you tell me who it is?"

I shake my head. I can't tell her initials. I also can't tell her I don't know because we agreed to no personal stuff. "I can't."

"Really?" she folds her arms and glares at me. "You really aren't going to tell me?"

"Not yet." I chew on my lower lip, hoping this will be enough.

She rolls her eyes. "Fine. Keep it to yourself."

"It's not … "

She throws a hand in my face. "Don't. It's whatever." Then she faces the front and ignores me for the rest of class.

# Chapter Twelve

*Tyler*

Between periods, I can't help the nagging sensation that I'm actually texting Layla Valentine. That alone should make me stop responding to her messages but I can't. It's also strange when I reach one of classes I'm bummed I have to slip my phone back into my bag. If it is Layla, I admit her texts definitely brings entertainment to my boring days here at school.

As I head to lunch, my thumbs press the letters on the screen. "Dude, who do you keep talking to?" Austin asks as we make our way to the cafeteria.

"Texting. Not really talking. Why do you care?"

"Whoa. What's up with the hostility? It was a simple question, bro."

I shake my head. Austin is cool but he's a total gossip. "Rachel wants me to sit with her today. Tell the guys," he says.

I laugh. "Pretty sure they'll know since her table is two down from ours."

He flips me off and heads to the lunch line. A hand slaps down on my right shoulder and I look up to see Jared peering over my shoulder. "Still milfing on that cougar?"

"She's sixteen." I don't want to tell him who I actually think I'm texting.

"Did you get a picture confirmation on that?"

"Nah. We're not doing personals."

"Your idea or hers?"

I make a face. "Mine. I don't need another stalker like Penny." Plus, if this is Layla, God only knows how she'd react if she found out she was texting me.

"Yeah. I forgot about her. Good thinking. But you do know you can find anyone you want on the Internet? You don't really need her name, just a number."

I feel my jaw drop. Jared smiles. "Dude, relax. Pretty sure if she hasn't shown up at your house yet, odds are she doesn't know or care about where you live. So, whatever happened to Penny, the nightmare?"

"She moved to the West Coast, thank the lord. I didn't even kiss her. Can you imagine how much worse it would have been if I had?" Just thinking about it gives me the shivers. Penny was what I like to call a jersey-chaser. If you were being scouted by colleges and she caught wind of it, she was on your doorstep.

She brought me homemade cookies every day. I brought the first batch into the locker room with me and some of the guys asked me who the cookies were from. Because cookies in a locker room will bring a crowd. As soon as I said, "From some girl named Penny," they all backed away and told me to toss them. Quickly.

I thought that was the stupidest thing ever. No one tosses cookies unless there was some illegal substance in them and you had to take a drug test. Which in my case would have sucked since we get random drug screenings. I lifted a chocolate chip cookie to my mouth and this big ass linebacker named Brad Johnson smacked that cookie out of my hand and tossed the rest in the trash.

Then it was like a campfire intervention or some shit. They all told me horror stories about Penny. They warned me never to engage. Never even to wave at her. She'd go away in a few weeks.

But she didn't go away. Apparently, Penny loved being ignored. She showed up everywhere I was. The mall. The country club. The lake. She even showed up at my family reunion. She told my mom we were dating.

My mom was a few sheets to the wind, and thought Penny was cute. I hopped on my bike and went to Jared's house. I was lucky he was home.

Later that night, I returned to my room and realized my favorite shirt was missing from my room. Yeah, that crazy chick was in my room. But before things really got out of hand, her dad got a job offer and she had to move. Worst three months of my life.

My phone buzzes in my hand but I ignore it for a second. "So, who did you look up?"

Jared pales. "I plead the fifth."

"For real? You got her number and searched Juliet up like a creepy stalker? That's just sad as hell man."

Jared and I get into the lunch line and he groans. "I don't have her number. I, uh …"

"Dude, her mom's from the billboards around town. Just go talk to her."

He shoves me. "Shut up. You know what I'm going through. I can't just ... never mind."

I glance down at my phone and read "Faye's" text.

```
Faye: My ex made his English paper
about me.
```

Wow, Adam really is such a douche. I don't type that though.

```
Me: Awkward.
Faye: Horrible. He basically called us
Romeo n Juliet.
Me: Uh wow. They died.
```

Biggest toolbag ever. I mean writing papers about them, referring to Romeo and Juliet of all things is just bad.

```
Faye: Yeah. My sis loves that crap.
Not me. I don't want 2 b compared 2 some1
else. Real or not.
Me: I feel ya.
```

Jared makes a noise and I lift my gaze from my screen. "What?"

"Well, I know you guys aren't doing personals, but I'm curious why even talk to her?"

"I don't know. I like talking to her. Why not?"

"Well if it's not going anywhere, why bother?"

I get what he's saying because it's basically true. If I tell "Faye" hey, by the way I'm Tyler Richardson pretty sure she won't speak to me again. "Who says it has to go somewhere? Maybe I just like talking to her because she doesn't know who I am. She isn't talking to me because she needs my dad to give her a letter or recommendation or to see if my sister will use her as model for her next book cover. It's kind of nice just being no one."

He shrugs. "Okay. As long as you know what you're doing. Seems to me you're getting in pretty deep. That's all."

"It's only been a few days."

My phone vibrates against my palm. Jared raises a brow as we put pizza and fries on our trays. "Right."

I roll my eyes.

♥

A football sails through the air and right to Mark. He catches the pass and then our defense snatches him up before he reaches the thirty-yard line. Coach Black blows the whistle and yells at us to come in.

As I run toward the huge group of guys forming a large circle, out of the corner of my eye I catch a glimpse of a girl being tossed into the air. She twists and then comes crashing down into a body of girls positioned underneath of her. Off to my left, I see Adam take off his helmet and stare at the cheerleaders too.

"Richardson! Kent! Do you two want to join the cheer squad, or are you a part of this team?"

"This team," I say.

Adam mumbles, "This team."

"Good! You can talk to them later. We've got a game to prepare for and unless one of those girls has a secret play to distract the whole defensive line so you can run into the end zone each time, I suggest your attention be on me and not them!"

Jared lightly shakes his head. He knows me too well and it stops me from responding with, "Well, now that you mention it, Coach, how about we get the girls to flash their fine assets. I'm pretty sure the whole stadium will be distracted and we could easily walk right into the end zone each time." But Jared's dad would blow a gasket and probably kick my ass. And just as I start to set my focus on Coach, I notice Jared straighten.

I want to glance over my shoulder to see what has him looking all serious. Then I see Mark, who's standing next to him, beam and wave. I give them both a look but a hand comes down on Mark's helmet and he instantly drops his smile. "Uh sorry, Coach," he mumbles.

"You guys aren't focused. Give me four laps around the field. Helmets on," he yells at all of us.

Some of the players mutter curses. Some say, "Yes, sir." As for me, I sigh and set off running.

# Chapter Thirteen

*Layla*

After practice, I notice my sister coming down from the stands. "Hey, what are you doing here?"

"I … um … I was invited."

I smile at her. "Yeah? By who?"

Her cheeks turn cherry red. "Mark."

I cast a glance at the boys running laps. "Good for you. Are you hanging here for a bit, or are you heading back to the house?"

Adaline comes up behind her, a deep scowl set on her face. "Please, Juliet, can we leave this hell hole? He waved at you like three times and he helped earn the team laps."

"Knock it off, Addy. God, why are you constantly ragging on him?" my sister snaps.

Adaline looks down at her shoes then sighs. "He's not a good person, Juliet. He'll hurt you."

"How do you know that? He doesn't have a rep like most of the guys on the team," my sister says. She looks back at me. "Right?"

"I haven't heard anything."

Adaline glares at me. "You know what, Juliet? I didn't want to do this, but if you date him, do not bring him to our lunch table. Do not even try to ask if I want to go hang out with you two for a double date or something. I refuse to take part in this." Then she plows past me.

My sister stares off at her friend with her mouth hanging open.

"What's up with her?" Rachel asks as she sidles up next to me but motions toward my sister.

"Nothing," I say.

Rachel glances over at me. "Are you giving me a ride today?"

"Yeah." I hand her my keys. "You can listen to the radio, I'll be there in a minute."

"Yep." She skips off.

Juliet glowers. "I still can't believe you're friends with her."

I can't believe it some days either but Rachel has always been there in my corner. "Hey, don't judge. I don't get on you about *your* choice of friends."

"What's wrong with Addy and Chase?"

We start walking to the parking lot. "Chase is one of three things: First, he's really super into Addy and stays near you so he can hide his feelings. Second, he's gay and trying not to let on. Third, he's super in love with you but won't risk telling you so he settles for friendship."

"He's not gay, Layla! Even if he is, who cares?"

"I didn't say it was a bad thing, Juliet."

"He isn't in love with me, either."

That leaves the other scenario. But Juliet doesn't comment

on it and I don't bring it up. We reach my car. Rachel already has the windows down and the music blasting. Juliet narrows her eyes. "Really? You let her listen to that bubbly pop crap?"

"What's wrong with this song?" Rachel yells over the boys singing about love and wanting a girl to stay.

"Their voices are terrible," Juliet says loudly.

Okay. My sister did have a point. They were awful sounding.

"Hey, Juliet? Listen to this," Rachel says, and she flips my sister off.

Juliet snorts. "Real classy."

"Are we ready to blow this popsicle stand?" Rachel asks.

"Yeah." I look back at my sister, who is retreating to her Jeep. "See you at home."

"Um ... Yeah. I have to stop at the library for something. Tell Mom, will you?"

I nod and slide into my front seat. I turn the radio down a few notches and Rachel smacks my hand. "What?"

"That's a great song," she protests.

"No, it kind of sucks."

"Hater." She sticks out her tongue. "Wanna hit the mall?"

"Can't." I pull out of the parking spot just as some dumb silver SUV blocks my path. I blow my horn at Tyler Richardson.

"Wow! Hating on a lot of people today I see. What did Tyler Richardson do to you now?" she asks.

I tighten my grip on the steering wheel. "Existed. He's the one who said I couldn't drive."

"Well. In truth, you do kind of suck. I mean you've taken out how many trash cans? And remember that parked car in the mall?"

In all fairness, my view was blocked by these boxes of crap my mom put in my backseat. Yes, I was supposed to take them out before I went to the mall but there was a huge sale that had a special time when it started and ended. When we were leaving, it was really dark and I may have tapped a bumper pulling out of my parking space. "Hey! We swore never to mention that again." I shoot her a look of disapproval.

"Right. I'm just saying maybe you might want to go a little easier on him. You're the one who almost creamed him in the parking lot at school. You did totally slapshot his phone out of his hand. No offense Lay, but you've been kind of a B to the boy."

"He's not innocent. How would you like to be called *Princess* all the time? The way he says it makes me want to backhand him. Remember when he put a toad in my lunch box?"

Rachel giggles. "That was in first grade. You need to calm down."

I roll my eyes. She thinks Tyler is cute and can do no wrong. I, on the other hand, disagree.

His window lowers. I honk at him again, and he sticks his head out and blows me a kiss. Then he proceeds to sit in my freaking way. "Oh. My. God. I'm going to maim his precious Grand Cherokee!"

"Breathe, Layla," Rachel warns.

As if the whole universe is against me today, Adam comes strolling up with a blond sophomore named Selena in tow. "Whoa. What the hell is that?" Rachel snaps.

Tyler doesn't move, so I'm stuck watching Adam make

out with Selena right in front of my car. "You've *got* to be kidding me."

Rachel reaches over and blares my horn, then she pops her head out of the passenger side and shouts, "He has *STDs!*"

I cast a look at Rachel. "Why would you say that? Now people are going to think I have diseases!"

"Shit. Sorry. It was a knee-jerk reaction."

The sophomore jumps away from Adam. They both look over at Rachel and me. Adam's the first to mouth "What the hell?" Selena crinkles her nose and sneers at Rachel, then me.

"Oh, Thot is *so* getting kicked off the squad," Rachel says.

I press my forehead to my steering wheel. "I just want to go home."

"Tyler finally moved. Looks like he was waiting on Jared and Austin."

I lift my head, and sure enough Tyler is finally pulling away. What a jerk!

# Chapter Fourteen

*Tyler*

Did I want to block Layla in? Not really. I only meant to tease her a bit while I waited for Jared to hop in. Then Adam had to spoil it by making out with some hot sophomore in front of her which makes me feel like freaking dirt.

Austin's in the back snapping off play-by-plays like I couldn't see what was going down perfectly fine in my rearview mirror. Of course, when Jared got in, he smacked Austin and me. "Dude, come on. Stop being a total asswipe."

When I leave the lot, Austin says, "All right, I'm calling it. I think Adam will somehow win Layla back by winter formal."

Jared snaps, "Are you high? He's not getting her back. He totally just had Selena Jenson nailed up against her freaking car."

"Yeah, to get Layla jealous," Austin defends.

Austin is my boy but sometimes he can be a little dense.

Even though I may be wrong that Layla isn't Faye, I've gotta agree with Jared on this one. "Dude, he's never getting a shot with her again. I bet any money his car is going to be keyed and tires slashed by tomorrow morning."

"Fine. Think I have a shot?" Austin asks.

"Aren't you hooking up with Rachel?" I say.

He shrugs. "She's been avoiding me. I think that ship has sailed."

"No. I'm pretty sure girl code is a whole shitload stricter than guy code," Jared states.

"Nuh uh. Really?" Austin says.

"Uh yeah, bro. They won't even go near a cousin's ex or something bat-shit crazy like that." He may be right. I overheard my sister calling some girl a wran for taking someone's cousin's ex to something. I just assume that was girl code meaning don't date anyone's exes. Cousins, sisters, friends, friend's cousins. Whatever.

While I turn onto Brand Boulevard, a gigantic billboard plasters my view. "Looking for love? Call Angela Valentine at 4VALENTINE."

"Jesus. That woman is everywhere," I complain.

Austin smacks my right arm. "Almost like your family name."

"Hardy-har-har. You're so freaking funny." Honestly though, he has a point. Half of this town is run by my family including a dentist office, law firm, jewelry store, and three car dealerships. Yeah. My family kind of runs Riverside.

I pull up to Austin's house first. He eases out of the back seat.

"Thanks for the lift. See you tomorrow."

"Yep."

As we pull away, Jared laughs. "Sometimes I have no idea what he's thinking."

"Oh, you mean the stunt where he's thinking about asking Layla Valentine out? That's hilarious."

"Yeah. He didn't think that through."

"Pretty sure Austin only thinks with his dick. And those choices are very questionable."

Jared nods. "Dude, do you have to be home right now?"

"Nah. What are you thinking?"

"I want to get some fast food. Mom is trying out these healthy dinners and last night I swear to God she fed me dirt."

I bust out laughing. "No wonder why your dad was so pissed off at practice."

"I think my dad is just naturally a bastard."

I nod. "What are you thinking? Shakin' Shack, Moe's Burgers, or Blue?"

"Burgers. They've got good shakes too."

"Yeah they do. All right. Moe's, here we come."

♥

The last person I ever thought I'd see at Moe's is Layla. She does not exactly scream, "I'll totally eat alone and mack down a huge, fat, greasy burger." But there she was, sitting in the back by herself, near the jukebox.

"Hello, boys; just the two of you?" a girl probably in her early twenties asks as she rollerblades toward us. Moe's is like a fifties diner. The wait staff wears rollerblades vinyl records decorate the walls.

"Yes, just the two of us," I answer.

She leads us to a table not far from where Layla is sitting. She is currently scowling at something in her notebook then she erases, squints at, then scribbles something else down.

"What are you about to do?" Jared asks as he hands me a menu.

"Nothing. Why?"

He raises a brow. "I know you. Haven't you pissed that girl off enough today?"

"Please. People like Layla need someone in their life ruffling their feathers. Otherwise they'll think everyone worships them, and they can't do any wrong."

He shakes his head. "I have no idea how you come up with this shit."

I march over to Layla and plop right down in her booth. She looks away from her homework and up at me. "Someone must really hate me."

"What do you mean?" I smirk.

She glares at me. "What do you want, Tyler? I'm busy."

"I can see that. What's the matter don't like math?"

Her face instantly turns red. "Leave me alone."

"Not so fast." I glance down at her paper and shake my head. Everything on it looks jumbled and, well, like a toddler wrote it. Maybe she isn't the girl I thought she was.

"Wow, you have some shitty handwriting, Valentine."

She snatches all her papers up, and slaps them in her

book. "Go away, Tyler."

"In a minute." I clear my throat. "I just wanted to say I'm sorry for pulling a dick move on you and holding you up so you had to catch Adam moving on."

She narrows her eyes. "Are you finished?"

"Yeah." A woman sets down Layla's plate of fries and a big monster burger.

I swipe a fry from her plate and pop it into my mouth. The woman with the nametag Henrietta says, "Oh, I'm sorry, hon; did you need something?"

"No!" Layla screams, and I say calmly, "Nope."

"He's not staying," she says.

"Oh, okay. Well, did you need anything else, dear?" Henrietta asks.

Layla shakes her head. "Thanks."

The woman takes off and I stand. "Wow, Valentine, I'm actually impressed."

"About what?"

"You actually have some manners. Who knew?"

She scowls deeply again, and I chuckle as I make my way back to Jared.

"I swear you mess with her because you like her," Jared says.

I laugh. "Please. Dating her would be like dating a viper."

"Then why don't you just ignore her?"

I smile. "Because I find great joy in pissing her off every day." I glance at her again, watching her type into her phone. Suddenly my phone buzzes.

```
Faye: Have you ever had a day where
```

> absolutely everything went wrong?

Gotcha. Now what to do? Play this out a little longer or just ignore her text? I must be losing my mind.

> Me: Yeah. That's my life mostly from 6 to 10 every day.
> Faye: Well, looks like I'm joining the club today.
> Me: That sucks.

"Hello, I'm Margret. What can I get you two today?"

I order a milkshake and a cowboy big burger. Jared asks for a shake, and a breakfast bacon burger.

"Who are you texting?" Jared asks.

"Faye. She's actually kind of cool." Which texting version Layla is kind of cool.

Jared shakes his head. "I'm telling you, this whole weird thing you have going on is just going to blow up in your face."

He's probably right. "No, it isn't. It's not like I'm asking her to marry and run away with me, numb nuts. I'm just saying she's pretty cool through text."

"Whatever. I still think it's a mistake."

I slump back against the booth. It's just texting. I'm not going to fall for Layla Valentine. Right? Anyway, what the heck would Jared even know? He's just sulking because the girl he wants just waltzed in with Mark. Ah, shit.

# Chapter Fifteen

*Layla*

This day is a whole lot of suck right now. I'm trying to enjoy a big juicy burger because this is what I do when my days are crappy. I order a greasy burger with delicious bacon, melty cheese, fried onions, and all the most awesome fixings and stuff myself. Top it off with a chocolate shake and some fries, and my frown turns upside down. So to speak.

But of course, someone has to ruin even that! Stupid Tyler. What does he even want? Telling me my handwriting sucks and all that. Excuse me, I didn't know we had to be perfect. At least there is one guy who doesn't want to make me feel a thousand times worse.

Even that is sort of ridiculous. For all I know I could be talking to some twelve-year-old pretending to be my age. Or some thirty-year-old. Oh, God.

I pick up my burger and take a huge bite. The usual bursting-with-flavor taste is so bland and blah in my mouth. What's happening to me?

The diner door swings open and my sister walks in holding Mark's hand. Oh my God, she lied to me. That little sneaky brat lied to me. She said she had to do something at the library. I get out of my booth and march right over to her.

"You are such a liar," I say.

Juliet turns, and her eyes are the size of saucers. She drops Mark's hand and swallows. "He, um ... He didn't have a ride."

"You know what Jul, I don't know what shocks me more. You trying to hide the fact you've got a boyfriend, or you lying to me."

She excuses herself with Mark, and pulls me away from him and the waitress. I snicker as she manhandles me around the diner. As soon as we're closer to my booth she releases my arm with a huff. "Listen. It's not like that at all. This is new, and Addy is super mad at me. I just ... I just want to have what you guys have all had. Once. You know?"

"I get it. I'm not Addy, though. You could have told me. I'm happy for you. Seriously."

She frowns. "I just didn't want to rub it in your face. Because of he-who-shall-not-be-named."

"Jul. You really need to quit with the *Harry Potter* references."

She glowers at me. "That wasn't. That's you-know-who. Whatever." She glances over at my table. "Are you here by yourself?"

"Yes."

"Do you want to be? I can sit with you. I think I saw Jared and Tyler here. Mark can hang out with them."

"No. Go. I'm fine. Really. I'm done here anyway."

She folds her arms. "Really? Looks like you barely touched

your food."

"I'm fine."

She sighs. "All right, if you say so."

Mark keeps glancing back at Juliet and I hug her quickly. "Your date is getting antsy."

She looks back at Mark and then smiles at me. "I'll be home later. We can talk if you want."

I love my sister, but I'm not up for sharing my crummy day. Especially when she looks so happy.

In my room, I pore over my math homework while listening to some techno mesh-ups between hard rock and some new pop songs.

My phone vibrates next to my book. I pick it up and instantly smile.

```
R: Hey u. Miss me?
Me: Oh yeah. But I've got to get this math done.
R: Yeah. That's my best subject. Need some help?
Me: It's not the implications that's hard its figuring out what the numbers are. And making sure my brain isn't mixing them up.
```

```
R: I'm sorry. Maybe u can screen shot
the problems. I can tell u what they say.
Me: Okay.
```

I move all things that may have my real name on it and then hold my phone steady. I snap a few pictures and send him some screen shots.

It takes him a little bit to reply. Maybe I shouldn't have sent that. Did we just get way too personal? Crap. It wasn't like he got a glimpse of my legs.

I chew on the end of my pen cap as I wait for him to reply. What if he thinks I'm really stupid? He'll know just by looking at the problems I'm only in Algebra.

My phone vibrates.

```
R: R u doing all the problems on the
page?
Me: Yes.
R: Cool. I'll type them out 4 u. Ask
if u want me 2 clarify what I send.
Me: Okay.
```

R texts me the first set of problems and with my voice app it reads it off perfectly as if someone like my sister was reading it to me. I feel awful and quite stupid. He probably thinks I'm the world's biggest airhead ever.

```
R: Ready 4 the next 1?
Me: Yes, please. And thanks. I'm sorry
for sounding like an idiot.
```

R: Hey now. U aren't an idiot. I'm not dyslexic but I googled what it's like 4 a person 2 have it. I'm sry.

Me: Thanks. Most people just think I'm stupid.

R: Those ppl r jerks.

"R" continues to patiently type out each problem to me. It's honestly the sweetest thing anyone has ever done for me. It makes me swoon, and it also makes me a little sad. I kind of wish I knew a little more about him. Then I'm kind of glad he doesn't know more about me. Especially since lately I've been feeling like a complete loser.

R: Well, I should let u get 2 solving. Have a good night.

Me: You too. Thanks again.

# Chapter Sixteen

*Tyler*

**Me: Ever get so excited about something that every fiber inside u is electric?**

Shit. I probably shouldn't have sent that. She'll probably think I'm half mad or a total dipshit. Hell, she probably read the message and is now thinking, "Wow good call on the no personal stuff."

My phone jiggles in my palm and a smile breaks across my face. Then it falls as soon as I see it's not her.

```
Jared: You've got to keep me from killing him.
Me: Dude. Go over 2 Juliet n tell her u're in love with her then make a move.
Jared: I can't, okay? I can't do that yet. But so help me I'm gonna smash his face in.
```

Me: U need 2 calm down. He's not even worth it. I know we're all friends. He's goin 2 move on soon enough. Let it play out.

Jared: I don't want it to play out anymore.

Right as I'm texting him back another message comes.

Faye: Yes. I get like that when I finish a routine. One that took weeks to get down.

Me: A routine? What do u do that has routines?

I already know, but I need proof.

Faye: Cheer.

Me: Hmm I'd like 2 see that. Since I don't know what u look like though I'll have 2 pic it using the type of grls I like. Sry.

Jared: Dude I srsly need 2 get out of here. Just 4 10 mins.

Faye: What kind of girls would that be? Please don't say busty.

Me to Jared: On my way.

Me to Faye: Dark hair, green eyes, beautiful smile, smart, n full of life. If they have long legs I'm a total goner.

Shit! I probably shouldn't have said all that. Oh well. It's out there. It's not like she's ever going to figure out I'm the one texting her.

As I am heading toward the doors leading to the parking lot, I slam into someone. I reach out and right them quickly before they hit the ground. Her deep mossy-green eyes gaze up into mine then she scrunches her nose. "Ugh! Watch where you're going," Layla snaps.

"Where *I'm* going? You've got just as much blame here, sweetheart. I shouldn't have been checking my phone and walking, but what the hell is *your* excuse?" I know I sound like a real asshole right now, but this is not text Layla I'm talking to. It's the one who loathes my very existence for some reason. The one who always has to be a complete bitch to me.

"My excuse? I don't need one."

"Oh, right. I keep forgetting. The high and mighty Princess Layla is walking the halls; that means we should all part and let her pass."

"Go to hell, Tyler. You don't know shit about me." She shoves me and stomps down the hall.

I should stop texting her right now. I slip out the doors and head to my Jeep. Jared is seething next to it.

"You all right?"

"No. I'm not. Get me out of here before I murder my teammate."

I unlock the doors and hop in. "You know he's also your friend?"

"Right now, he's an asswipe who's pissing me the hell off. If he talks about how long it's going to take him to nail Juliet in the locker room ever again he will lose more than limbs,"

Jared snaps.

I definitely have to get him out of here before he changes his mind and murders our wide receiver.

♥

At the lake, we sit on one of the empty benches. I smack his arm. "You feeling any better? I kind of don't want to skip the rest of the day, man. We do have a game tonight. And I don't want to run laps before it either."

Jared sighs. "Why did he have to pick her? I mean … I'm trying to be cool with this. I am. Because he's not a total dick, and if she's happy then I'm happy. But why did he have to pick her?"

"To piss you off. Think about it. He's jealous. Always has been. Your dad's our coach. Where's his dad? Out of the picture. He's probably going to go to a third string college. We're going to be at the top division one schools. No doubts about that. I'm not defending his actions; don't for one second think I am. I'm just saying stand in his shoes."

"I know what you're saying, and I have. Every freaking day this week I've tried to look at this from his view. It's just … she's only thing that brightens my day. And now I have to watch my friend make her happy. The whole thing makes me want to hurt him."

"Still. He is your teammate and your friend. You've got to suck it up."

Jared growls and throws a stone into the lake. "You're right. Let's head back."

"You sure? You're good? No murdering tendencies in there?"

He laughs. "I'm good. Thanks Tyler."

"Anytime. Let's catch the bell before fifth starts." We hop back into my Jeep and I drive us back to school.

The rest of my day goes the same as usual. Nothing exciting, no drama. But most of all no Layla biting my head off for no reason.

# Chapter Seventeen

*Layla*

Out on the field, I toss my cheer bag and my book bag against the fence along with the rest of the girls' bags. We each decorate our eyes with little blue and gold stars in the outer corners. Rachel's shrill-fake laugh reaches me.

I quirk a brow as I stare at my friend acting ridiculous. "Tyler Richardson! That's who you want to score with tonight at the after party?" she bellows at Selena. Yes, the very same girl who was making out with Adam, practically humping him, on my car the other day.

Unbelievable. I can't stand Tyler. He's a jerkwad, but even I wouldn't wish this train wreck on him. Causally walking over to the silly girl, I say, "You can't have him. I hear he's taken."

"Who?" Rachel asks.

Selena blinks up at me. "Is he? He looks pretty single to me."

"Well, he's not. He's dating some girl from Fairview. Go

ask him if you don't believe me."

She smiles at me then walks over to her group of friends. Rachel shoves me. "What was that?"

"Nothing. I just ... Oh, come on. That one there is just working her way up a ladder."

"Yeah, and? She wants on Tyler's pole. Who cares?"

"She's only using him for popularity."

She puts her pom-poms on her hips. "So? It's Tyler. You hate him."

I cast my eyes down. "I know. I guess. I don't know." Okay. I can't admit this to anyone, but when I bumped into Tyler today he made me feel small. Unwanted. He also made me feel like I'm nothing but a total bitch. I'm not. If I could save him from a girl looking to boost her popularity, then okay. He can see I'm not as bad as he makes me out to be.

The stands begin filling up and Coach Mallard screams at us, "In line ladies. Shake your fear."

Ugh. I hate this cheer. It's the stupidest one we have. But we all get to make up one defensive cheer, one offensive, and one peppy one to get the crowds going. There are twelve of us on the squad, so we literally have thirty-six different cheers to choose from during the forty-eight minutes of each game.

"Get 'em up, Get 'em up, Tigers. Shake out your fear, and roar!"

Rachel makes her roar face, fangs out, mouth open and her nose wrinkled. I stifle a laugh as I shake my pom-poms to the left and right while going through another round of the cheer.

Once we're done I giggle. Rachel joins me and our coach gives us the stink eye. I glance back at the game, which is about to start. The guys are all lined up for kick-off. "Nick wants to hang out tonight," Rachel says.

"Aren't you with Austin?"

She shrugs. "I like Austin, but we're not serious."

"Did you talk to him about that?"

"Ladies!" Coach Mallard yells as she claps to get our attention. "Crush it."

Rachel nudges me with her elbow. I can't help smiling so big my mouth hurts at the corners. This is my cheer.

"Tigers, here we go. Here we go. Crush it like you want it more. Crush it, we need to score. Tigers crush it."

I spot my sister in the stands, wearing her "Want pie? 3.14 right here" shirt. She waves at me. I smile and wave a pom-pom at her. She looks so out of place.

"Wow, she even came to the game in her geek gear," Rachel says.

"Leave her alone. She's just being herself. If Mark doesn't like her geeky side then he can suck it!"

"Whoa. Chill. I'm just saying I'm surprised she didn't try to put in a little more effort. I mean he *is* Mark Whalan. He's not some librarian."

"Knock it off. I think it's cute. He likes her dorkiness."

Rach must see my mood, because she drops ragging on my sister and her choice of clothes.

We do another round of cheers.

We all seem to stop as the crowd erupts in cheers. I turn and watch Tyler pumping his legs, carrying the ball from the forty-yard line past the thirty-yard marker. He dodges a few guys from the backfield trying to tackle him. He spins around one and stiff arms another, and then bolts into the end zone.

I shake the blue and gold pom-poms in my hands and squeal out a "Wooo!" His eyes land on me and there is something in his gaze that makes me stop cheering for him.

He hands the ball off to the ref and pats his teammates who come running in to congratulate him.

"Good job, Tyler!" Selena shouts as he jogs past her.

He tips his head in her direction then runs to the sidelines. Wow, he's got a nice body. Too bad he's a jackass. And what was that look he gave me?

I'd like to say the rest of the game went differently. It didn't. Adam stood along the sidelines the entire game. He glared at me whenever our eyes locked. Mark kept throwing winks toward the stands when he caught something in the end zone. Jared looked like he was going to murder anyone who got in his way. And when Tyler would score he'd give me the coldest stare I've ever encountered.

By the time game was over I was exhausted, needed a shower, and did not want to go to anyone's house to drink or act stupid. Dragging myself and my bags out to my car, I check my phone. There are two unanswered messages waiting for me.

```
R: If ur team plays 2night, good luck.
R: We won. How did ur team do?
Me: We won.
R: Headin 2 any parties?
Me: No. Car, home, shower, and my bed.
R: That doesn't sound fun. I get it
though. Have a good night.
Me: You too.
```

"Layla! Where are you going?" Rachel asks.

"Home."

She makes an ugly face at me. "Seriously? Fine. I'll get a ride from one of the boys. Call me tomorrow."

I smile. "Okay." I tuck my phone into my bag then unlock my car. As I'm putting my bags into the backseat a shadow falls over me. I turn and squeak.

"Jesus! Adam! What the heck?"

"Take me back, Layla. Please. I'll do whatever you want. I miss you."

I shove him away. "You don't miss me! You certainly don't care. The only thing you're mad about is not getting my virginity! You're not getting it. I'm not going back out with you. And you can try to win me back with every pathetic, sleazy attempt you want but it won't work. You cheated on me. I'll never forget that. I'll never forget how you texted her the entire time we were on a date."

"Baby, please!" he reaches for me and I smack him.

"No! Don't call me Baby! That name is reserved for someone who gave a shit about me. It's meant to be an endearment from someone who adores me. The only person you adore is yourself!"

Adam starts to say something but a voice interrupts us. "Layla, you alright?" Jared asks.

"I'm good," I say with a smile. "Good game tonight."

He watches Adam for a bit. Tyler comes up next to him. I can't help but stare as his hand runs through his hair, pushing damp strands out of his eyes. "What's the ... Are you taking him back?" Tyler asks.

"Yes," Adam says while I growl, "No!"

# Chapter Eighteen

*Tyler*

Layla's face looks murderous.

She pushes Adam and he stumbles back a bit. He looks hurt but her words cut through the air like a knife. "You cheated on me! Get a clue. Never. Going. Out. With. You. Again! Done. So done!"

"Baby," he says. She gets into her car and slams the door shut. Adam is such a dipshit though, and tries to get her to roll down her window.

"Jared, looks like we're going to have to pick up dumbass here and take him away before Layla calls the cops."

"Shut up!" Adam yells at me. "She loves me."

"No, bro. I'm pretty sure you pissed her the hell off," I say.

Jared walks over and grips Adam by the back of his neck. "Let's go, man. Tyler here is heading to Melanie's house. I hear Selena is going to be there."

"I don't want Selena."

"If you start crying I'm going to personally punch you in

the nuts," I warn.

"She wouldn't let me claim her."

I take it back. He's about to get punched if he keeps talking like that. "What did you say, man?" I ask.

He shoves me and tries to wriggle free from Jared's grip. "You both heard me."

"Don't be a prick, Adam. Anyone can see you aren't ever winning her back. I don't care if you lick her shoes and shower her with rose petals," I say.

"Eff off, Tyler," Adam screams.

I reach my Jeep and Jared pushes Adam into the back. "He's right, man. You're such a dumbass."

"Whatever."

I shoot Jared a look. Why did we decide to help this idiot? We should have let Layla run over his foot or call the cops. Anything would have been better than listening to him sob.

We arrive at Melanie's in record time. We all pile out and head into the house. It's full of people already. As I pass the stairwell someone hands me a cold beer. I hand it off to Adam. "Drink up."

He doesn't argue; he just pops the top and walks off. I look around at the same shit that happens every weekend and I hit Jared's chest. "I'm not staying."

Jared grumbles as Rachel Little bounces over to us. "Hi Jared. Great game. You're amazing." She looks over at me and gives me a weird look. "Good job, Tyler."

"Yep."

I start to shift away but then Rachel snorts. "Oh lord. This cannot be happening."

I follow her stare and notice Mark and Juliet dancing.

Well, more like Mark trying to show Juliet how to grind and then her looking uncomfortable and as out of place as her t-shirt shirt in a house full of girls in skimpy clothes.

Jared looks over at Rachel and snaps, "What's wrong?"

"Look, my best friend might be that dork's twin but that doesn't give her the right to be here. She doesn't belong at all. Look at what she's wearing, for God's sake. That right there is a huge sign she'll never fit in."

Jared shrugs. "I think she looks pretty freaking hot. Personally, the whole I'm-totally-smart-and-don't-give-a-shit-what-people-think-about-me look really does it for me. Showing a ton of skin leaves very little for the imagination."

She gapes at him. "You're joking."

"He's really not," I say. "You ready to go?"

"Yep." Without another word to Rachel he stalks out the door and I follow.

My phone buzzes before I slip back into my Jeep.

```
Faye: I swear the universe is against me.
Me: Y is that?
Faye: Just jerks in general.
Me: Yeah. Hey. I'm bout 2 drive my friend home. Won't text 4 bout 20 mins. Wanted u 2 know I'm not ignoring u.
Faye: Wow that's really sweet. Drive safe. Talk to you soon.
Me: Talk 2 u then.
```

Jared groans. "You're not getting hung up, huh?"

"I'm not. I like talking to her though."

"Bullshit. When have you ever texted a person, let alone a girl, this much?"

I continue to drive with the music cranked up. Hopefully it will make Jared drop this interrogation. It doesn't. "Wow. You really are into her. How can you be into someone you've never met? You don't even know what she sounds or looks like. What do you really know about her?"

"Enough." I make a turn on Hobson Street. "I don't know what this is. All I know is I like texting her. So what?"

"I just don't get why you haven't stopped. You know it's not going anywhere."

"How do you know it's not going anywhere?" I can hear the harshness in my voice.

Jared grumbles. "You told me that you guys wouldn't get personal or whatever. Therefore, that means you won't meet her. What the hell is the point of texting someone you won't meet?"

"Why are you jumping all over me? This has nothing to do with me texting Faye. It's all about you trying to get Juliet to notice you. Well, I hate to break this shit to you, but she probably has noticed you. And as Rachel so eloquently pointed out, she's not exactly in the same class of people as we are. So that means she wouldn't have made a bold ass move even if she did like you. Mark saw that shit and swooped in." I probably shouldn't have let all that loose, but man, he's really pissing me off.

"Let me out here. I'm going to walk."

"Oh, don't be such a pansy. I'm taking you home."

He slaps the power button on the radio. "Whatever,

man. I'm trying to point out sooner or later this whole veiled relationship is going to blow up in your face."

"I know."

"What?"

"I know it's going to eventually end." I am not stupid. Soon one of us will start seeing someone. That thought right there bothers me more than I want to admit. Which is crazy because it's not like I can actually ask her out. In person Layla hates my freaking guts.

I pull up to his house. "Thanks for the ride. Sorry for being a prick."

"It's cool man. I'm sorry too. You'll get her soon."

"Maybe." He gets out and shuts the door.

♥

My phone has rested in my hand for about twenty minutes now. Maybe I should stop texting her. There's a knock on my door. My dad enters my room looking like he's already had one too many whiskeys. His blue eyes are the same as mine, only bloodshot and glazed over.

"How did you do?" he hiccups.

"Good. We won." He would know if he ever went to a game. I don't dare mention that. He's too busy. His absence gives me: my Jeep, the roof over my head, and every other luxury around here. I'm happy, I'm blessed. But would it be so terrible if he saw one game?

He bobs his head up and down. "Good. Good."

He rocks on his heels. His usually pressed suit is in disarray. His black tie is undone and falling away from the collar. "No parties?"

"There were a few. I just decided to stay in."

"Back in my day there was a party around every block. Me and my buddies went house to house. And the ladies? You couldn't keep them off of us. I had one every night." He laughs as if recalling this shit is somehow funny. "Bet you know what I mean. Don't get serious or tied down until you're thirty-five."

Yep. This is the type of crap my dad slurs at me. He brags about his past and then tells me to be a player for a long time. He also tells his office buddies how great I am at football, how I'm going places. Yet he doesn't really know; he's never watched a single game.

Mom used to come when I was younger but she stopped around eighth grade. If I do make it big, guess who's getting thanked? My friends, coaches, and maybe my girlfriend, if I get one of those. It certainly won't be my shitty parents.

He makes his way to the door. "Well, we have a charity event tomorrow. Some damn thing your mom is making us do. Starts at noon."

"I know." It's for underprivileged children, but of course he can't remember that.

He steps out of my room and I text Faye.

```
Me: I hate my family.
Faye: I'm sorry. I can't complain too
much about mine.
```

Me: Mine r entitled dickwads! My dad is always busy taking on clients or some shit. My mom is more worried bout lookin great in the public eye n hosting all these events. None of them really know I exist.

Me: Sry 4 the rant. He just came in2 my room n basically told me 2 go screw all the grls in the world. Then said I shouldn't get married til I'm old. Meanwhile he's drunk. Again.

Me: Again sry I'm ranting u probably don't want 2 hear bout any of this.

Faye: That sounds awful. Don't be sorry for unloading on me. u've listen 2 my crap about my ex. I say rant away.

Me: Thanks. I really hate that they don't attend my games. Yet they brag 2 whoever is in their little circle of tightwads n rich jackasses how gr8 I am. How would they even know? They never come.

Faye: Wow. My mom might not understand cheering but she makes as many games as she can. I'd be so sad and ticked off if she didn't come to any of them.

Me: Yeah. I'm not asking them 2 come 2 all of them but 1 would b freaking nice.

Faye: If our games didn't fall on the same days I'd totally come see you play. Everyone needs support.

I want to tell her she does see me. I can't. Not yet.

Me: Thanks. So ... r there any big dances coming up at ur school?

Faye: A few. I don't plan on attending. Kind of funny. Last year I would have been crying about not having a date or attending a school dance.

Me: What changed?

Faye: It's just a dance with someone you'll eventually forget right? Someone who will become that guy you went to this with or that with. It'll be nothing. OMG I'm sounding like my sister.

Me: She sounds pretty smart. N yeah I get it. Every1 is gettin on my case bout stupid crap l8ly. Like when do u plan on taking ur ACT n SAT? What colleges r u looking at?

Faye: I know. It's like the future isn't just a we will see thing. It's like you have to know all the answers and your plans now. In the meantime I have enough trouble passing Algebra.

Me: Exactly. Hey, um ... do u mind if I call u?

Faye: I uh ... I don't know. Do you think that's a good idea?

Me: Yes. Maybe. Do u think it's bad?

Faye: Idk what if I sound like some

```
beast 2 u or something? Will u stop
talking 2 me?
    Me: I'm pretty sure u won't.
    Faye: Um ... okay.
```

I hit dial and wait. Two rings in and I hear a faint sigh then, "Hey."

"Hi."

"Um ... so ... you don't sound like a beast," she says then laughs. Holy shit, I think I love the sound of Layla's laugh. I hardly hear it when she's around me.

"Not yet, I try to keep all that hidden," I tease. My cheeks hurt from grinning. What is wrong with me? Why do I keep grinning like an idiot? Thank God she can't see me, she'd probably think I was nuts.

"Do you usually go to parties after your games?"

"Sometimes. I just wasn't feeling it tonight," I say.

"Me neither. I don't think I can take any more sympathy stares, or people whispering behind my back about what must've happened between me and Douche of the Year."

"That is a great name for him." I laugh. "So how's that been going?"

"The rumors, or avoiding my ex?"

"Both, I guess."

I hear something rustle then she groans. "It's been crappy. I mean in class I can tell there are a lot of people who are so happy we broke up. Then there are those who just want to feed off gossip, so they gloat about it and make up reasons. I don't tell them the truth because I'm tired. Why should I? What's it to them anyway? Ugh, then there is this one boy in my school who's constantly being a total jackhole. Like somehow my very existence bothers the living hell out of him. But I guess I shouldn't care because he's like a huge class clown."

Damn it. This is why I can't tell her it's me she's talking to. She thinks I'm a jackass yet, she's the one who treats me like garbage.

I clear my throat. "He sounds like an asswipe."

"He is. I guess you can be that if your father has his face and family name plastered all over and all the money in the world. Why would you have to take life seriously? He'll have a job and all that money to play with probably right after he graduates."

Is that how she really sees me? No wonder why she hates my freaking guts. I don't want to break the news to her that I would probably get nothing more than a janitor's job at my father's firm if I didn't go to college. Even though we have money my father constantly reminds us all that our family built our legacy from nothing. And we need to earn our keep.

"I know people like that." I knew a whole bunch of country club brats that fit that description.

"Yeah, they suck."

"If you could change one thing what would it be?"

"For my dad to be here. He died when my sister and I were in middle school."

I don't think anyone in town will forget that day. Mr. Valentine was super fit. He ran every day. People in town swore he never drank or smoked. Not once. Mr. Valentine was always nice, and he always got the baseball team ice cream even when we lost. One day on his run he collapsed just outside of town. My uncle was the one who spotted him on his way to work and called 911. The funeral was huge, pretty sure everyone attended.

"I'm sorry for your loss."

"Thank you. If you could change one thing what would it be?"

"I'd want a do over. One whole day."

"Is there a specific day?" she asks.

I smile. "Nope. Can't tell you that."

She laughs. "That seems a little unfair."

"Might be, but I'll tell you eventually."

"Why not now?" I can hear the pout in her voice.

I chuckle. "Because that's a waste of a good surprise. Besides, how else am I going to get you to keep talking to me?"

She huffs. "Oh fine."

"What is your favorite type of dessert?"

"Ohhh that's a good question but you have to answer first?"

I can't help but laugh again. "White chocolate chip cookies."

"Really? No pies or cakes your favorite dessert is cookies?"

"Yep. What's yours?"

"Ummmm ... I love turtle cheesecake the most."

"Cheesecake is weird because I don't know if it's a cake or a pie. You have crust like a pie but it's called a cake. When you look it up, it's vaguely considered both. Which do you think it is?"

"You know I've never thought about it. I just think it's delicious. Is that a category?"

Phone Layla is funny. Way better than the one I see every day at school. I wish this version of her would actually greet me one day instead of the typical Ice Queen that's been in my presents for most of my life.

"For you it can be."

She giggles. "That's awfully nice of you. Oh hey, my sis is home. I need to ask her how her first party was."

"Oh, cool. She's younger than you then?"

"No; she's older. She's a very shy person."

Usually the girls I know can't stand their family. I like how Layla cares about hers. It's refreshing actually.

"Well, I hope you have a good night Faye."

"You too."

We hang up and I set my phone on my charger. What the heck am I getting myself into?

# Chapter Nineteen

*Layla*

Oh my goodness, R and I talked on the phone. His voice was so sexy rumbly deep. I almost told him my middle name is Faye. Almost.

Of course, now that I know what his voice sounds like I can't help picturing what he might look like. Ugh! This is a bad thing, right? I can't fall for a faceless voice. This is *not* how this is supposed to work.

Juliet opens my door and slips into my room. There is a glow to her. I smile. "Hey, how was it?"

"It was good and weird."

"How so?" I ask.

She takes a seat on my bed and then stares up at my ceiling. While she does this I quickly inspect her neck for stray hickeys. What? I want to be sure Mark takes it slow on her. She may be older than me by a few seconds but that doesn't mean I shouldn't look out for her. "We were walking around, saying hi to his friends. That was fun. Girls were staring at me like they wanted to skin me alive. That was weird. Oh, then Mark wanted to dance with me. I thought oh cool slow dancing sounds fun. But that wasn't what he was trying to do. He wanted to bump and grind me. It was just too weird having him press all his you-know-what against me. I felt uncomfortable. Then Tyler and his friends Jared and Rachel we're gawking at me."

"Oh, don't worry about them. Rachel, well, you know how she is. Don't pay any attention to her."

She closes her eyes then looks down at the floor. "I know. It's just … it's different. I see Mark and I think, why does someone like him want to bother with me? I know I'm pretty. I know I'm smart. But honestly, we have hardly anything in common. He hates books. He isn't into the same kind of video games as me. He's also, you know, super popular. Me though, I'm like the uber dork. And don't try to tell me I shouldn't say that about myself because I can say it and be happy about it. I totally am an uber dork. I'm not ashamed to admit it."

"As long as what you say about yourself makes you happy then I'm not complaining. And who cares if you hardly have anything in common with Mark, right now? Maybe you two balance each other out. You know? Maybe you'll find things you have in common. Maybe you won't. Maybe he'll open you up to a new side of yourself you've never seen before. You just have to try."

She lifts one corner of her upper lip. "Oh my God. You've been reading mom's crappy pamphlets again, haven't you? Don't you know those things are full of shit?"

"They are not."

"Um, yeah, they totally are, Lays. If those things were so

awesome at love advice I would have gotten myself a boyfriend years ago. But they are just trash. Only yuppies whose destiny it is to become spinsters believe that crap. Why? Because they're so desperate to change instead of becoming a lady with a billion cats."

"I hope you know those BS-filled pamphlets actually let you eat dinner every night."

She groans. "Now you sound like Mom."

"Whatever. If I wanted to sound like Mom I would give you a twenty-question quiz that rates your date with Mark."

"Right. And since when is going to a party actually a date?"

I laugh. "Oh, you're so … " My phone buzzes next to me. I snatch it up and beam a smile.

"Who is he?"

I look away. "Who's who?"

"The guy making you all lusty-eyed and stuff."

I shrug. "He's just a guy."

"Right." She tries to snatch my phone away but I have quicker reflexes.

"Come on, Lays. Tell me."

I sigh. "All right, fine. Don't make fun."

"I won't."

"I don't really know."

She gives me a weird look. "What do you mean?"

"So, remember when Adam and I went out on a 'romantic' dinner?"

Juliet nods.

"Well, he was sexting a girl. I decided to text her and warn her that he was a two-timing jerk, and that she should stop sending him naked selfies 'cause he probably had more than one girl giving him pics. You know?"

She nods some more.

"Well, I didn't text her from his phone. I should have, but I didn't want things getting deleted or him spinning the story so it sounded like I was making it all up. So, I decided to text her from my phone. But with my dyslexia I, uh … fudged up the numbers and I ended up texting this guy named R."

She bursts out laughing. "I'm sorry, what? Like Roger Rabbit?"

"It's the letter R. Probably his first, or middle name. Or his last name. Or maybe his name is full of R's. Anyway … I don't know what's wrong with me. We just text each other and it's nice. Today though, we actually talked on the phone."

Juliet's eyes bulge. "Layla, have you completely lost it? He could be a fifty-year-old predator looking for some young fun."

I narrow my eyes. "He is not. He's our age. He thought I was old too."

"Do you even watch Dateline's *To Catch a Predator*? That's how this all starts! He pretends to be your age only to suck you in. Oh my God, Layla, you can't text or call him again."

"What? Why?"

"Because he could be some pervert. Please tell me you haven't exchanged photos?"

Juliet's getting so riled up she's putting me in a bad mood. "I haven't sent him my face. He doesn't even know my first or last name! He goes to our school."

She shakes her head. "That doesn't make it better. There are over a thousand kids at our school. For all you know he could be the school's janitor and he's waiting to get you alone so he can take you in the hall closet and butcher you. Then we'll find your body parts scattered all over the place."

I point to the door. "Go away."

She frowns. "I'm not trying to be mean. Could you do me a favor?"

"What?"

"Promise me you won't text that person anymore until you at least get more than an initial from him."

"Fine."

She gets off my bed and leaves my room. As soon as my door is shut I text R.

```
Me: My sister thinks you're some fifty-
year-old janitor who plans on killing me.
    R: Damn she caught me. Looks like the
jig is up.   :-)
    Me: LOL. But for real am I going to
get more than just your initial for your
name?
    R: Yes. Not 2day tho. I still think u
may have stalker tendencies, LOL.
```

I snort. In reality, do I really want to know his name? Isn't this better?

```
    Me: Please ... Pretty sure you might
the one with stalker tendencies.   :-)
    R: Dang. Caught me again. Srus tho I
really liked talking 2 u 2night.
    Me: Me too.
```

My smile widens.

```
R: What school do u go 2?
```

Crap! I can't tell him what school I attend yet. He'll put all the pieces together and know who I am.

```
Me: Huntersville
```

Close enough.

```
R: Oh cool. We don't play u guys til
conference time if we both make it. How's
ur team doing so far?
```

Ah shoot! This is what I get for lying. I hope their website is up to date. I quickly look it up on my laptop and then type out.

```
Me: Eh. Okay. We lost 1 game.
R: Cool. We're undefeated.
Me: That's awesome!
```

Of course, I already knew this. I just wish I could find out who he is. But what if I do, and he's actually a total jackass? The fear of kind of knowing enough about him makes curious, I will admit to that. It also scares the crap out of me.

```
R: Yep. Well my battery is low n I'm
beat. Chat 2morrow?
```

```
Me: Sure. Night.
R: Sweet dreams.
```

Those two words had me swooning. He wished me sweet dreams. I put my phone on my charger and flip my light off. R might be a mystery, but it's no mystery how he's starting to weave himself into my heart. Is that such a bad thing? Is texting someone you never see who somehow makes you happy really so wrong?

# Chapter Twenty

*Tyler*

I've been contemplating calling her since I woke up. I don't know what's wrong with me. Her voice, though, is something I crave to hear. Almost as much as I crave getting little text messages from her. Which is really screwed up because face-to-face we fight like cats and dogs. Whatever this is will never work.

Screw it. I hit call and listen to it ring.

"Hello?".

"Hey. I wasn't sure you'd answer. What are you doing right now?"

"Um ... well ... I've gotta start cleaning. Today is the day we scrub down the house. Then I'm heading to the mall."

"Cool." Really, though, I feel sweaty, and sick. Is she going to the mall to pick up guys? Shop? See a movie? We're not dating. Hell, she doesn't know I'm R yet, because if she did, I'm pretty sure she'd slap me or stop talking to me or both.

"Yeah. Shoot, my mom is calling me. Can I talk to you a little later? Say around four?"

"Oh, I don't know about that." She deeply sighs and I chuckle. "Kidding. I'll answer. Have fun cleaning."

"Yeah, I'm not a fan of cleaning bathrooms."

"I don't think anyone is, babe."

"Um … Okay. Bye."

Crap, why did I call her babe? "Bye," I say causally so it doesn't draw the attention back to the word I probably shouldn't have said just yet. The call ends and instead of feeling happy I feel miserable. I look around my room and groan. I definitely need to get ready.

As I'm getting dressed my mom calls me. "Tyler?"

"Yeah?"

"Are you almost ready?"

"Just buttoning and tucking." My mom hates when I say this. She says it reminds her of dirty romance novels. I have no idea what that is supposed to mean but ever since she admitted that I make extra certain to say it. Because for one, this gets back at mom and all her embarrassing Tyler-in-diaper stories she tells everyone at the club. And two, it's funny.

I hear her grumble. "Tyler, please don't say that."

I open my door and smile at her. "We ready to roll?"

She looks annoyed about something but she doesn't say what. She goes down the stairs and I follow. She stops in the kitchen. "Where the hell did he take off to?"

"Dad's missing?" I ask.

My mom scrunches up her face. "Yes. I tell him a certain time and the man always disappears. You know what? I'm not waiting this time. Let's go. The car is all packed up. Could you drive though, hon? I had a little nip in my coffee this morning."

Of course she has. She would have to, being married to my dad, who's probably hiding in his office working on another case. He does this kind of shit all the time. There's always a high-end client who really needs him. Whatever. She continues to stay married to the asshole.

She's not exactly a saint either. She can't go an hour in the morning without alcohol. By noon she's three sheets to the wind. God forbid we have guests over. When my mom's drunk she likes to air out all our dirty laundry to anyone who'll listen. This is another reason my dad doesn't attend the events she hosts.

I take the keys from my mom and slide into the Lexis LX. Once mom is buckled in I pull us out of the garage and down the drive. As we're heading to the country club my mom complains, "He knew how important this was. I suppose getting his clients what they need is way more important though."

Jesus. Here we go. "Tyler, when you get married, promise me you won't become a prick. Promise me when you make a vow to a person you'll keep it. Promise me when you say you'll be there, you will actually be there and not disappear on your wife!"

"Yeah, mom." Just stop talking about this.

"And he wonders why I'm not jumping into bed with him."

"Mom, TMI." She needs to stop talking about her and my dad's sex life before I projectile vomit all over the steering wheel.

"Sorry. I'm sorry. You're completely right. I shouldn't be talking about any of this with you. I don't want you to think badly of your father."

It's a little too late for that. I don't tell her this though.

I pull up the Windemfield Country Club Estates and a valet comes rushing out. He's dressed in club colors, maroon and black with a gold crest on his left pocket. My mom smiles as she practically stumbles into him.

I roll my eyes. This really couldn't get any more humiliating.

"Hello, Mrs. Richardson," he says to my mom in an overly cheerful voice.

My mom pats his cheek. "You're cute. If only I were twenty years younger."

I take it back. It just got more humiliating.

"Sorry, man." I hand off my mom's keys and walk toward the restrooms.

After I use the bathroom, I make extra sure to avoid my mom. This is the shit about my life no one knows about. I can't trust anyone not to talk about it. Well, Jared would be the only person. I learned a long time ago how people love to gossip about the rich, especially when it comes to my family. When I was in first grade I told one person during morning period I wanted to kiss a certain girl. By lunchtime everyone knew. They all giggled at me except for the girl. That girl was Layla Valentine. She told me never to speak to her again. Of course, I didn't listen. I did everything I could to get her attention but ended up making her cry. Yes, she actually punched me in the face at recess.

Austin comes toward me. He's decked out in some suit pants and a nice dress shirt, but his coat and tie are missing. "Hey, man. I was wondering when you'd show."

"Here I am."

"Your mom said you were using the bathroom."

I nod. "Is it boring as hell in there?"

He glances back at the ballroom. "Yeah. The girls here are from Blackhawk and Huntersville. Some are decent looking but mostly they look like future gold-diggers."

"Huntersville?"

He nods. "Yeah. A few chicks are from there. Their moms are friends with someone from here. Good causes, yadda yadda. I started zoning out."

Hmmm. This is my chance to prove my suspicion that Faye is in fact Layla. "Right. Which ones were they?" I ask.

"Why are you interested in girls from Huntersville?"

"Cause I am. Point them out."

We walk into the ballroom and he gestures to a table in the far back corner. I walk over and plop down in the empty chair at their table. Austin joins me, probably because there are no other dudes at this thing, and he wants to know what's going on with me.

"Hello again," one of the blonds say to Austin.

He smiles. "Hey. This is my buddy Tyler. His mom is the one organizing this event."

"Oh," the blond says. "That's so wonderful. You know, it's sad when children don't own shoes."

"Or purses," the redhead next to her says. Three girls nod together.

"Uh, right. So, you ladies go to Huntersville, right?" I ask.

They nod again. The black-haired girl says, "Yes. Do you go to Riverside?"

"Yeah. Um, do you girls know a cheerleader named Faye?"

"Faye? Nope. I don't think there's anyone at our school

with that name. Did you mean Faith? We have a girl on our cheer squad named Faith."

Faith?

"Um … did she date an Adam DiAngelo?"

"No. We don't have anyone by that name at our school either," the blond giggles.

Bingo. I get why Layla lied about her identity, so I'm not mad. It's just crazy that out of all the numbers in the world to send a text to, she got mine. How do I continue to go about this without her figuring out who I am?

When I move away from the table and head toward the one I'm supposed to be sitting at, Austin slumps down next to me and starts in. "All right what was that?"

"Nothing."

"I call horseshit! It's about the girl you've been texting, huh?"

"What?" I glare at him. How does he know about this? I certainly never told him.

He rolls his eyes. "I saw some of the messages you were sending each other when we were heading to lunch Friday." I scowl at him and he shrugs it off. "So, are you going to tell me what's up?" he asks.

"Nothing."

"Well, obviously you caught her in some lies. Where did you meet her?"

I'm not about to tell him that Faye is some figment person Layla Valentine made up. He already spreads enough rumors as it is. Last thing I need is for Layla to find out I'm R before I can convince her that we could be great together. Maybe it's best I lay off texting her so much.

# Chapter Twenty-One

*Layla*

He didn't call. He hasn't texted me for the rest of weekend. Monday morning my phone lies restless in my palm. I don't understand.

I need to get to the bottom of this. What if he got a girlfriend at his mom's lunch event? Maybe he doesn't feel the need to tell me if he did because we're just accidental text buddies. It's not like I proclaimed he was my boyfriend. How could I? I never had a face-to-face conversation with him.

"You're doing it again," Rachel says.

"What?"

She shakes her head at me. "You're being super quiet. What's up?"

"Nothing."

"That's it. I'm calling an intervention. There is something going on with you."

I absently spin my combination and pop open my locker. "Don't be ridiculous I'm just not in the mood to talk."

"See, that might work on your sister, but it doesn't work on me. I'm your best friend; you spill things to me. So spill!"

"There is nothing to spill."

She snatches my phone away. "Hey. Give that back!"

"It's him, isn't it!" She enters my passcode, which I totally regret giving her, then she snaps, "Who's R?"

"No one! Give it back."

"No. Tell me who he is and I'll give it over."

I glare at her. "Fine. He's a wrong number, okay? Happy?"

"What do you mean? You've got like over hundred texts here. If it's a wrong number how come it didn't end after you figured it out?"

"Because I like talking to him. But it doesn't matter anymore because he obviously lost interest." I snatch my phone back and she frowns.

"So, if you never met him, and have no clue who he is, why do you care?"

I sigh and grab my books from my locker. "I don't know. I guess I just liked that he never made fun of my dyslexia. I liked him not knowing me as Adam's girlfriend. He made feel like a normal person."

"Okay. So did you ask him what's going on?" she asks.

"I texted him four times and he didn't respond. I pretty sure that means he's done. Right?"

Rachel throws her arms around me and gives me a squeeze. "It's going to be okay Lays. Oh, I know what will cheer you up. A date to the winter formal."

"No."

"Yes. Come on. We haven't missed a dance since freshman year."

"I know." She tugs me down the hall. "I just don't think I'm up for it."

"Please. I'll find us dates. Please just say yes."

She clearly isn't going to give this up, so I nod. "Fine."

Rachel squeals and jumps up and down. I wish I could get her to stop. people are starting to turn our way and stare. "Okay. Okay. Quit."

She stops hopping and smiles. "This is going to be great! You'll see." She breaks off and goes to her first class.

I truly doubt her words. I feel like nothing will be great for me again. Ever since my breakup with Adam everything has turned to crap. The only bright side were my texts from R and now I don't even have those anymore.

My mood is gloomy at best. I glance at my phone but there are still no messages waiting. It might as well be dead in my hands. I swipe a tear strolling down my cheek and enter first period.

At lunch. I can't take it anymore.

```
Me: Are you mad at me?
```

Nothing. No dot-dot-dot waiting. Nothing.

I'm not going to cry. Why am I getting so worked up over someone I've never met? It's not like we had soul-touching conversations. I just … I want him to tell me why. If he found someone, I'm okay with that. My heart doesn't like that idea, but at least I'd know it wasn't something I did.

Rachel sits down beside me. "Hey. Stop the moping." Then she looks at my phone and takes it away. "This is depressing you. I'm going to do you a favor and take this from you for the rest of the day. Out of sight, out of mind."

"What if my mom calls?"

"When has your mom ever called during school hours?"

"Never. But it could still happen."

She rolls her eyes. "Listen. If your mom calls I will tell her you went to bathroom and left your crap behind. I have your phone because I mistakenly thought it was mine. Then I'll get her to call the office or excuse myself from class and give it back to you."

"I don't think this is a good idea. I know you're trying to help but I really just want my phone back."

"Well, you aren't getting it back. Not until after cheer practice today. If you're worried I'll lose it or something I'll give it to someone I know you trust."

"What? No. Don't hand it off to Juliet."

Too late. She calls Juliet over. "Come here, Spaz-o."

Juliet glares at her and heads over to our table. "Rachel, please don't call me that," my sister says, her voice was actually nice.

Rachel looks annoyed. "Whatevs. Your twin needs your help, she's just too proud to ask. Hold on to her phone until the end of the school day."

"No. Why do you want me to take your phone?" Juliet asks me.

"I don't," I say.

She looks over at Rachel. "Why?"

"Because it's making her depressed waiting for messages that aren't coming."

Ugh. Leave it to Rachel to tell my sister all about my problems. Awesome. Just awesome. Now Juliet is glaring at me. "I told you it was a terrible idea to keep texting him. Hand it over."

Rachel slides my phone over to my sister and Juliet stomps over to Mark and his friend's table. I hope Juliet doesn't tell anyone about this.

"So, about our dates. I was thinking a senior or sophomore for you."

I push my chicken Caesar salad away then rest my head on the table. "Why can't I get someone from our grade?"

"Um ... because most of them are friends with the dumbass who cheated on you."

Speaking of Adam, right then he enters the cafeteria and comes over to our lunch table. "I need to talk to you, Layla," he starts.

I look up at him. "Go away."

"Yeah, you ass. Get moving in another direction. For the twenty millionth time, she doesn't want to talk to you."

Adam smiles at her. "Hey Rachel, do me a favor and shut up. Unless you want me to tell Layla about you and me last weekend. Oops."

I look over at my best friend, who suddenly pales. "What is he talking about?"

"It's nothing."

Adam takes a seat next to me. "It's not nothing."

His words practically smack me in the face. I stare at Rachel. "You're joking, right?"

"Lays, look." Rachel says. "I was super drunk and I was actually telling him off, and then one thing lead to another and I don't know what happened." Adam snickers.

I can't comprehend this. First, he cheats on me. Then my best friend hooks up with him. And the only person I want to talk to right now isn't talking to me. I push away from our table and storm out of the cafeteria.

"Layla! Come on!" Rachel shouts. I don't look back.

# Chapter Twenty-Two

*Tyler*

Juliet joins our table at lunch. When Rachel calls her over to her and Layla's table I snap at Mark. "Do you really have to rub it in Jared's face every chance you get?"

"What? I'm not doing anything wrong. You guys bring your girlfriends over here all the time."

"You're a real dick sometimes. I swear you're just trying to get Jared so pissed off he smashes your face in. And you know what, I won't stop him. Neither will Austin."

Austin looks up from his tray and says, "I want no part of this shit."

Mark rolls his eyes. "Fine. We'll sit somewhere else."

He starts to rise, taking Juliet's things with him, right when Jared approaches. He casts a glare at the items in Mark's hands and says, "I gotta go study."

Jared leaves and Mark sits back down. I shake my head. "You need to … " I don't finish because Juliet sits down beside him.

"You look mad," Mark says to her.

"Oh, it's my sister. I have to carry her phone so she doesn't text someone."

I have a feeling she's talking about me. If that's the case, believe me, I want to text her but I won't. I just have to keep my mind off texting her back.

Rachel's shrill voice cuts through my thoughts. I look over at her table. Layla is rising while Adam is glowing with giddiness. "What did I miss?" I say.

"Oh yeah. I forgot you all bounced early. Rachel hooked up with Adam. Guess he just told Layla," Austin says.

"That's jacked up," I say. This information makes me want to text her back all the more. Provide some sort of comfort to her. But if I want to win her over as Tyler, this is what has to be done.

She storms past our table and heads out of the cafeteria. Juliet rises and Mark looks at her. "Where are you going?" he asks. What an idiot.

"To my sister. She clearly needs me. I'll talk to you later."

She marches over to Adam and Rachel. All the sudden I hear, "You're nothing but a rat and you. Stay the hell away from my sister!" Then she darts her leg out and kicks Adam right out of his chair. His ass slams to the ground and he glares at Juliet.

"You little troll!" he screams.

Mark, Austin, and I all stand up and walk over to Juliet. "Don't even think about it," I say to Adam as he gives Juliet a murderous look.

Juliet moves around us while mouthing her thanks. I fold my arms across my chest and glower at Adam. "Austin, I think you should go get coach."

"On it," he says.

Adam snarls, "What the hell is wrong with you Richardson? This is between Layla and me. All of you should just stay out of it."

"We've all tried that, man. You're crossing lines, and now it's affecting all of us," I snap.

"Yeah. It's one thing to pick on us guys, but harassing girls is not cool," Mark says.

"What seems to be going on here," Coach Black bellows from behind me.

I shift and face him. "Adam isn't fit to be on the sidelines with us. He's not even fit to wear a uniform, Coach. He broke three of our rules of respect to his teammates, this school, and the students."

"Is this true Adam?"

"No. He is just sticking his nose where it doesn't belong. He wants my girlfriend," Adam states.

I laugh. "Layla isn't dating you, bro." I want to say, 'and yeah, I want her' but I finish with, "You're delusional. Coach, he's harassing her. Every day we see it. She begs him to leave her alone but he doesn't. He's at her locker, follows her to class, finds ways to stop her in the halls. We should have said something sooner."

"He's right, Coach. And just a few minutes ago he acted like he was going to attack my girlfriend, who happens to be Layla's sister. She told him to stay away from them."

"Adam. Let's go," Coach Black says.

Adam looks like he'd rather do anything then walk off with Coach. It's his own fault. If he knows what's good for him, he better stay away from Layla. Otherwise he might find himself waking up in a hospital with a bunch of broken bones.

# Chapter Twenty-Three

*Layla*

My best friend hooked up with my ex. I'm hiding in a bathroom stall, tears streaming down my face as my body is racked by all the emotions coursing through me. Rage, betrayal, heartache. My insides knot so tight I feel physically ill.

The bathroom floor is disgusting, but I don't think about it as I crouch down and bring my knees up to my chest then drop my head down and cry. Above my sobs, I hear the bathroom door swing open, followed by voices.

"Oh my God, did you see her sister go all cray-cray on Adam?" one voice says.

"I know. I mean, I know you're dating Mark Whalan and all but you're still a nobody. Way to commit social suicide for you and your man by kicking his teammate off his chair. That whole family is psychotic," a whinier voice says.

Juliet kicked Adam? I smile. Juliet always has my back, no matter what. I stifle my tears and listen some more. "Well, there is one good thing. We can totally get her kicked off the squad now."

"Definitely. I bet her friend Rachel would totally help."

Rachel might be a shitty friend right now because she thinks with other parts of her body and not her head. But there's no way she'll try and get me kicked off the cheering squad, right?

I stand up slowly to prevent from making a sound and give away my position in the bathroom.

"Do you think I should get Adam or Tyler to take me to the winter formal?" one girl asks.

I push open the door. Both girls look back. It's Selena and her friend Jessica. "I think you should leave Tyler alone. As for Adam, have fun with that. If you guys are together even a month he'll find someone to screw on the side. I mean, that's what he's famous for. But stay away from Tyler. He doesn't need your filthy popular-pole-climbing paws digging into him!"

Selena glares at me. "You're so last season, Layla. Get a life. I can have any guy I want in this school. If I wanted to, I could totally take your sister's man for starters."

"Do it. Juliet will have you on the ground in a matter of seconds. When she does let you up, you'll be shopping for wigs to cover up the many bald spots you'll have."

Suddenly the door opens again. My sister stares at me then she looks over at the other girls. "Hi." She turns to me. "I was looking for you."

"It's fine. I was just leaving. Oh, and ladies. If you try anything, just know I won't wait for karma to get even."

Juliet studies me as we walk out of the bathroom. She

hands me an antibacterial wipe and I use it on my hands. I toss it in the trash and we continue to walk to my class in silence. Before we reach my classroom, she places her hand on my shoulder and turns me.

"What was that back there?" she asks.

"Which part. The bathroom or the cafeteria?"

"Let's go with both. Although I think I got the gist of the cafeteria."

I nod. "Adam has been bothering me since we broke up. He keeps wanting me to take him back. I keep refusing. Apparently, the party I skipped and you went to, he and Rachel hooked up."

"She's a slut," Juliet grumbles.

I squeeze my eyes shut then open them slowly. "Yeah, well, I will deal with it. I was crying in the bathroom and those two sophomores from the squad were in there talking smack about both of us."

"So? People do that all the time. They think I can't hear them but I do. Who cares?"

"I care. Especially when one of those trolls says they're going to hurt you because they can. I'm not going to let someone do that."

"What are you going to do? Raid my closet, dress up, and pretend to be me? No one would be able to tell the difference until you tried to take one of my classes."

"I wouldn't. I'd get them back in other ways."

"Listen," Juliet says. "I can handle myself. It's fine."

I smile. "I know you can but I've got your back too."

She laughs. "Yeah, well, I had yours today. I knocked Adam on his ass."

"Thank you."

"I know you slapped him a few times but you should really kick him, possibly consider taking out his knee or something."

"Right. His dad would totally sue mom." I frown at the thought.

"Yeah." We walk the rest of the way to my class.

Right before I enter she hugs me. "Lays, here." She places my cellphone in my hand. "I know you probably don't want this right now, but I think you might need it sooner than later. Especially with the day you're having."

I take it. "Thanks." Although having a blank screen in my hand isn't exactly comforting.

# Chapter Twenty-Four

*Tyler*

I spin my phone on my desk. We're going over all the bones in the body in Biology 2 today. I stare at sheets before me, as my mind slowly wonders. Mr. Yars is so boring. His tone, demeanor, everything is just so monotone and slow.

I'm about to fall asleep, which wouldn't be a first for me. I strain to keep my eyes from glazing over. I turn in my seat and notice Layla at the door. She knocks a few times and Mr. Yars says, "Enter."

She walks over to the desk and asks, "Mr. Yars, I missed some things second period, would you mind if I sat in this class and took the rest of the notes? I have a pass from Mrs. Hatlock that it's okay to be here." She hands over a yellow slip and Mr. Yars waves her off.

"Go take a free seat. Same rules apply to you this period as they do when you have me at second."

She nods and scans the room. The only free seat is at my table because Harris is out sick.

She heads over and plops down in the chair beside me. I haven't sat this close to Layla since I was in sixth grade. Her scent hits me hard, and damn the girl smells delicious. Toasted marshmallows and something else. Pumpkin pie?

Whatever it is has me perking up. I smile at her but she doesn't respond. Right. She hates me.

She flips her notebook open and I glance at it then say, "Whoa." I can't help it, it just spills out and she instantly glares at me. I knew with her dyslexia her spelling would be a little bad but dang man her notes look like flipping Chinese.

"What?" she says as a blush spreads across her cheeks.

I turn the notebook toward me but she snatches it back. "Stop," she whispers. "Please."

"I'm not going to make fun of you," I say.

She grits her teeth. "I can't spell well."

"Okay. Do you want me to go over what's really on the board? Because if you write any of that crap down you're going to get an F." I know that sounds horrible but I can't sit here and watch her struggle. It's killing me.

"You don't have to help," she says. I can hear the stubbornness in her tone.

"Well, too bad." Damn girl is going to be the death of me I can feel it.

I take notes and make sure that I get every bit down for her even though she's sitting beside me and writing away. As soon as the class bell rings I kick her bag out of the way to distract her so I can steal her notebook. Some of her things go sailing across the floor. Do I feel like shit after doing it? Yes. But she would have never handed it over willingly. Not to me at least.

She glares at me before taking off to retrieve her bag. "You're such an asshole!"

I smile. As soon as she turns her back I grab her notebook and shove it in my bag. She'll thank me later.

♥

I decide that my hand would probably fall off if I hand-write all the notes for her, so I type them. It actually doesn't take me as long as I thought it would. I even add in helpful tips that I use to remember certain things. Like you can remember all the muscle type tissues if you just remember CVS: cardiac, visceral, and skeletal.

About an hour later I print off two copies, one for me and one for her. She'll need this anyway because we're allowed to use notes for our end-of-the-year exam. I staple the pages, tuck them into a folder, grab her notebook and head out the door.

Fifteen minutes of driving and I'm at her house.

The big red door opens to a woman matching the billboards all over town. Short brown hair and big brown eyes. Yep, it's their mom. "Hello, can I help you?" she asks.

"Hi Ms. Valentine. My name is Tyler Richardson and I was wondering if I could talk with Layla a moment?"

"Um … sure. She's up in her room. Just go on up the stairs and it's the second door on the right."

"Uh … okay." I enter the house and she closes the door.

"I'm in the middle of dinner and profiling, sorry."

I've never had a mom just invite me inside their house so openly. They usually make me wait on the porch or something especially if I'm not picking up their daughter for a date. Before I think too much of it I head up the stairs. Juliet comes down the hall and she stops in her tracks. "What are you doing here?"

"I came to see Layla."

"Does she know that?" she asks as Chase comes out of Juliet's room.

"Uh ... Does Mark know about *that*?" I ask and motion to Chase.

She laughs and so does he. I don't see what's so funny. Chase says, "Dude we're best friends. Mark knows that. He's in her room right now." Chase hands her an empty plate. "He devoured all the cookies."

She smiles. "Yeah, he does that." She takes the plate then points to Layla's room. "She's in there."

"Right." I shuffle past them and knock on Layla's door.

"What?" she shouts.

I figure that's the universal sign to come in, so I do. She's sees me and yells, "What the hell?" Then she covers up her chest area, which is slightly exposed. Her bra is covering up most of the bits.

I throw up my hands and swing around. "Sorry. Shit. Sorry. I was just. I typed them." I wave the folder over my head but don't turn around.

Suddenly her door plows me in the face. I cup my hands over my face and scream as shooting pain blossoms around my nose. "Ah Whuck!"

"What's going on? I heard screaming," Ms. Valentine says. "Oh, oh goodness. Are you okay? Crap. Is everyone okay in here?"

"I'm fine," I mumble through my hands, which are pressed against both sides of my nose.

"I'll go get you some ice." She takes off right as Layla mutters, "I never said I was okay."

Next thing I know Layla is yelling, "Damn it Tyler! I was changing! You can't just go barging in people's rooms. Who even told you to come up here?"

"Your mom. Can I turn around now? I'm afraid you might stab me in the back with some scissors or something."

She laughs. Holy shit, that laugh. I love it.

"You can turn around."

She sits on her bed cross-legged. I walk over to her and take a seat in the chair. Her mom reenters the room with an icepack. "Here you go. Are you staying for dinner?"

Layla answers, "No!" I say, "Sure."

Her mom looks puzzled. "Layla, don't be rude. Would you like to stay, Tyler?"

"Sure."

Layla glares at me. I smile at her. Yep, this is going to be great. Her mom quickly leaves the room and shuts the door. I'm actually a little shocked because usually parents are always leaving doors open.

"Why are you here again?" she asks.

"Notes. Here." I rest the icepack on my face and hand over the folder and her notebook.

"You took my notebook? You really are a total dick. You know that?"

"I typed out all the notes we've taken since August out for you."

I move my icepack so I can look at her. She glares. "I don't need this."

"Geez. Would it kill you to say thank you?"

Layla frowns. "I'm sorry. Thank you. I just … I don't like feeling stupid."

"You're not stupid. You just really suck at spelling. So what?"

She sets the notes aside and scratches her legs. "You're right, it's nothing. Thanks," she says, but her tone and the way she keeps digging her nails into her legs. She really doesn't openly tell people she's dyslexic. I don't get why she would be so forthright about it to "R" but no one else.

"Want to go over them? I also put in some easy study acronyms that I use."

Layla opens her mouth but suddenly her phone rings. She picks it up and then drops it. "Sorry. Um … "

"You can answer. I can step out if you need some privacy."

"I don't. It's just Rachel and I'm not talking to her right now."

"I get it."

"Why are you here Tyler? You could have given this stuff to me at school."

She's right. I could have given her all this at school. The thing is I think I needed to see her and make sure she was okay. Usually Layla steamrolls everyone, like she doesn't have emotions at all. She scowls, puts on a fake smile for the crowd. They think it's genuine but I'm pretty sure it's fake as hell. At least now it is. Last year, not so much.

"I don't know but it looks like I get dinner."

She smiles. "Yeah. Be prepared though. My mom might be the best matchmaker but her clients definitely aren't following her recipes."

I frown. "So … I should probably think about stopping somewhere after this?"

"Yes. Unless Juliet is cooking." She shrugs and picks up the packet of notes I gave her. "So, your extra notes are from you or the book?"

"Both. I made up the acronyms."

She flips through a few pages then sets it down. "Thanks. I'll look at this later. I have to do some math right now."

"Okay." She must have a lot of homework. I've been home for as long as she has and I finished my work and typed those notes within an hour.

"What?" she asks.

"Nothing." I stand up. "I'm going to see if your mom needs help in the kitchen."

She looks up at me. "Really?"

"Yeah."

"Why?"

"Because it's polite. And I know a thing or two," I say.

She shakes her head. "Pretty sure my mom would not approve of toad."

I raise a brow. "Toad?"

"First grade you put a toad in my lunch box."

I bust out laughing. "That was a frog. I think it was our class frog, Herme. Oh, shit. Is this why you hate me so much?"

"Might be." she glowers at me. "You've done nothing but

torture me throughout school. You give me dirty looks. You call me Princess, yet you know nothing about me. I'm far from being a princess!"

I look around her room. Her walls are decorated pink and white. She has a white bedspread, white furniture, and pink lampshades. "Uh, your whole room screams princess."

"It does not! It says I'm a lady."

"Oh, I'm sorry. I didn't know you wanted to play the grandma card, but okay: your whole room screams I'm an old lady. Let me go find my cane."

She narrows her eyes. "Get out! And take this with you!" She throws my notes at me and then looks back down at her book.

Ha. She's not getting rid of me that easy. I leave the notes on the floor where they landed and walk out of her room. I don't know why I'm in the mood to rile her up, but I am.

# Chapter Twenty-Five

*Layla*

Tyler Richardson is the most aggravating person on the face of this earth! Why couldn't he just be polite, hand me the notes, and go about his day? Why must he insist on digging underneath my skin like a bad rash?

Okay, maybe I shouldn't have mentioned the toad incident. But he made it sound like my ignoring him and being annoyed by him these past eleven years was all my fault. Um, no! He's had a hand in it more than a few times.

"Stupid Tyler," I grumble.

I pick up my phone with no intention to text R but my fingers were already working through the letters.

```
Me: I'm sorry you're mad at me. I
don't know what I did but please text me.
R: lied. I saw some ppl who go 2
Huntersville n I asked bout u n ur ex.
```

> Me: Oh. Ok. Faye is my middle name.
> R: All right. But that doesn't explain ur boyfriend not really existing.
> Me: I made up his last name. You said no personals and that was getting personal.
> R: Ok. I'm sorry I was mad. I just deal with enough liars.
> Me: I'm sorry too.
> R: I missed talking 2 u n I hate 2 do this but I'm really busy can I call u l8r?
> Me: Sure. I missed talking to you too.
> R: Good. I'll call u l8r.

I don't respond. I wish he could talk to me now but at least he's not ignoring me. I can't believe he was asking about me. I mean, sure, I still lied because I don't go to Huntersville. Oh man, is he checking to see if I really exist? Maybe Juliet is right and he's really a stalker.

No more personal info. If he texts me back about being caught in another lie because no one has Faye for a middle name I'm cutting this off. Cold turkey. Might have to change my number too, but I'll get to that later. Right now, I have to work on math.

"Juliet, Layla, boys—wash up and come downstairs. Dinner is ready," my mom calls.

I slam my books shut, pick my notes up off my floor, and set them on my bed. Then I head to the downstairs bathroom since the upstairs one is occupied. As I open the door, Tyler walks right into me.

"What the hell!" I yell.

"Hi to you too, sunshine."

"What are you doing here?" I demand.

He smirks. "Well, I believe I was invited to dinner."

"You were not. I uninvited you the moment you started being a jerk."

"News to me, sweetheart. Now, if you'll excuse me."

I block his path. "Absolutely not. This isn't a game. I don't want to be angry the entire night."

"Then don't be." He smiles and lifts me up.

I'm so flabbergasted by this action I sputter. "W-what a-are you doing?"

"I'm moving you out of my way, half-pint. And now, I'm off to the dining room. See you there," he says with a wink and practically skips off.

I march into the bathroom, wash my hands, and enter the kitchen. Mom says, "Please ask your guest what he would like to drink."

My guest. Oh, I'll show him—he's so not my guest. Calling me sunshine, sweetheart, and half-pint. He's about to get a swift kick in the head. Smirking as if he's won this round. HA. Tyler Richardson, welcome to the new and improved Layla Faye Valentine. She doesn't take your shit and cry to her mommy. Nope. She dishes it out and takes her punishment for misbehaving.

I smile sweetly to Tyler. "What do you want to drink?"

"What do you have?"

"Almond milk, milk, water, and lemonade."

"Lemonade is great. Thanks."

I stalk off the fridge and fill two glasses with lemonade. Then I walk over to the table, where Tyler is spooning mashed potatoes on his plate, and dump both glasses on his head. He remains seated, a scowl on his face. My mom screams, "Layla Faye! How dare you? What is wrong with you? Apologize this instant and go to your room for the rest of the evening!"

"Sorry," I say in a bitter tone. My sister is snickering at the other end of the table and Mark is covering his mouth too. Chase just looks down at his plate of food. Tyler, though. He looks up at me like he's confused.

I roll my eyes, no longer worried about him or the rest of this evening. Tyler can totally kiss my butt. I make my way to my room and sit on my bed. My stomach growls and I groan. Maybe I should have eaten a little before doing that. Ugh. Now I'm going to have to wait until everyone is in bed before I can sneak some food.

# Chapter Twenty-Six

*Tyler*

I'm sitting at the Valentines' dinner table, shocked because Layla Faye dumped lemonade on my head. I don't get why she's so pissed at me.

Maybe she's never going to come around to liking me, only "R". What will she do to me when she finds out that I'm the one she's been texting?

Ms. Valentine hands me some towels while she continues to apologize for her daughter's craziness. She calls it a "little fit."

"No worries." I wipe my face and hair. My shirt and pants will remain wet and sticky until I get home. "I probably deserved it." I know I didn't but I say this so she'll quit fussing over me.

She sits down and looks at Juliet. "I hope you don't throw fits like this."

"I won't," she mumbles, and shoves a forkful of potatoes in her mouth. "Mmm. Mom," she swallows. "These potatoes are amazing."

"Tyler made them."

"Shut up," Mark says. "Richardson, I didn't know you

could put Betty Crocker to shame."

I wink. "I keep my apron next to my Batman gear."

Chase and Mark chuckle. Juliet just snorts. "Thor is better."

"You prefer hammers and gods over a human with kick ass gadgets?" I ask.

"Yes," she says.

Mark frowns. "But Batman is just as cool."

"Is he? He seems like a jerk. Yeah, his parents died and his butler raised him. But he doesn't say, 'Hey Alfred I'll totally get my own tea.' Alfred is always asking him, 'Is there anything else you need, sir?' Then he treats Robin like a kick toy too. So, he is a jerk," Juliet says.

"Wow! I never really thought of Batman that way, but I can see that," I say.

Chase doesn't add to the conversation, he just eats. Ms. Valentine doesn't seem to be paying much attention either. Mark glares at me. "But that's not really Batman. That's Bruce Wayne."

"They're the same person. One just wears a suit at Wayne Enterprises. The other wears a bat costume and fights crime. Both seem to treat Alfred like a butler and not family, like they try to make it seem," Juliet says.

"She's got a point," I say.

"You both are nuts," Mark snaps.

Juliet shrugs. Chase shakes his head. "I think Spider-Man is pretty cool."

"Yeah, he is. I like Wonder Woman too," I admit.

"What? Spider-Man?" Mark sounds completely offended.

Chase nods. "I think he's pretty cool."

"Me too," Juliet says.

Mark glares at Chase and then shovels food into his mouth. If I didn't know any better I'd think Mark was jealous of Chase.

I finish my plate, wash it, and head back to the table, where Juliet, Mark, and Chase are arguing about something else. Ms. Valentine is no longer at the table. So, I fill a fresh plate with potatoes, beef roast, and fresh green beans. I grab a fork and head up to Layla's room.

I open the door without knocking. She's sitting on her bed staring down at her book. She looks up at me and then at the plate of food in my hand.

"Here." I set it down on her desk. "Don't tell your mom. I think she might ban me from the house."

She stares at me. "Why are you bringing me food?"

"It's a peace offering. I'm sorry for upsetting you."

She nods. "I'm sorry for being a bitch and dumping drinks on you."

"It's cool. My shirt and pants are clinging in all the right places, don't you think?"

She laughs. "Definitely." She moves off her bed and takes a seat at her desk. I glance over at her math homework and frown.

While she eats I take a seat on her bed and check her answers.

"What are you doing?" she asks with a mouthful of food.

"Well, girl with no manners. I'm checking your work. You know you got the right answer for two and seven if those were really the numbers from your sheet."

She pales. I notice her swallow then she says, "Oh. Um. I guess I wasn't paying attention."

This is not the same girl from the phone. This girl will

not admit to her problem. Is it because she thinks I'll think she's stupid? Maybe she's actually figured out that I'm really R, the guy who's been texting her, so I apparently already know. Nah. She hasn't given me any signs she knows that.

"The first number is seven, not one. In problem number two, the letters are supposed to be A and C, not B and O, although that's really funny," I grin.

She chews on her bottom lip. "Okay. Um, and the numbers and letters are right on the others except for problem seven?" She reaches for her paper but I pull it away.

"Eat. Please. Your growling stomach is making me think of starving children in some third world country."

Layla narrows her eyes and turns to her plate of food. She eats some beef and then mumbles, "Wow."

"What?"

"This is good."

"I know."

"Mom never cooks this well. It's always dry and overdone."

I smile. "You're welcome."

"What do you mean I'm welcome?"

"I cooked dinner. You're welcome," I say with a wink.

"No, you didn't. Did you? Where did you learn to cook? Don't you guys have a maid?"

I scowl at her. "Mary Ella teaches me things. I'm not going to have a freaking maid for life you know."

"What, they won't travel with you to college?"

"Ha ha. So funny. No."

She places a heap of potatoes in her mouth and moans. God, her foodgasms are doing things to me. I glance down at her homework again to keep me from thinking dirty thoughts.

# Chapter Twenty-Seven

*Layla*

Holy smokes, can he cook. It's so good I keep embarrassing myself by letting out loud moans. He glances over every once in a while. My cheeks are completely on fire.

This is bad. He probably thinks there is something seriously wrong with me. At least my stomach isn't growling anymore. I'm also ashamed about my behavior earlier. He didn't have to make me a plate and sneak it up into my room for me, but he did and I'm not sure why. Maybe he just did it so he can prove he's a great cook, which, okay, sold.

Whatever the reason, I don't care. I wish he'd stop looking over my work though. Usually Juliet checks it. Well, I haven't had her looking at it lately since R. Still, I'm not comfortable with Tyler looking it over. He hasn't flat out said I'm a total dipshit or anything. I just don't want him looking at it and questioning why numbers and letters are all crazy.

Sure, I could tell him the truth, like I usually do when someone asks, but then it's always followed by that same look. Which is like aww poor you or uh huh that just means you're stupid, honey.

I finish the last bite of food then stare at the empty plate for a little longer. Tyler clears his throat, drawing my attention to him. "So, you wanna take a crack at this stuff?"

"Um ... okay." Why isn't he looking at me like I'm a total dumbass? Even Adam used to give me those looks.

I walk over and sit down next to him. I stare at my paper filled with numbers and words and take a deep breath to calm my mind.

"You okay?" he asks in a gentle tone.

"Yeah, I just ... It takes me a minute to, uh, read through a problem."

He smiles. "Want some help?"

"No. I, um ... got it."

He sighs. "Layla, it's okay to ask for help. I'm willing to do it."

"I know. I just don't want you to think I'm stupid."

"I don't." he nudges me. "Come on. I'll just read off what each problem is supposed to say and you do the math. Cool?"

I smile. "Okay."

Maybe I'm wrong and people like R do really exist: kind, patient, and willing to help. Tyler didn't say he'd work through the whole problem, just that he'd read them off so I got the right things down. First time Adam tried to help me with math he called me an airhead, then he said, "I got this babe," and did all the problems for me. That's nice I guess, but at the same time it made me feel stupid. I know math. I just got confused on the numbers.

"So great job on the first problem, you got that down

perfect," Tyler says. "Problem two is supposed to be one X plus five Y, quotations, eight minus seven, quotations three equals six, quotations seven X minus four Y quotations."

I copy down the problem he reads off and start to work it out. Then we continue through the next set of problems. In no time, I'm finished with Math and we move on to the notes he typed up.

Ten minutes into it, though, he glances down at his phone and says, "Shit. Sorry, I have to go. We can work on some of this tomorrow. I mean, if you want to."

"Okay. That sounds like a plan."

"Sweet. I'll just take this with me so you don't get in anymore trouble." He grabs the plate and leaves my room. My heart pitter-patters against my chest as he closes the door behind him.

What the heck is happening to me?

♥

Rachel doesn't come by my locker in the morning. I think she knows better. She doesn't sit by me in lunch. Not that I care. My sister and her boyfriend do though. So does Adaline, but she mostly gives Mark dirty looks.

"So, you and Tyler hooking up?" Mark asks.

Juliet elbows him in the side and Mark grunts. "What?"

"Don't answer that sis," she says.

"Wait, you and Tyler Richardson?" Adaline says.

"No. No. No. He just wanted to hand me some notes I missed in Bio 2. Nothing more," I say. There are enough rumors in this school about me I don't need to add to them.

Mark doesn't look convinced. Adaline does because she knows about my problem.

"That's nice. He seems like a good guy, even if he likes to goof off half the time," Adaline says. "I think that's something that runs in all male DNA though."

My sister smiles. "I think you're right."

"This is unfair. Three girls against a dude," he says with a scowl.

"Oh, get over yourself," Adaline snaps.

He grumbles something but I can't really make it out.

Lunch is very quiet after that. Tyler and I see each other in the halls but he seems to be avoiding me too. I guess our moment of a truce ended as soon as he walked out of my room. I can't dwell on it. It's not like we were really meant to be friends anyway, right?

My phone buzzes in my hand.

```
R: I have this theory that some of our
teachers r actually aliens.
Me: Really? Like your science teacher?
R: Nah. He's 2 boring 2 b an alien. I'm
thinking my history teacher might b 1.
She zones out all the time. Mid-sentence.
Then she'll b like Huh. Where was I?
```

He apparently has Mrs. Webber. She totally does zone out mid-sentence. I giggle as I walk to my next class. I round a corner and wham! Adam collides into me. "What are you ... Layla. Huh, never thought you'd be so absentminded walking the halls."

"I was ... um ... never mind."

"Texting. Wow. You. The I hate texting queen. Who are you talking to?"

I draw my phone close to me. "No one."

He tries to pluck it from my hands but I kick him in the shin. "Leave me alone!"

"You ran into me!"

I shove him and move around his limp form. I look back to make sure he isn't following and run down the hall. Arms wrap around my waist and a deep voice says, "Whoa, Princess. Let's not make it two for two."

I blink up at Tyler. Fiery heat blossoms across my face. He smiles and it's slightly dazzling. How come I never noticed that before? Someone passing us in the hall whistles as if we're making a huge scene or something. It's enough to snap my attention back and pull out of his tight embrace.

"Sorry. Um. I. Ahum ... I was just ... getting to class."

"I see that. Little tip: you should watch where you're going." He winks and then moves past me. Breath I didn't even realize I was holding slips out as I watch him leave.

I text R before waltzing into my last period class.

```
Me: LOL. I have a teacher kind of like that.
R: I just reached my class. Talk 2 u after my practice is that cool?
Me: I can't. I have a meeting after my
```

practice. I'll text you when I'm out is that okay?

I step into class even though I'd rather talk to him.

# Chapter Twenty-Eight

*Tyler*

As soon as class ends I head to my locker, grab the books I need, and make my way out to my Jeep. Off in the distance I spot Adam and Layla arguing by her car. He keeps reaching for her bag and she keeps squirming to get away from him.

Instant rage blasts through my veins, causing my muscles to flex and my hands to clench into fists. There are at least three hundred people in the parking lot and no one has even made an attempt to help her.

I grip Adam's shoulder, spin him away from Layla, then slam my fist into his jaw. He spits blood out on the ground and stares at me. "What the hell is wrong with you?"

"Stay away from her! We've already warned you about this," I growl at him.

He takes a swing at me but I dodge it, grab his hand and twist it behind his back. Adam screams, "Why do you even care? Do you want my woman, Richardson?"

"First of all, I'm not yours," Layla yells. "Second, it's not your concern anymore who wants me. But I'm pretty sure he's the last person who would. Just leave me alone Adam."

Her words cause me to fumble a little with the task at hand. My grip on Adam loosens enough that he wriggles out of my hold and pushes me back. "We were brothers. That's what the football team is: it's a family. You pissed all over that the moment you and your other backstabbing tools got me sidelined. Second string, what a freaking joke. Then you dicks had to pull one better and make up some bullshit story to get me kicked off the team."

"Wait," Layla cuts in. "You got him kicked off the team?"

"Coach made the decision. Did I push it along? Maybe. Adam, I don't give a shit if you're pissed off at me, Jared, Mark, or even Austin. I don't give a shit if you're mad at the whole planet. You did this. The only way you can correct it is by leaving her alone. She's not property. She's not someone you can just magically stake a claim in. Can't you see she's terrified?"

Layla is trembling by her car. Adam glances at her then over at me. "She's scared of you. She was just fine before," Adam snaps.

"Bullshit! I don't corner women in parking lots."

"What's going on over here?" Jared asks from the sidelines.

I turn to Jared. "This one here keeps ignoring what we told him." I jut a thumb in Adam's direction. "Before we all become extremely late to practice, I was going to offer Layla here a ride."

"She has a car," Adam starts. "It works fine. She doesn't need your help, Tyler. Just piss off."

"Layla," I say.

She nods. "My battery died this morning, Juliet had to give me a jump. I was waiting for her to do it again but she already left. I keep forgetting about her side project for her science class. She gets to bail after sixth period."

Layla takes a step toward me and Adam blocks her. "No. You aren't going to keep avoiding me, Layla. We need to talk."

"There is nothing to talk about, Adam. For the millionth time, just leave me alone."

"You heard the lady. Go on Adam before I have to hit you again," I say.

He shoves me and Jared jumps between us before I can take another swing at Adam's face. "Knock it off. Layla, go with Tyler. Adam, stay put."

Layla sidles up next to me and we walk off to my Jeep. I open the front passenger door for her and she blushes. "You don't have to do that kind of stuff," she whispers.

"What? Open doors or put Adam in his place? Because neither can be helped. I was taught to stand up for the right things and to always open doors for ladies." I wink at her. "Plus, my mom would totally kick my ass if she ever found out I'd ignored what was going on in the parking lot or didn't open a door for a girl." I lean in close because I'm selfish and I want to smell her toasted marshmallow scent. "My mom actually terrifies me."

I pull back and her face is the color of a Red Delicious apple. Goodness. I never knew I could have such an effect on her.

Once she's in the seat I shut the door. Jared runs over and hops in the back while I slide into the driver seat. "If we hurry, we might actually make practice on time," Jared huffs.

"How come you never ride with your dad?" Layla asks.

I use the mirror to judge Jared's face. His lips are drawn into a hard line. His eyes blaze a bit then he snorts, "Because he's an asshole."

"Oh. I'm sorry. I guess. He just seems nice in school. Maybe a little stern, but he doesn't come off as a prick or anything," she amends.

"Well he is," Jared says.

"Yep, and Jared doesn't want to be seen as Coach's pet," I joke.

He laughs at my sad attempt at humor. I glance over at Layla and she's staring at me as if I've lost my mind. I smile and return my attention to the road. "Plus, Jared just likes my ride better."

"Very true," he confirms with a nod.

"Thanks for the ride and the help with the other thing in the parking lot," Layla whispers.

I shrug while slowing to a stop at the red light. "It's no problem. You need to tell Coach that Adam keeps harassing you," I say.

"He's right. My dad will take care of it," Jared says.

"Look, I get it. I just don't want any more trouble. It's hard enough listening to what everyone has been saying. It's even worse knowing that they're only on his side."

I grip the steering wheel a little tighter. "Who the hell would be dumb enough to be on his side?"

"All the girls who think he's the next Abercrombie & Fitch model. I mean, look at my own best friend. I thought she was on my side and she hooked up with him."

"That's a poor example because Rachel only hooks up with football players and there are just so many of us on the team. Every dude knows this," I growl.

"And have you guys hooked up with Rachel?" She asks.

Jared mutters, "That's never happening."

"I'm with Jared on that one."

"Don't you guys find her attractive?" she asks.

Jared is quick to the punch. "No! There's only one person I find attractive and it's definitely *not* her."

"Who is it?" she asks.

"That's classified info and you don't have clearance," Jared says.

I throw the vehicle into park and hop out.

"So, what about you? Do you find her attractive?" she asks as she exits and rounds the front of my Jeep.

This feels like a loaded question. If I answer yes will she think I'd actually pull the same stunt as Adam? If I say no would she ask why?

As I'm about to answer her Coach bellows, "Where the hell have you two been? Get in and get changed before I have you running laps all practice!"

"Shit," I mumble.

Jared and I hustle down to Coach. I don't expect Layla to follow but suddenly her voice breaks from behind me. I whip around and Coach stares at her then glances between Jared and me. "What's going on?" he asks.

"It's my fault they're late. They came over to help me out because Adam cornered me in the parking lot. I'm sorry," she says.

Coach Black shakes his head. "That damn kid is really

becoming a pain in my ass. Thanks for letting me know. You two get in there and get changed. We're going to have a team meeting about this right now."

I glance back at Layla and she smiles. "Thanks again." She walks off to her own practice.

# Chapter Twenty-Nine

*Layla*

Practice was, well, strange. First, I got a lecture from my coach whom I had to inform of my reason of being late. She stormed off to find Coach Black to confirm my story.

A few minutes later she looked paler, and she mumbled instructions to us. After practice, she pulled me aside and made me promise to tell her right away if something like this happens again. Something like what, exactly? Adam demanding I speak to him? Some ex-boyfriend begging for my forgiveness? Some douche cheating on me?

It weirded me out. I nod though, and then walk toward the parking lot searching for my car. Then it dawns on me I didn't drive here. Shoot. Now what was I supposed to do?

"Come on Princess, I got you covered," Tyler's voice sounds off behind me.

I turn and smile. "Um ... you don't have to."

He shrugs. "I know. But seeing as most of the girls left and I doubt you want to hop in a car with Rachel or the psycho twins over there, I'm your best bet." He opens the door for me.

"I can call Juliet."

"And wait while she drives all the way out here? Seems pretty silly."

It was silly. But I can't get into a car with him again. People will see and draw conclusions. They'll begin a rumor that we're dating now. It's hard to refute such claims when he's pulling stunts like opening doors for me.

"Layla, come on. I'm not going to kidnap you. Just driving you back to your car. Then taking Jared home."

Jared walks up to us and smiles. "Are we waiting for someone else?" Jared asks.

"Nope. Just waiting for Layla here to hop in."

"Oh," he opens the back door and slides in. I sigh and take a seat up front. Tyler smirks at me as he shuts my door then gets in the driver's seat.

Ten minutes later we're at the school and I stare in shock at my car: it's covered in rose petals. Tyler swears next to me. "Wow, he's officially gone off the rails."

I grumble, "I'm going to be here forever cleaning that up."

"No you aren't. You can't clean it up. This has gone far enough. This is proof he needs help," Tyler says. "Stay here."

He gets out of the car the same time Jared does. Jared pulls out his phone and snaps some pictures.

Tyler hops back in and says, "There are photos of you two glued all over it. Plus those petals. It's like he made your car into a trip down memory lane float. Do you have any clue what that idiot wrote?"

I shake my head. I can't spend the rest of the evening

scraping this crap off. I have homework to do, and that's already going to take up most of my night as it is.

Hot tears well up and gathers at my lashes. "I can't." I stare at my car.

Tyler's arms wrap around me and suddenly he pulls me into a hug. I shift and sob against his shoulder. "It's going to be okay Layla. I promise. I'll take you home and if you want I'll tell your mom why. Everything is going to be okay. We'll clean this up tomorrow."

"People will see it."

"Yeah. They'll see how completely screwed up Adam is."

"My mom is going to kill me. She doesn't even know about this. If she finds out … " I start to tremble as the fear and panic race through my body. She'll blow up at the school for not informing her of this sort of problem. She'll be furious with me for not telling her what's been really going on with Adam. All she knows is we broke up because he cheated, not that he's been stalking and harassing me, plus has now gone completely crazy.

I pull back and watch his gaze drop to my lips. Is he going to kiss me? My heart slams against my chest, and tingles fill my stomach and zip through my body. Do I want Tyler to kiss me? Yes. As the excitement of the possibility of his lips pressing to mine courses through my body a door opens and Jared says, "Sent all that to my dad."

I return all the way to my seat and glance over at Tyler. He runs his hand through his hair and puffs. "Awesome."

"Did I miss something?" Jared asks.

Tyler smiles. "Nope, not a thing. All right; let's get out of here."

What? Wasn't he just about to kiss me? Whatever. Calm down. It's just Tyler for goodness's sake. He usually gets under your skin and makes dumb comments that make you want to slap him. It's Tyler Richardson. *You don't want to kiss Tyler.* So why do I feel like my whole world just crumbled in an instant?

Once he pulls up to my house I hop out, say thanks, and run inside. I quickly notice my mom isn't home. This only darkens my mood. I storm past her stacks of pamphlets scattered on the entryway table and spot one I've never noticed before: *Getting to know the real you.*

I leaf through the pages and some of the advice is so obvious it's truly laughable. No wonder Juliet says these pamphlets are loaded with gullible garbage. "You have to be honest?" I can't believe people read this crap.

I'm half tempted to throw out the stupid paper when the last section jumps out at me.

*Hiding from your true inner self makes it hard for another person to fully open up to you. If you can't be honest with yourself, how can you expect another person to fully accept you for who you truly are? Opening up and showing all of your good, bad, and ugly will not only help your future relationships, but help you learn what you truly want and not what you think you want.*

Is that what is happening with me? I certainly was delusional enough to think Adam was perfect when if I really look back at things he was an asshole. The boy never opened doors. He always made fun of me. Is that even how I ended up in a relationship with Adam? Was I looking for something that I really didn't want? No. That's ridiculous. No one knows what they really want besides the basics. Like, hey world, I don't want a cheater, a douche, or some kind of creepy stalker. I want someone kind, sweet, and who has a sense of humor. If he looks great too, hey, that's a bonus. I thought Adam was all that, but I was wrong.

The side door leading to the garage swings open and my mom walks in carrying some grocery bags. "Hi Mom. Need some help?"

"Hey honey. Where is your car? I didn't see it when I pulled in."

I walk past her and out to her car. I busy myself grabbing some bags then head inside. "Oh, um ... I left it at school."

"Why? Did you forget to put gas in it again?"

Do something one time and I swear it's the first thing that's always on her list. I roll my eyes and groan. "No, Mom."

"Well, then why is it at school?"

I need to come clean. I take a deep breath. "Someone glued crap all over it. I would have been there all night trying to get it off."

"What?" she loses her grip on some of the bags. I dive toward her and snatch them up before everything falls to the ground. "Is it some crazed fan?" She examines me from head to toe then asks, "Do you know who would do such a thing? Is there something you've been keeping from me?"

"No, Mom. Don't freak out."

"That's a little difficult, considering." She enters the kitchen and places the bags on the floor. "Layla, what's going on?"

I pull out some bananas from a bag and hang them on the fruit basket. I stare at the countertop instead of looking at my mom. "You know Adam and I broke up. What you don't know is he's been trying to get me to go back out with him ever since. He stalks me at my locker, he blows up my phone with texts and calls, and now he's glued memorabilia of some sort on my car."

"I thought you told me he cheated on you? Why would he turn your car into a love float?"

"He did cheat on me. I don't know why he did it. He probably thought I couldn't exactly ignore him. I'd have no choice but to respond to him."

"Well, you aren't. In fact, we're going to change your phone number. I don't want you near someone so completely off balance."

I don't exactly want to change my number; it took me forever to remember the one I have.

"Don't change my number. I blocked his calls."

She huffs. "Fine. I'm calling the school. I don't want him in any classes with you."

I nod. I don't really want her calling the school either, but I have to give in to something. "I'm sorry. I just wanted to handle this on my own. For the most part I thought I did."

"I understand your need to be independent. I also get coming to me is an out-of-the-world concept. But sometimes, Layla, I need to know things like this. We'll figure out how to collect your car from school. Get it checked out."

"Thanks Mom."

"I'll call uncle Harvey. He might be able to tow it here. I want him to look it over, make sure Adam didn't do anything else to your car."

"Pretty sure it's just the gigantic scrapbook display all over my car."

She frowns. "I swear the world is a crazier place than it was when I was your age."

I nod because I really don't want to relive her high school days with her. She picks up her phone and calls my uncle. While she's doing that I make my way to my room.

My bed seems to call to my tired muscles. I slump down on the mattress and then lie back. A deep sigh leaves me. I pick up my phone and text R.

> Me: How was your day?
> R: It was interesting.
> Me: How so?
> R: Apparently I'm going 2 b a DD at some party this weekend. But I never said I was going.
> Me: Wow. Who offered you to be a DD?
> R: My 1 friend.
> Me: So if you don't go?
> R: His butt won't have a ride 2 or from. How was ur day?
> Me: Sucked.
> R: Want 2 talk about it?
> Me: Not really.
> R: I'm sry u had a crappy day. Anything I can do 2 cheer u up?
> Me: Just keep talking to me.

My phone rings. It's him.
"Hi."
"Hey," his sexy voice rumbles.

"What are you up to right now?" I ask.

"Well, I'm currently talking to this pretty cool person and heading to my house."

"Oh. You text and drive?" I will never speak to him again using text messages if he does. That's my biggest pet peeve ever.

"Nope. I just hopped in my vehicle and called you. I hung out with my teammate for a little bit."

"Good. I can't stand people who text and drive."

He laughs. "Me neither."

"How was practice?"

"Uneventful, I guess. Just a whole lot of running and reviewing plays." It sounds like he's completely bored with this conversation. To be honest I'm bored with it myself.

"I'll, um … let you go," I say.

"What? Why?"

"Oh, uh … I have homework to start on. So … I'll just talk to you later."

"Hey, wait. I … I thought you wanted cheering up?"

I sigh. "It's okay. I feel better. Really. I'll talk to you later." I hang up the phone and set it aside. I don't know what is wrong with me. Adam's words pollute my thoughts. *No one will want you. You're boring. You don't do anything.*

Sure, he said it in the hallway right before I slapped him, but still. Did he have a point? Could anyone really want me for me? Is my personality boring? I can feel the words cutting deeper.

A knock pulls me out of my daze. "Hey honey. Someone is downstairs for you," my mom says.

I get off my bed and head down. As I reach the bottom step Tyler smirks at me. "Hey."

"Hi. Um … what are you doing here?"

"I wanted to talk to you."

I raise a brow. "Okay, about what?"

"Look, I know Adam has been giving you crap lately and acting like a major tool. So, I wanted to let you know that if you need someone in your corner feel free to let me know."

I laugh and bob my head. "Right. Cause we're best friends."

Tyler frowns and takes a seat on our living room sofa. "No, but I think we should try."

"Try being friends? I don't know. We're usually at each other's throats." My mind wanders back to that almost-kiss. Did he want to kiss me?

"I think it's because we don't really know each other," I states.

"Is that it? Or is it because you tend to make everything into a joke?" I don't want to feel rejection again, so yeah, I'm deflecting and putting up walls.

Tyler smiles. "Look, it's true. Here's the thing, though: I really like seeing the bright side in everything. The world is pretty grim without laughter. So I crack a few jokes, play a couple of pranks, turn serious things into something to laugh at. It doesn't mean I don't care."

I fold my arms. "Doesn't it? I appreciate the rides and the notes. I also appreciate you jumping in to help control the Adam situation. I don't need a hero, though. And this whole nice act you got going on is just that: an act."

"It's not, though. I'm a good guy, Layla. I'm a great friend. So, what do you say. Friends?" He sticks his hand out.

I clasp his hand and a spark runs through me. I quickly

withdraw mine and nervously lift the corners of my mouth in a smile. His blue-gray eyes bore into me as if he can read all my unspoken thoughts. I clear my throat and move toward the bookshelf on the opposite side of the room.

"So ... I think I'm going to head home," he says. "I'll see you tomorrow. Unless you want my help with something before I go?"

Do I want his help with math again? I sort of do, but it feels a little wrong to rely on it. He's already helped me with Adam; that should be enough for one day.

"No. I got it."

He gives me a look that says, "I don't believe you try again." I smile again and he says, "All right. You know, agreeing to be friends means you have to be honest with me. Looks like I'm just going to have to offer my services in your mom's kitchen again." He slowly stands and I glare at him.

"Don't do that. Ugh. Fine. You can help."

He beams a smile like he just won the lotto. "Lead the way, then."

# Chapter Thirty

*Tyler*

I told myself to stay away. Ease into this slowly. I mean, we're talking about Layla "Faye" Valentine. Most of the time I can't believe they're one and the same. The girl in those texts and phone calls is sweet and funny, and doesn't hate me. The girl sitting across from me in her pink and white room looks like she's about to freak out and run for the hills any second now. Like she's waiting for me to be an absolute asshole or something.

"Layla, you need to relax."

"I am relaxed," she says with her brows bunching up in the middle.

I shake my head. "You're really not. If you grip that pencil any tighter it's going to snap."

She looks down at her pencil and drops it with a frown. "We can take a minute if you need it," I say.

"I don't." Layla flexes her hand and I can't take the space between us anymore. I get up out of the chair and move next to her. She starts to scoot away but I grab her hand and massage it.

"W-what are you doing?" she asks.

I crack a smile. "I'm giving your hand a rubdown. You need to relax."

"I um ... mmmhmmm."

"Yeah?"

"Shut up and keep ... oh yeah."

I almost laugh but keep massaging her hand. Her eyes flutter shut. I move my fingers gently up her arm and then knead her shoulders. She moans softly.

She leans forward. I want to keep working her muscles until she melts into me but I can't. I have to stop this.

I pull my hands back and smile at her. She's not smiling back though. She looks annoyed, or shocked. I'm not really sure which it is but neither is good. Layla tugs at the hem of her shirt and inches away from me. She does it so casually, like she's trying to hide the fact she's putting space between us. It's almost amusing.

"Thanks for the, uh ... yeah. What's number ten say again?"

I snatch her book from her and begin reading, "Y plus ten. Minus eight Y plus B to the fifth power equals six minus Y to the third power. Plus Y minus twenty B."

Her pencil sketches out the problem then she taps her eraser against her chin. It's one of her tics; I want to label it her thinking tic. She pauses and I stare like a creep. A knock on her door helps break my attention from her.

Juliet enters the room before Layla tells her to come in. "Layla, I have a huge problem and I ... oh ... uh ... I didn't know you had company."

"It's cool," I say and stand up. "I can step out for a second. Do you mind if I get something to drink?"

Juliet smiles at me. Layla answers, "Sure. Can you bring me back a bottle of water please?"

"Sure. As long as you promise not to dump it on my head."

Layla blushes. "I s-said I was s-sorry."

When she's nervous and stammering it's cute as hell. I'm not about to tell her this though. I just nod and glance over at her sister. She looks perplexed, as if she's trying to figure out what exactly is going on between Layla and myself. "Juliet, would you like anything?" I ask.

"I'm good. Thanks, Tyler."

I walk past her and leave the room. I probably shouldn't do it but I have a feeling whatever is happening is about Jared or Mark. If that's the case, I want to know what's up beforehand so I at least have a game plan on how to handle it. I lean against the door.

"Juliet, why are you so upset?"

"I'm probably crazy. I think Mark might break up with me."

"Why would he break up with you?"

I hear sobs and then Juliet whimpers, "There was some girl hanging all over him after school. He wasn't pushing her away. He didn't even notice I was even there until I said 'hey' to him."

Ah, shit. I make my way downstairs and pull out my cell.

"Hey," I say as soon as he answers.

"I can't talk long, man. My dad is making us run drills."

"Jared, screw your dad's drills for like three seconds. Listen, you might be getting your wish."

He huffs. "And what the hell would that be?"

"The one where Mark messes up and breaks Juliet's heart and you get the girl."

"Wait. What? Dude, I hate Mark right now. I do. But if she's happy that's all that matters. I want her happy. What did he do?"

"What *doesn't* Mark do? He flirted with a girl."

"Shit! I got to go." Before I can say another word, he hangs up.

I snatch some drinks from the Valentines' fridge and head upstairs.

As I'm about to enter Layla's room the doorbell rings. I press my ear to the door and the girls seem to be still talking and haven't heard the bell. I set down the drinks and head down to the front room.

I swing open the door and Chase raises a brow at me. "Uh, hey Tyler. What are you doing here?"

"Hanging out with Layla. What are you doing here?"

"Going to play some Wrath of Death with Juliet. Like usual."

I take a step back and eye Chase. "Whoa, Juliet is into video games?"

"Uh, yeah. Kind of our thing. She also likes Harry Potter, and doing those mud runs." He steps around me and makes his way upstairs.

"So are you, like, into her?" I ask. I know my question and tone make me sound like a total asshole, but I need to know how much competition might be out there for Jared.

Chase whips around on the steps and says, "Just friends. More like brother and sister."

"Ew. Okay. So no banging there at all."

"What the hell, Tyler? No. And if Mark is asking you to do recon, ask him to do it himself. I don't appreciate the acts on and off the field. He can swear to Juliet he's cool with her and I being friends, but the prick has found every way possible to have me injured. It's bullshit!"

I nod, even though I'm pretty sure if things are as bad as they sound Chase isn't going to have to worry about Mark. We head upstairs and Juliet steps out of Layla's room and startles. "Chase! Hey! Who let you in?"

"I did," I grin. I walk into the bedroom with the drinks.

Layla stares at her work and doesn't seem to notice I even entered the room.

"Here you go," I say, plopping down beside her with a bottle of water.

"Oh, thanks. Sorry about that. Girl stuff."

"Right. So, you going to Kelly's party this weekend?"

She shrugs. "Probably not."

"Why?"

"I just … I don't want to."

"Because of Adam, or Rachel?"

She shrugs again. "Both, probably. Plus, I just don't want to go."

I know it's both. We've texted about it. Why is she closing me off in person, but on the phone, she's an open book? I don't get it.

# Chapter Thirty-One

*Layla*

Tyler has come over my house for the last three days. It's confusing too. He hasn't tried to kiss me again. I don't know why, but when he looks at me my heart stutters. When his minty breath wafts in my direction I hold my breath. Why?

Logically speaking I shouldn't want or feel these things for Tyler. He says crazy crap that drives me nuts and he annoys the hell out of me. Then he touches me and my skin is ablaze. My thoughts fizzle out and all I can wish is that he won't stop touching me.

But I'll get text messages from R and my heart will start up in a frenzy. Butterflies swarm my stomach and my skin gets tingly. It's crazy. How can two people, one I don't really know and the other I usually generally despise, cause these feelings?

Juliet storms into my room and finds me staring at myself in the mirror. "What can I do for you this early in the morning?" I ask.

"What did you get me involved in?" she practically screams at me as she thrusts her phone into my face.

"I can't … " I'm about to say, "read this," but one glance at her and I know that's not the right thing to say at this moment.

She scowls at me. "Why am I getting text messages from this person telling me to watch myself because of you?"

I frown. "Don't worry I'll handle it."

"Will you? Because to me it doesn't look like you've been handling anything lately. Your boyfriend cheated on you with who knows how many girls. Now he stalks you, possibly going to throw a whole parade in your name. Your best friend probably screwed your ex. And you've been hanging out with the one person you loathe most in the world. My goodness, maybe you are right, and you're actually handling things," she finishes with an eye roll.

"I told you … "

She throws her hands up. "Stop! Just stop it right now. I'm happy, Layla. I'm not the loser twin anymore. People see me walking with Mark and they actually say hi to me. I don't know what you did to piss off whoever this might be, but I need you to handle it."

"I'm going to make sure nothing happens to you. It's just some crazy girl on the cheerleading squad. She's trying to get me kicked off. She's a popularity seeker. That's all. She probably thought if she went out for cheer she would automatically become the most popular girl. Who knows. What I do know is this: those types of people will do anything to get what they want."

She folds her arms. "So basically, this is somehow your

fault. Great. Just fantastic! I'm not you, Layla. We may look exactly alike but I'm the nerdy one. I don't want people to look at me like I'm the genetic freak of the family anymore." Tears slip down my sister's face and my heart clenches.

"I'm sorry. Juliet, I'm truly sorry. I'll fix this. I got your back."

She swipes her tears and sniffles. "Whatever." I watch her flee my room and I crumble against my vanity. One eyelid is perfectly done with makeup. The other is bare. I stare at myself a little longer then I reach for the makeup-remover wipes.

I take a soft, moist towel and rub it across my eyelid. Once all the purple and pink shadow stains the wet cloth, I toss it in the trash, and leave my room.

♥

I had forgotten how awful the bus is. I didn't want to ask Juliet for a ride considering how much my mess is now screwing with her life. Plus, this shit with Selena made her cry and that's not acceptable.

Some freshman with terrible acne, sweating so profusely I'm not positive if his hair is wet from a shower or greasy from lack of bathing, is currently breathing in my direction. I cringe a smile and look down at my lap.

"You're pretty. Are you new?" He sniffles deeply, like he's inhaling me. Gross.

I feel my eyes bug out. "I'm not new."

"I know everyone. I never seen you before."

I nod. I'm not about to take the bait.

He switches seats and sits across from me. "So. I'm Joe. I can show you around the school." He giggles his raspy squeak.

"Look, I'm sure you're sweet and all, but I really do know where I'm going."

"I know you do, Juliet. I was just so excited to see you on the bus. I like you a lot."

I sink my teeth into my bottom lip. He thinks I'm Juliet? Oh, goodness. This bus ride literally can't get much worse, can it?

"I'm not Juliet," I whisper back.

"Right, you're the other one. I get it. You could have just said no thanks. No need to make up lies."

"I'm not making up anything." I pull out my student ID and he snorts.

"You could be returning that to your sister. It's fine. No need to try to make me feel better. I knew I had no chance in hell."

There is no arguing with crazy. The outcome is always terrible. I shift toward the window and squeeze my eyes shut.

When we pull into school I hop off the bus so fast you would have thought the thing was on fire. I nearly collide with Rachel right as I take off down the walkway. She smiles at me. "Hey."

I don't say anything back to her. This is the longest I've gone without speaking to her. Sadly, it hurts. The words swimming inside me are bursting to come out but I swallow them. I'm not ready. I start to pull away and she cries out, "Come on,

Layla! I said I was sorry! What more do you want me to do?"

I keep walking away. I know she's sorry. It was a mistake. I get it. But I also firmly believe she's capable of restraint, no matter how drunk. I need more time.

In my distress, I accidently shoulder another person while entering the school. I mumble, "I'm sorry."

"Wow. That's got to be a first. Hold on, let me pull out my recorder. Can you say that again?" Tyler jokes with a grin.

I roll my eyes. "No."

"Nice look. Run out of makeup?" he jokes.

"No."

"Wow. One-word answers now. What's going on? I thought we were moving past hating me," he says.

I can't help myself; I smile at his stupid comment. "Maybe. Maybe I just don't feel like talking."

Tyler escorts me to my locker. "I'm not going to give up just like that. Tell me."

I raise a brow. "All right, mister nosey pants. Some chick is trying to ruin my sister because she's got it in her head I'm in the way of her becoming super popular. Oh and P.S., the same girl wants you too."

He burst out laughing. "I'm sorry. What?"

"You heard me the first time."

"It's just so utterly stupid I wasn't sure if you were pulling my leg or being serious. Who's the girl?"

"I am serious. And why should I tell you her name? Don't you want the extra fan mail?" I reach my locker and start twisting in my combination. It pops open and I glance over at Tyler.

"I really don't need any extra fan mail." He nudges me.

"Come on, give me some kind of hint. What sort of stalker is in my near future? Please don't tell me she's a grade-A, five-star clinger."

I snort at the thought of Selena being labeled a five-star clinger. "Sophomore."

"What? That's all you're giving me? Come on, Princess, that's barely shit to go off. A hint is more like her name starts with an F."

"Her name doesn't start with an F. Unless you want to label her something like F-buddy."

He grins. "Are you jealous?"

"Please! I can't get rid of you fast enough," I tease. Although, the thought of him wanting Selena makes me disgusted. Why do I even care? This is Tyler Richardson we're talking about. He doesn't like me like that. I don't like him like that. I mean, I think I don't. My body is throwing me off, giving me feelings that I should have for someone nice, and sweet.

I need to derail this subject. "Aren't you going to your locker?"

"In a minute. Trying to get rid of me so quickly?"

I shake my head. "I just thought you needed your books. Your hands are pretty empty and that backpack looks really light."

"It is." He leans against the lockers and smiles. "I notice you took the bus today. Juliet not giving you rides now?"

"It's not that. It was … my choice."

I notice the sprinkling of scruff along his jaw. I wonder what it would be like to kiss it. I shake my head quickly. Why do I keep having these silly thoughts about what it would be like to kiss Tyler?

He stares at me and I blink. "What?"

"I was saying right, like you chose not to wear makeup today."

"I said that ... " He presses his finger to my lips and I close my mouth.

"As I was saying. It's fine be what you want and all that jazz, but if you want I can come by and get you."

"That's silly. Aren't I way out of your way?"

"You're closer than you think," he says, and my heart slams into my chest. I quickly turn away as I feel my cheeks burning.

After exchanging books from my locker, I take off down the hall without responding. He probably thinks I'm cuckoo-bird crazy or reverting to my old self, which involves ignoring him as much as humanly possible. I'm not ignoring him. But I might be a little crazy, because my body and mind are not reacting how they should. Not at all.

I slip into my first-period class and busy myself. There are already plenty of seats filled and people talking amongst themselves. So, when he finally strolls by my room, I immediately turn to the girl next to me, Erin, and start laughing as if whatever she said was the funniest thing ever.

Apparently, this was a terrible idea on my part because Erin just glares at me with watery eyes and sobs, "Why do you think my brother being shipped off overseas is funny?"

"What? No. I was laughing at something else."

"It doesn't seem like it."

Her friend Nancy shakes her head. "You're such a bitch, Layla."

I face the front of the room and glance down at my desk. *Way to go.*

Ms. Prez strolls into the room and announces, "Class, be seated and quiet down. We've got a lot to cover today in History."

I flip open my notebook and click my pen. Before the tardy bell rings, Adam taps on the door. One of his eyes is swelled up and bruised. A gasp escapes me as I take him all in. Who in the hell beat him up and why do I even care?

He hands Ms. Prez a note. His eyes scan the room. As soon as his good eye lands on me it narrows and his jaw clenches. I swear I can hear his teeth grinding from three rows back. "Well, Adam, here is the rest of the work for this week."

Ms. Prez hands him a stack of papers and he grins at her. "Thanks, teach."

He glances my way one last time and my body freezes. It isn't until he finally exits the room that my body starts to unwind and the knot in my stomach uncoils.

Ms. Prez rambles on about something and I barely catch on to what exactly it is until she says, "What are your thoughts on this Layla?"

Crap! "Thoughts on what?"

"Exactly. Please try to pay attention. I don't stand up here just to hear myself talk. Learning this information is important, class, it will be on the test tomorrow."

Everyone snickers. I get that I'm not exactly listening to her excessive babbling but did she really have to call me out on it? What about Zack in the far corner of the room? He's sleeping, for goodness sakes.

# Chapter Thirty-Two

*Tyler*

I screwed up. I thought we were getting somewhere. I thought flirting with her wouldn't be so bad. Turns out I totally misread her signals. It shouldn't really surprise me, because when have I ever been able to read Layla Valentine correctly? Never.

I pull out my phone during first period and send her a quick text.

```
Me: Hey beautiful. How's ur morning
going?
```

I slip my phone back into my bag and look up at the board. Mr. Zino, my Algebra 2 teacher, is scribbling some problems on the board while he says, "This will all be on the test."

As I'm taking notes a blond girl enters our room. She beams a smile at me and waves. I lift my hand to be nice. She looks familiar but I can't exactly place her. Mr. Zino pulls away from the board and says, "Can I help you?"

"Yes, I have a few office slips here," the girl says.

She looks at me again and winks. Where have I seen her before?

"Tyler? You're wanted in the office. Take your things with you," Mr. Zino says.

Shit! What could this be about? If it's about beating Adam's ass in the parking lot, he deserved it. Coach didn't seem all that mad when I told him what I had done. I haven't pulled any pranks lately. In fact, I make sure not to do anything during football season. It's my go-to rule.

I shove all my things into my backpack and make my way out the door. "Hi!" the blond girl says as she pops out in front of me.

"Hey."

"I'm Selena." She twirls a piece of hair around her finger and says, "You played such a great game last week. Are you pumped for the Blackhawk game?"

"Uh … yeah."

"I can't wait to perform my new cheer for you this Friday." She winks at me again, and that's when everything all clicks.

I shake my head. "Ah, you're Adam's little plaything from a couple of weeks ago."

"I'm not his plaything. I'm totally free," she says as she follows me to the office.

"Oookay." I start to turn toward the office doors and she pulls my arm. "What are you doing?"

"I broke you out of class to talk to you, silly." She flutters her eyelashes and walks her fingers up my arm.

It actually does nothing for me. I'm not even slightly turned on. In fact, I'm annoyed she gave me a fake note. I need to be in Mr. Zino's class, not skipping it with this girl who is clearly pissing me off.

"I know you probably don't want to hear this but I love you," she says.

I blink. "I'm sorry, you what? You don't even know me."

She shakes her head. "Sure, I do. You're Tyler Richardson. You're sexy. You're the greatest receiver ever. You have fantastic hair and abs."

I need her to stop. "You just named all the superficial and vain shit about me. Do you have anything else or are we done here?"

"Why are you being so mean?" she sticks her lower lip out.

I restrain from rolling my eyes. "Selena, is it? I'm sure deep down you're probably nice. I'm just not interested."

"Why not?"

"I'm seeing someone." It's not technically a lie.

She folds her toned arms. "No, you're not! I haven't seen you with anyone. Why are you lying?"

"I'm not." Sure, Layla and I aren't officially anything. Hell, I can't even really say we're friends, but I'm working on it. It's a little complicated. What if she likes R more than she likes me? I know we're the same person, but I'm pretty sure she doesn't know that. When I found out Faye was Layla, hell, I almost stopped talking to her immediately. But I truly like Faye, and she is Layla—just a side of her I never see.

Selena keeps staring at me like she's waiting for some sort of revelation. I keep glancing around the empty halls for an escape. There isn't one. Damn girl has me cornered by a set of lockers near the office.

"Well, who is she then?"

"Why do you need to know?" I ask. Yeah, I'm the master at avoiding questions with questions. My sister says it's the most annoying habit I have. I say it's a great life skill for getting out of situations with my pants still on, so to speak.

"Because I told you I'm in love with you."

I scrunch up my face and shake my head. "You said it and you gave me some really piss-poor reasons that show how little you know me. Sorry, but I don't think you're actually in love with me."

"I'll prove it." As soon as I'm about to protest she plants her lips on me. Someone gasps loudly.

I break from her lips and turn to see Layla with her hand over her mouth.

"Layla," I call out.

She turns on her heels quick and bolts down the hall. Great. Just fantastic! This is exactly what I don't need right now.

Selena looks smug. "I think we should hit up Kelly's party this weekend, after you score a billion touchdowns and kick Blackhawk's ass!"

I need to shut this shit down right now. "No! I don't want you cheering for me. I don't ever want your lips on me ever again. You're not only bad at it, you're so bad I felt like my dog could do better." Her eyes well up with tears, and yes, I know I should probably stop. But she did just ruin my happiness with someone I really care about. Bring on the rain of tears. "While we're at it, never try busting me out of class again to feed me some bullshit about how you're so in love with me."

She sniffles. "But I do. You're a jerk."

"Awesome. I need to get back to class."

I storm down the hall and back into First Period, which is now ending in less than ten minutes. I hope someone in class at least took some notes that I can borrow, since Mr. Zino informed us that everything we discussed today will be on our test tomorrow. Fan-flipping-tastic.

I hope to see Layla at lunch so I can at least talk to her. Tell her that what she saw this morning was nothing. She'll probably say it doesn't matter because it's not like we're dating or whatever.

But I need her to know it was nothing. Unfortunately, she's not in the cafeteria. I wait and wait. Maybe she'll arrive late. She's not late though. She's not coming.

"Juliet, I hate to put you in the middle of something, but can you relay a message to your sister for me?"

She raises a brow at me. "Uh. No."

"Please." I'm not above getting on my hands and knees and begging. And I will if my pleading doesn't work. Her gaze drills me.

"I'm not a messenger. Just text her like everyone else."

"I, uh … can't." Because I want to play off this cover as

R a little longer. It would kind of blow my plans if I text her right this minute. "Hey Layla, sorry about what you saw in the hall. It really was nothing. P.S. I really think we should grab some food sometime." That would look real strange coming from my pseudonym.

"Lemme guess, your phone died didn't it, genius?" Mark says.

I shrug. "You got me. Can you relay the message for me Juliet? Please."

Her shoulders lower. "Fine. What is it?"

Maybe saying it aloud in front of my boys isn't a good idea. "Uh, right. I'll give it to you in a second." All the guys at the table observe me and I shake my head. "What?"

Austin pipes in, "Nothing. It's just, since when the hell do you want to relay a message to Layla Valentine?"

"Mind your own business," I growl.

Mark, being Mark, laughs. "Oh, he's been hanging out with her a lot lately."

"Really?" Austin asks. I certainly don't answer. Mark smirks. Juliet kind of nods and then Jared approaches our table.

"What did I … miss?" he asks, his eyes landing on Juliet.

"Nothing much, man. Just Richardson here might be macking on Layla Valentine," Austin answers.

"Shut the hell up!" I yell. I don't know why his crap is ticking me off, but right now I'm not in the mood. Yes, I like Layla. But it's not so simple. It's kind of complicated. I don't need it getting any more complicated with stupid rumors either.

I snatch up my notebook and write: *I will see you later. We need to talk.* Then I pass the note to Juliet.

# Chapter Thirty-Three

*Layla*

My sister thrusts a note into my palm during the switch between Sixth and Seventh periods. I stare at the paper as if it's offending me. "What's this?"

"I don't know. I was just told to deliver it."

Students pass us on both sides of the busy hallway. Some seem to glance our way but mostly they just keep walking. I glare at her. "Who told you to give this to me?"

She is closed-lipped on the matter and shoulders into me as she pushes down the hall. I sigh and head to my class and unfold the note. It takes me a full fifteen minutes to read the words. When I finally figure it out I'm beyond mad at him. He was in the hall with Selena. He was flirting with Selena. He freaking kissed her.

Thinking about his lips pressed to hers makes me nauseated. I shouldn't even care. It's just Tyler. So what if his facial stubble is a little sexier than I thought it was before. Who cares if I like his deep rumbling chuckle. Big deal if I really like his help with my math problems. He's still Tyler

Richardson. The same guy who poured orange juice under my chair to make it look like I peed my pants in the fourth grade. The same guy who taunted me throughout elementary school and most of junior high. The same guy who gave Adam a ton of shit for dating me from day one. He's an ass.

There's no other word for it. What kind of guy says, "Hey, we need to talk," to a girl after kissing another one earlier that day? A true jackass, is who. Of course, if he's a jackass so am I, because what kind of ding gets worked up over someone who's been mean to her most of her life? An idiot, that's who.

"Layla?"

I look over and notice Rachel sitting beside me. "Hey," she says. "Are you okay?"

I nod even though I don't feel fine at all. I also just realize our teacher, Mr. Vander, isn't here today. We have some old lady who's wearing what looks to be someone's curtains as a jacket and rug as her pants. She also doesn't seem to give one rat's butt if we're not sitting in our seats or learning anything. The TV in the corner that broadcasts our daily school announcements is currently on a local channel. On the TV is some soap opera I've caught my mom watching when I was home sick a few times last year.

I sneer at the TV as a couple fake-passionately kiss and another man walks into the room and yells at them. The woman turns and pretends to be shocked by being caught. The two men act like they're going to throw down over this woman.

Rachel snaps her fingers in front of my face. "Layla, come on, it's me. I can see you're upset. What's wrong? Please talk to me."

"I think I'm insane." I must be. I'm snarling at a fake

relationship on TV. I'm upset that a guy who basically has been the bane of my existence since the beginning of time is possibly in love with a girl trying to ruin my life. Yes. I'm officially insane.

She shakes her head. "No, you aren't. Why would you think that?"

I shouldn't be talking to her, for starters, but it feels good. I missed talking to her. "I think I like two people. One of them I've never met. The other, well, he's taken by someone who just wants him to boost her popularity status."

"Okay. Well, how about you start from the beginning with the one you've never met and work your way to the other."

Before I even realize it, I'm telling her everything. From the texts between "R" and I and down to Tyler popping into my life. And me liking him there instead of hating it like I should. By the time I'm all finished, Rachel and I stare at each other.

"Layla, I really want to give you a hug right now, but I feel like you haven't totally forgiven me yet."

I nod as tears stream down my face.

"I get it. My advice about the two boys, I think you should hear Tyler out. Then you need to text this other person and meet him. If it's real, you'll know. If what you feel with Tyler is stronger, then you'll know who to fight for. You know?"

"You don't think it's silly?" I ask.

"What?"

"Falling for someone you've never met and getting emotional over a guy like Tyler?"

She shakes her head. "I think things happen for a reason."

"So, what are you going to do?" she asks.

"I don't know. I'm worried if I open up to either, I'll lose both. Or worse, what if they both want to give this a try? What do I do then?"

"You're not marrying them. You're not even dating them. Just go hang out with Tyler one day and mystery man on another. Find out who you like more."

I chew on my lower lip. "I guess."

"Layla, you need to quit worrying so much. Just relax and have fun, live in the moment."

That's her lifestyle motto. Maybe that motto is to blame for her crappy decisions, which lead to her hooking up with my ex. I frown at the thought.

"Stop, Layla. I told you a million and one times, I'm sorry. I can't take that night back, but if I could you know I would."

"I know. It just stings still, you know? I see now what a real jackass he is, but he also was my first long term boyfriend. He had his sweet moments. We made some good memories. But his betrayal and how he treated me, how he continues to treat me, really hurts. I know I didn't give him my V-card. He shouldn't be a total tool to me. He shouldn't have cheated on me. He should have done the right thing and broke up with me if his sexual needs were so overwhelming. You know?"

"I do. I'm sorry I hurt you too. Really."

I sniffle a little but manage to smile at her.

As I'm walking outside with Rachel, Tyler pushes off his Jeep and stalks over toward us. "Layla, you got a second?"

Rachel nudges me and I sigh. "I'll wait for you, okay?" she says, then she yells, "Jenna, wait up!"

She runs after Jenna, our head cheerleader. Tyler smiles at me and I look down at the ground. "Hey." His fingers skim the bottom of my chin and he tilts my head so I can see him.

"What do you want?" I sound defeated which I truly hate. But damn those blue eyes boring into my soul.

"What you saw in the hall, it was—"

I cut him off. "I don't care. Do what you want, Tyler. We're just ... I don't know what we are other than acquaintances, because we're not friends. We're not dating. Heck, a few weeks ago I disliked everything about you. No worries. I gotta get to practice. You don't have to wait for me, I've got a ride and, um ... you don't have to come over to my house after." My heart squeezes as I push out every word. Keeping him at a distance for now is the best solution.

His eyes narrow a bit. "Yeah. Okay. Glad that's all straight. Later." He pivots and marches off to his Jeep.

My entire body aches all over. It's for the best though. Selena will leave Juliet alone, which means Juliet won't be mad at me anymore. I won't be confused about liking two boys. And we can just move on like nothing ever happened.

# Chapter Thirty-Four

*Tyler*

What the hell happened? Couldn't she see what I was about to tell her? She just stomped on my heart and threw it back at me like, "Eh. Here you go."

She wouldn't even let me explain. Don't bother coming over to her house? Well, I'm sorry, but Princess Layla is going to see I don't give up that easy. I don't care if it ticks her off either.

I drive to the field and suit up in my practice gear. I'm in a mood. A very bad one. Most of the guys can tell too, because not one of them has said a word to me. They fan out when I approach the water cooler, or after a play, and in the huddle, I notice some of them are practically jumping on Jared's helmet so they don't have to stand by me.

"All right, that's it! What is going on with you?" Jared bellows at me from the huddle.

"Nothing!" I've never gone to blows with Jared but I'm about to.

He takes off his helmet and slams it to the ground. I do

the same and then he charges me. Our pads press against each other and he yells, "What's up with you today? We're a freaking team, Ty! Act like it! You just plowed right into James here like an effing truck and there isn't any need for it."

"He was in my running lane."

"Oh, so we just take out our teammates. It's practice, dude. Find another route. We can't afford to be busting up our own guys!"

I shove him. "Get out of my face."

"I'll get in your damn face if I want to. Settle down or go sit down!"

"You're not the coach! You're just his son. That doesn't make you the damn boss, Black."

I feel arms wrap around my shoulders, jerking me back. I see some of the guys containing Jared. I don't know what the hell is wrong with me. Well, I take that back. I know exactly what's pissing me off: that damn shit Layla said. *We're not even friends.* The hell we weren't. What the hell have I been doing over at her house for the past few days? Why would I offer to pick her up or take her home? If we weren't friends, why would I help her with her math problems every day? It's bullshit!

"That's enough you two. You got energy to kill someone, go run it off! Ten laps around the entire field. And if that doesn't straighten you two out you'll be running the stadium stairs. Got me?" Coach Black bellows at us.

Jared glares at me and shakes his head. "Thanks. You're a real awesome best friend!"

I bow my head and begin my laps. Damn Layla is screwing with my head. Football is the one place I'm in complete control. I don't have to act a certain way. I don't have to pretend or fake a smile and act like everything in my life is perfect. That is, until today. I no longer feel in control and it's costing me big time. My best friend thinks I'm a total asshole and probably wants to strangle me. I need to snip the strings on this Layla shit and move on. This is not worth the trouble it's already causing.

Jared and I are neck-in-neck on the first lap and I'm breathing pretty easy. "Hey man, I'm sorry. I just lost it back there."

"Whatever man. I don't know what the hell is wrong with you lately," Jared puffs.

"Layla. Okay? I have a freaking thing for Layla."

He falters a bit. "Valentine? Are you kidding me?" I don't say anything. "Oh, that's just rich, man. You know you can't go after her." We round a corner, and before I can ask why the hell not, he says, "Jesus dude, we're trying to keep unity on the field. How do you think Adam is going to feel when he gets wind you want his ex?"

"Screw Adam. He shouldn't have cheated on her."

Jared laughs and my anger returns. What the hell is so funny? I contemplate shoving his ass right into the railings. "You do realize how hilarious this is, right?" He's still chuckling. I don't find this funny. "A month ago, you couldn't stand her. I had to beg you to give her a ride back to school." This is very true. "You were okay with her walking back. You do remember that, don't you? Now you've got a huge thing for her? What the hell changed?"

I stop jogging and he stops too. "Come on. We have to keep going or my dad is going to make us run stairs," he says.

"She's the girl I've been texting."

"Hold on. Does she know?"

I shake my head. "Don't tell anyone." I start jogging again. "All these pieces started adding up, and I don't know man. The more I texted her, the more I started to like her."

Jared doesn't say anything; so, I continue. "But she blew me off before the start of practice. It's like she's back to her ice queen ways and I can't stand it."

"Just tell her."

I laugh. "That will go over real fantastic. 'Hey Layla, call me some time, I think we should go see a movie or something. Oh, you want my number? You already have it, babe.'" I cringe. "She'll probably punch me in the face and call me every name in the book." Even as I analyze all the worst possible scenarios I realize I sound like a lovesick chick. Shit!

I can see Jared biting back a laugh and I actually don't blame him. I'm freaking pathetic. "So … basically either way you're screwed." We slow down on our last set of laps. "You can't text her because she'll hate you. You can't confront her because she'll freak out." We pass the goal post on the opposite end. Jared pants out, "And Adam will be even worse than he is now. You can't stop texting her entirely either, because chances are she'll figure out it was you then she'll really hate you. Either way you are screwed." He shakes his head. "I told you this would blow up in your face eventually."

"I know!" I yell at him as we finish our sixth lap. "Now you get it."

"No. Now you are getting a taste of what I'm going through. Because the only way this gets really shitty is watching her fall for someone who isn't you."

That won't happen. "I just have to cut ties."

"That's one step. You won't feel better though." We're

jogging the straightaway past the home side benches. "Then you'll see her move on and you'll take a backseat if you aren't doing the same."

"Are you done?"

"No. It's only going to get worse from there, man."

We make another lap and I'm getting tired. "Why does it have to get worse?"

"Because you're going to be stuck in the same bullshit bubble that I'm in. There will be so many times you'll want to tell her and show her how happy you could make her." I almost yell back 'we won't be the same.' I'll eventually tell Layla how I feel. "But you can't without destroying her first and it kills you. In your situation there is no Mark, just you and your texting secret identity."

Damn. Maybe there was a little more holding Jared back than I realized. But he hasn't killed Mark yet. Doesn't that mean he's holding himself together a little better than he thinks? There has to be some sort of trick. Because if she screwed me up this much by just blowing me off without letting me get a word in edgewise, making me so mad I can't think straight, how the hell am I going to handle her finding someone else? I'll explode.

My thoughts must be all over my face because Jared says, "Yeah, it totally sucks."

"How the hell do you not kill him every day?"

He makes a noncommittal grunt. "Don't know. Focusing on football. Keeping busy. Trying to avoid being around them as much as possible. It's hard not to lay him out every day on the field, or drill him with the football so hard he ends up unconscious."

"I'm sorry."

We're finishing up our last lap. "Me too. Keep your head in the game."

"How much shit are you going to get at home over this?" I ask with a frown.

"A lot."

♥

I figured I needed to take on some of the punishment since this is technically my fault Jared's in deep water. We're currently in his backyard busting our asses doing drills through the obstacle course his dad has set up. Seriously, this shit looks like something from a movie about people training to be Marines or something. Pretty much the only thing we don't have to do is crawl through a mud pit.

We do have to run between sets of tires, around some cones, and carry the football through these thickly padded steel poles set so close together you can barely get past in full gear. We should though, and we need to do it without dropping the ball. I fail three times.

Jared doesn't. I have a feeling he's run this crazy shit twenty times a day, every day, since eighth grade. By the time we're done, I almost pass out on the lawn. How the heck does Jared put up with this crap after practice and still manage homework? I'm about dead.

Jared has sweat dripping off the tips of his hair and nose. "You all right down there?" He asks with a grin.

How the hell can he possibly be smiling at a time like this? "No man. I might need a stretcher to haul me out of here."

"Thanks. For doing the drills with me."

"You do this shit every night, don't you?"

"It's not so bad once you get through it a few times."

"He's insane. You do realize that?" I ask, glancing back at his dad to make sure he's out of earshot.

Jared frowns. "Comes with the territory I guess."

"Boys! Time to come in," Coach Black yells.

I push off the ground and follow Jared into the house. "Wash up for dinner," Mrs. Black says. "Tyler, are you staying?"

"No, ma'am. I have to get home to my homework. Thanks for asking though."

"You're always welcome," she says with a pearly smile.

I leave the house feeling exhausted and guilty as hell. I knew Jared was pushed hard by his dad. Hell; sometimes his dad would get shitty if Jared was staying over my house. I thought it was because he thought I was a delinquent or something. No wonder Jared never asked Juliet out where would he even find the time to take her out? Not with his dad monopolizing like this every day.

When I finally pull into my own driveway I slide my phone out and sigh. "Here goes nothing."

```
Me: Would u b my d8 2 my school's
winter formal?
```

Layla doesn't respond right away. It's too late to take back the message. Crap. I should have eased into this. Damn it. I just blew it.

# Chapter Thirty-Five

*Layla*

I stare at the message on my phone. Tingling little wisps of flutters fill my belly and dance along my skin from head to toe. I chew on my lower lip.

"What's wrong?" Rachel asks.

"I just … "

"Is it math, or those feelings for Tyler and mysterious texting boy?"

"Well, R just texted me. He wants me to be his date for the school dance."

"Oh, my God! Are you serious? Let me see!" she yanks the phone from me and smiles so wide I swear her face is going to crack. "What are you going to say?"

"No. I can't. I mean, for one he'll know I was lying to him. Two, what if this is too good to be true?"

Rachel wrinkles her nose and nods. "You're right. I mean, what if this person turns out to be catfishing you. And really he's an old man."

"What? Don't be silly. We talked on the phone and he did not sound like an old man."

"There are apps that can disguise your voice, you know."

The more she tells me this stuff the more I don't want to see him. Wow, Juliet was right. This was a really bad idea.

```
Me: I can't. I'm going out with someone
this weekend and if things go well I
don't want to hurt his feelings. Sorry.
R: No worries.
```

My heart instantly stings. How could I possibly go from feeling all blushy to miserable in a matter of ten minutes?

"Are you okay?" Rachel asks. "You look really pale and awful right now."

"Why do I feel like I made a mistake?"

She shrugs. "You didn't, though. Look, you don't know this person. He could be a total fake. Maybe he's not really on the football team. Heck, maybe he's a freshman nerdball."

What does that matter? I wouldn't care if he is a freshman. I wouldn't care if he doesn't really play football. However, I do think he would care who I am. And hell, what if he just doesn't like me? Just look at Tyler, he admitted to disliking me. What if this person does too?

It's just better to leave this alone and not know.

Rachel hugs me. "It's going to be okay. You'll see."

"I know." But really my insides don't feel like that. They are aching in places I didn't know one could even hurt.

She gets off the bed. "I have to head out. I'll call you later. 'Kay?"

"Yeah. Sure." Oh, my God, I sound like a robot. I better snap out of it soon.

Rach smiles and then leaves.

I fiddle with my phone. *No. It's better this way.* I drop it on the bed and walk out of my room. *Out of sight out of mind, or however that phrase goes.*

As I descend the stairs, I hear laughter pouring out of the kitchen. I peer around the corner and see my mom and sister sitting at the table, flipping through some photo albums.

"Oh, remember this one?" My mom coos and points to a photo. My sister giggles.

"Layla was so mad." Then Juliet frowns. "Mom, I know you say we sometimes need our own space to work stuff out and all, but I'm worried about Lays."

Mom turns to her and sighs. "Me too. Ever since she and Adam broke up she's been bit of a frumpy, grumpy girl. I want to butt in and help but I also want her to work through whatever is going on by herself. I don't want to be that mom. The nosey one who needs to know your entire business."

"Mom, I don't think she'd mind so much this time."

What the hell, Juliet? I'm so mad at my sister for suggesting such a thing. I don't need help. So, I've been a little edgy. So, I decided to dress like a mess. Who cares? A few days of it doesn't mean I need my mom to come in and fix things. Maybe I'm more of a mess than I realize though. Still, I can fix this. At least I'm fairly sure I can. I grab my coat and purse then rush out the door.

Once I'm outside though I realize I'm sort of screwed. My car is still in the shop, Rach just left, plus I ditched my phone in my room, so there goes calling for a ride. But I need to get away from the house. At least for a little while.

I walk to the nearest bus stop.

I've been walking in and out of stores for the past thirty minutes. My mood hasn't improved.

As I approach a store called Gowns by Design, the pit in my stomach worsens.

This is ridiculous. I should be able to step into a silly dress shop if I want to. So, I rejected the first person to ask me to a dance since Adam and I broke up. Big deal?

I step into the store and browse the beautiful gowns hanging on the racks. Different materials such as silk, satin, and glittered rhinestones slip through my fingers. Usually I want to try on every dress in the store. Today, I want to bury my face in glittery sequins and bawl my eyes out. Why did I have to be such a wuss? Why didn't I say yes?

*Because secretly you want Tyler to ask you.* That's ridiculous. He's clearly made his choice. He kissed Selena in the hall. Enough said.

Screw it. That's exactly what I'll do.

I leave the store and rush back home to tell R everything.

# Chapter Thirty-Six

*Tyler*

My phone has been going off with text messages for the last hour, all of them from Layla. She's telling me who she is and that she attends the same school as me. Everything I already knew. Problem is she still turned down my offer to take her to a dance.

I've never actually been dissed by anyone but her. Seems so fitting that even in our little secret texting life she would reject me too. Freaking wonderful.

I'm not responding to her. She can blow up my phone until she's blue in the face. I won't text back. Instead, I go to bed.

The next day as I'm shutting my locker, a sweet marshmallow scent fills my nose. "Hi Tyler," Layla says in a cheery voice.

Seriously?

I pretend I don't hear her and start down the hall. She pops in front of me with a raised brow and waves, "Hi Tyler."

What a joke. The idea that she thinks she can come up to me and act like we're friends after the shit she pulled yesterday. Un-freaking-believable! She touches my arm but I shrug her hand off and continue moving down the hall. I only take about four strides before she yells, "Really? Fine, be a jerk."

"One to talk, cupcake," I mutter.

"Uh. Did I miss something? I thought you were into her?" Jared asks as he bounds up beside me.

"I am. She's clearly not feeling me."

"Didn't look that way a few minutes ago. You completely brushed her off."

"She did it twice to me, once at school and last night. Look at this shit." I show him my latest text from her.

Jared laughs. "She doesn't know this is you."

"It doesn't matter. It says right here she's going on a freaking date this weekend."

"Sorry man."

I turn to face him and shrug while walking backwards. "Plenty of fish in the sea, my friend."

He gives me a keep-telling-yourself-that-man look. I ignore it until my back bumps into something and I hear, "Hey, watch it!"

I swivel around and my eyes land on the twin of the girl who took my insides and twisted them all into knots. "Sorry Juliet."

"What's it with you and us Valentines? You trying to tell us we need to get knocked down a few pegs?" She laughs but I just stare at her. Does she know I like her sister?

Jared chimes in, "Hey Juliet. Don't you have Mr. Walker for Fifth?"

"Yeah. That assignment yesterday was so hard. How did you do on it?"

"I spent almost two hours on it," he says with a frown. I step back and try to move away from them. No need to stand around like a third wheel.

I spot Mark coming down the hall; I still have a debt to pay to Jared for yesterday's practice laps.

I hurry to Mark and deflect him. "Hey man. Got a minute?"

"What's up?" Mark asks.

"It's about the dance coming up. Are you getting a limo?"

His face instantly pales. "Do you think she's going to care?"

"All girls care." I grab him by the shoulders and start walking him to my First Period class. "I got it covered. I just want to know if you're in." It's sort of a lie. I mean, I'll pay for the limo. I just haven't gotten the thing yet.

"Cool. I was going to ask Juliet this week."

"Yeah, you should. Before the playoff game."

"I know, we're going to rock it."

Selena comes bouncing toward us in her uniform. "Hi Tyler! Hi Mark!" she says in a bubbly voice.

"Hey Selena," Mark says. I see his eyes sweep down Selena and back up again.

"Bro, why are you checking her out? You've got a girlfriend," I whisper.

"I can still look," he says.

Selena is now in front of us twirling a blond curl around her finger. "You guys look so handsome. Are you two excited for the big game tonight?"

Tonight, is the Blackhawk game. Not only are they our rival, it's also the last game of the regular season. Then it's the start of the playoffs next week. Usually I'm pumped for games, and especially *this* game, but today I actually don't give a shit.

"Yeah," I say.

She winks. "Can't wait to cheer for you boys." She walks past us with a giggle. Mark scans her and I roll my eyes and head down the hallway.

"Dude, I think she's into you," Mark says.

I shrug.

"You need to get laid or something," he says.

Probably, but I'm not going to admit it. I'm almost at First Period, so I say, "See you at lunch."

Mark looks at me like I'm crazy. "Yeah, okay."

I slip into class and drop down into my seat near the back. My phone dings.

```
Faye: I'm sorry. Please talk to me.
```

# Chapter Thirty-Seven

*Layla*

My day sucks. I mean it really bites the total big one. It's last period and R hasn't responded to any of my texts. At this point I might need an intervention or have my mom confiscate my phone. Not that the texts I've sent are stalkerish or make me out to be a total psycho. Well, at least I don't think they do.

Why won't he talk to me? Is it possible I did something wrong and now that I revealed who I am it's changed his perspective of asking me to the dance? Like he doesn't want anything to do with me at all? It shouldn't bother me. It does though, and I really miss our conversations. Somehow, someway, I completely blew it.

Not only am I dealing with this, but now Tyler is giving me the brushoff too. What was that all about? I thought we were friends. I get he's not really into me. I get that Selena is his type, though I cannot for the life of me understand why he would be into Selena. Is he blind? Can he not see she's using him?

She probably has no idea what kind of things he even likes, like what his favorite band is. Not that I'm really much better but I bet I know a heck of lot more than she does.

Someone snickers beside me in class, drawing me away from my current thoughts and back into reality. Ms. Clements stares at me. "Layla, I'd like to see you after class."

Dang it!

The final bell rings, dismissing everyone from class except me. I wait until everyone leaves before I approach Ms. Clements's desk.

Her beady eyes lock with mine. "Layla, I don't know what's going on with you lately but it's troubling me. Your work as of late is subpar. You aren't taking notes. Do you know I called your name seven times before you even snapped out of your daydream? Exams are coming up soon and I really need you to focus."

Nothing like getting a lecture for being below average to top off an already crappy day. She frowns at me. "Here is a copy of the notes. Do not let this happen again or I'll be forced to call your mother and set up a meeting with the school's counselor."

That is the very last thing I need. "I'm sorry Ms. Clements. It won't happen again. I promise. Thanks for the notes."

"Be sure to study them. You only get one pass in my class."

She dismisses me. I gather up the rest of my things and as I exit the classroom spot Tyler and Selena just outside the doorway. She's walking her fingers up his arm and he's not making any attempt whatsoever to dissuade her affections. A slow burn creeps up my throat as my stomach twists in knots.

Hot tears threaten to spill. I blink rapidly to hold them at bay. A few slip out as I bow my head and rush down the hall away from them. It feels like a thousand needles have pinpricked my heart when I reach my locker. What is wrong with me?

It's just Tyler. Stupid, annoying, likes-to-make-sure-he-has-everyone's-attention Tyler. I shouldn't care at all. But I do. He's the first person besides Rachel and my sister who doesn't make fun of my dyslexia. He doesn't look at me with pity either. He doesn't try to make me feel dumb, and I love that.

When Adam found out about my dyslexia, he laughed, like with tears springing from his eyes. Then when we went out to restaurants he would say, "Oh, should I read the menu for you?" As if I was a toddler. I hated how much he belittled me, but I wanted to give him a chance. He didn't know what I was going through so he didn't know how to handle it. At the time, I thought maybe that was his way of helping, but it just humiliated me. I never told him though, so he never knew. I can't exactly fault him for that.

"Hey," Rachel says, pulling me from my thoughts. "Are you okay?"

I shake my head. "I think I'm in love with him but he likes someone else."

She yanks me into a hug and says, "It's going to be okay. Let's just cheer our asses off tonight. Go to a party. Find you someone to flirt with and have a good time. It'll help you forget about whoever is bumming you out."

"It's Tyler. I love Tyler. Oh, God, what is wrong with me?"

She leans back and smiles. "Well, what about mystery guy?"

"He won't talk to me. I told him who I was and he hasn't responded. See," I say as I dig out my phone and hand it over to her.

She lets me go and looks through the texts. "Oh, whoa. Maybe there is an explanation. His parents could have taken his phone away from him because he didn't do a chore or something."

I shrug as I take my cell back. "Maybe. But wouldn't a mom or a dad text back saying he lost his phone privileges or something?"

Rachel shakes her head. "Whenever I have to turn my phone over I punch in a new password and give it to them. My mom will see the messages, but she won't be able to respond. Send him this: *Sorry if you're grounded. Hope you can talk soon.* This way he won't think you are crazy for blowing up his phone with those messages," she says.

I chew on my lower lip. "Okay."

"If he ends up not being grounded then he's a total jerk and you deserve better."

The corners of my lips sink. As much as I want to let her words empower me, there is a deep pain in my chest at the thought that R wouldn't want me. It's just another kick to my damaged ego.

I voice text the message and push send.

Rachel and I head out into the parking lot. For the first time ever, I don't feel like cheering at a game. Especially not one where the one person I want is going to be looking for someone else on the sidelines.

I shouldn't be upset. I should be happy. How can I possibly be happy, though, knowing the person he wants is so wrong for him?

As I make my way to Rachel's car I hear my name. "Layla!"

I turn and spot Mark and my sister going toward her Jeep. They wave me over. I have no idea what those two want. From the way they're huddled next to each other, I don't think it would be wise to go near them. They look all delighted and in love, and I'm pretty sure my mood will bum them out.

Juliet locks stares with me. Reluctantly I approach.

"We were going to head to the Pizzeria. Wanna come?" Juliet asks as Mark pulls Jared over to us.

"Yeah. Come on. You're in, aren't you Jared?" Mark says.

I glance up at Jared and note his grim expression. A slight tug on my left arm pulls my attention and I notice Rachel standing beside me. "Someone say Pizzeria? I'm in. Lays you're in, aren't you? You love their pizza," Rachel chimes.

Of course, I love their pizza. It's the best in the town. Only an idiot with no taste buds whatsoever wouldn't like it. But then *he* joins the group with *her* clinging to him like post-it and my stomach sours. "I, uh … don't think so. Sorry."

I backpedal away right as Tyler says, "What's going on?"

"We were trying to get a group together to head to the Pizzeria. Everyone's in except Layla," Mark answers while he stops me from leaving.

Great. Now everyone is going to know something is wrong and ask me about it. Tyler looks at me with a raised brow. "Not feeling pizza or something?" he says. I swear it's like the whole swarm of people around us melt away and it's just us.

Why can't he see that thing suctioned to his side like an

octopus is the reason I don't want to go? Surely, he can see. I blink quickly as I feel a fresh bout of tears start to bubble up in my eyes.

Darting my gaze to the ground I stifle the urge to express what I'm really feeling and answer, "Not today. I've got to catch up on some homework." A sharp pain forms in my chest and I swear I'm about to fall over and die.

Rachel grabs my arm and pulls me away before I can embarrass myself any further. Clearly Selena won. I need to come to grips with that fact really quickly or this is going to be one of the crappiest days not only of the year but possibly my whole life.

We're about halfway to Rachel's car when a deep voice speaks from behind. "Hey, uh, Layla?"

I turn and swipe away a few tears. "What's up, Jared?" I try smiling but there is no point. I'm a mess and there is no sense in hiding it now. He can return to his friends and tell them some rumor, like maybe I'm missing Adam or something.

"Are you two going somewhere else to eat?"

I glance over at Rachel. She smiles like always whenever Jared is around. Big and flirty. Most of the time it makes me laugh, how bad she has it for him, but this time I can't even muster a smirk. "Yeah, well, I don't know about Rach, but I was going to grab a burger instead."

"Ugh! Burgers. Can't we get Chinese?" Rachel whines.

I shake my head. I need a burger and a shake but she is driving.

"I'm down for some Moe's if that's where you're going?" Jared says.

Rachel groans. "Fine. But only because it's two against one. Need a ride, stud?"

Her flirting knows no bounds. "If you don't mind."

"You can take the front," I say. I know Rachel wouldn't want him sitting anywhere else, even if he looks like he'd rather be. As I slip into the backseat I can't help but notice Jared staring off into the distance at something.

"Pick the tunes," Rachel says to him.

Jared looks half dazed. "What?"

"Music. You pick what you want to hear."

"Ah, that's cool. Listen to whatever you want." He shifts in his seat as Rachel pulls us out of the parking lot and onto the main drag. "It's Tyler bugging you, huh?" he asks me.

"What? Why would you think Tyler is bugging me?"

Rachel groans. "Seriously Lays, he pegged it. Don't sit there and deny why you turned down gooey, warm mozzarella for dead, sizzling cow served on a bun."

I thought she was on my side. Some friend she is. I roll my eyes. "Yes. Fine. I admit it. Your buddy basically told me off this morning, and then Selena was practically dry humping his leg most of the day. It's been so stellar all I want to do is drown my rejection in a huge shake and eat a bacon burger with a mountain of fries."

"You should talk to him," Jared suggests.

"I kind of tried that today but he blew me off. And again, I'd like to point out he's already taken by some sophomore skeeva."

Rachel giggles. Jared shakes his head. "He's probably just doing it to make you jealous."

"Did he tell you that?" I demand.

"Nope. I'm not allowed to speak for him. But I think he does like you too. Why else would he even care if you weren't going to the Pizzeria?"

"This way he can eat somewhere else? Maybe he wants alone time so he can take his new toy back to his palace. It doesn't matter." I know I'm turning into a silly sap. The words are already out there though, so judge away.

"Oh, for God's sake! You are sounding like a child. Knock it off. We're getting you a damn shake, a burger and some fries, and then we're going to cheer. After the game, we're going to a party and we're going to find you a man."

I inwardly wince and notice Jared cringe. Even he thinks it's a terrible idea. I'm not Rachel. I can't just hop from person to person with no feelings involved.

Before I can make an argument, she pulls into Moe's.

# Chapter Thirty-Eight

*Tyler*

I'm about two seconds away from losing my shit. How could he do this to me? There's a bro code. I know I said that pursuing her was no longer an option when she endlessly rejects me. Still it hasn't even been twenty-four hours. Jared was supposed to go with us to the damn Pizzeria, not hopping rides with the one girl I want and her best friend.

When I see him later today I'm going to put my fist through his face for lying to me. I thought he was into Juliet, but what if this entire time he's been secretly into Layla? I'm going to kill him. Friend or not, he's dead.

Selena's disgusting perfume is only making my mood worse and my head is pounding. I don't want to be a total dick right now, but God I want to shove her away from me. She's been clinging to my side ever since Third Period. Normally I'd take this all in and use it to my advantage, showing the girl who ticked me off that I've moved on just fine. I can't take it anymore. In fact, after I saw Layla hightailing it down the hallway after she spotted me and Selena, I wanted to ditch Selena. This girl doesn't seem to take the hint. I'm not into her at all; she just followed me around all damn day.

"So what kind of pizzas should we get?" Mark asks.

Juliet mumbles something but the music is loud and the place is packed and I couldn't hear a word she said. Mark, who's sitting next to her, bellows out her request. "You guys good with sausage and cheese?"

I nod. Selena makes a strangling noise beside me. "Meat? Ewwwww! No thanks! I just want a salad," she says. "Baby, will you order that for me? I have to use the ladies room. Oh, and get me a water. And make sure it's bottled, not tap."

First, I do not like being called Baby. Second, is she joking right now with the water? We're in a pizza joint, not a country club. And third, she wants salad only, like a damn rabbit. I can't. Nope. Sorry. Three strikes.

She scoots out of the booth, finally giving me a breath of fresh, nontoxic air. Austin rubs his temples and grumbles, "I think your girl bathed in that shit she's wearing."

"One, not my girl. Two, I know. Try being suffocated by it in your car."

"Bro, seriously how are you still alive?"

"Not sure but I so need pain relievers soon."

"I'm not going to be able to stomach anything. It's like walking into a department store and getting doused in the face with that shit," he complains.

I agree. Between her strong scent, worrying about what Jared and Layla are doing together, and wanting to kill Jared for it, I don't really think I'm up for pizza. I pull out my phone and stare at the screen.

Layla sent me over a dozen messages. None of them I responded to. I told myself I wouldn't but I can't help myself.

>  Me: Hey. Sry. I misplaced my phone but found it.
> Me: So Layla, how was ur day?
> Layla: Crappy. I missed u. Sorry if that's 2 much.
> Me: Nah it's cool. I missed u 2.
> Layla: Good. What r u up 2?
> Me: Getting pizza. How about u?
> Layla: Burgers and shakes. It's my go 2 when I'm having a bad day.
> Me: Y was ur day bad?
> Layla: It's not a big deal. So, what # r u?

Yeah, I'm not telling her this. I want to know why her day was bad. Did Jared do something? I'll kill him.

> Me: I'll tell u what position I play if u tell me y ur day was bad?
> Layla: Really? We're going 2 b like that r we? Fine. It was a lot of things.
> Me: Yes we r. Go on.
> Layla: LOL. I got a bad grade on my bio quiz. One of my friends is in luv with a girl who's completely wrong for him. I thought I could pretend & b happy about it but I can't. Now he won't talk 2 me.

```
Me: Who's the friend?
```

Please do not say Jared. I won't be able to sit in this booth a second longer if she types that.

My phone dings.

```
Layla: Tyler.
```

Wait. What? She's talking about me? Yeah, I gave her the brush off because she rejected me, but who the hell does she think I'm in love with? She's gotta be talking about someone else.

```
Me: Richardson?
Layla: Yeah. Don't say anything. I know u 2 r teammates.
Me: Lips r sealed.
```

What the hell? Selena slides back into the booth and I wish she hadn't tagged along with us. Mark the dumbass invited her. I really want to continue texting Layla and find out who she thinks I'm apparently in love with. I can't though. Not with Selena hooking her arm through mine and staring at me with doe eyes.

"What?" I ask.

"Nothing. You're just so perfect."

I have the urge to roll my eyes. She can't be serious right now. She doesn't even know anything about me. How can she sit there and say crap like that? Does she think this is something I want to hear? Do I really look like I need my ego stroked?

She walks her fingers up my arm. I wish she wouldn't do this. I swallow hard and glance over at Austin. He's looking at his phone. "Hey, did you watch the game yesterday?" he asks.

"Broncos and Chargers?" I ask.

"Yeah. I'm glad Denver picked up Caleb Morgan. He's a great QB."

"I still can't believe he went into the draft as a sophomore. Most people wait it out, you know?"

"Who's Caleb Morgan?" Selena asks.

I glance back at her. "New quarterback for the Broncos. He played for the Jets for a while."

"Oh."

Austin nudges me and pulls up a video on his phone.

We watch the replay of Caleb's eighty-yard pass to his receiver, winning the game with only seconds left on the clock. It really was the Hail Mary of all plays.

"Tyler? Have you thought about the dance any?" Selena asks.

"Uh ... nah." Because that's the truth. The things I have been thinking about are: how much Selena's perfume bothers me, Layla hanging out with Jared, and why Layla thinks I'm interested in someone other than her.

Selena frowns. "Well, are you?"

"Am I what?"

"Going to think about it?"

I want to tell her no, but that will make me sound like an asshole. "Yeah, I'm going to think about it. My mind needs to be focused on the game tonight though. Cool?"

She bounces in the seat with a smile and bobs her head.

Our waitress comes over to our table and takes our order,

saving me from conversing with Selena for at least a few minutes.

The waitress reads off what she wrote down. "I have uh o-one l-lar-rge p-p-pep-p-peroni. One l-lar-rge s-s-sausage. One s-salad w-with r-ra-n-nach. Is that it?"

Juliet suddenly smacks Mark in his arm and snaps, "That's not funny."

"Why isn't that funny? The waitress read it off like she couldn't read at all."

"Maybe she has a learning disorder. Does that mean it's okay to laugh at her?" Juliet looks livid and I missed most of what happened.

Mark smirks. "It's hard not to laugh at it. I thought it was funny. Why are you so upset?"

"Don't worry about it."

"All right." Mark looks over at the rest of us.

Selena pipes up, "I thought it was funny."

I glare at her. "Why would you think that's funny?"

"You didn't find it amusing that the girl was stumbling over our order?" she asks.

"No." I tell her, then look across the table at Juliet. She's still fuming.

She stands up. "You know what, I'm not hungry. Can someone give Mark a ride to the field? I feel ill."

I look over at Austin. "You take him." I toss my keys at him. "I'm going to make sure Juliet gets home okay."

Austin gives me a funny look. Selena pouts, "What about me?"

"Austin can take you to the field too."

She scoots out of the booth to let me out. Mark stops me

before I can make my exit though. "Hey, thanks for going. I think she needs some space from me right now, otherwise I'd go."

"Sure. Whatever." I don't want to tell him I'm doing this for him, because I'm not. I'm doing this for Layla, and because her sister's in tears and probably shouldn't be behind the wheel right now.

I hurry out of the Pizzeria and catch up to Juliet before she hops into her Jeep. "Hey. Let me drive."

She turns and swipes a few tears from her face. "How will you get to the game?"

"Well, I was thinking that maybe you wouldn't mind me driving us to Moe's."

"Oh, uh. Okay."

She hands over her keys and we get into her Jeep. I stare down at the shifter and laugh. "Holy shit. This is a stick."

"You don't know how to drive one, do you?"

"You're actually in luck. I was debating on getting a standard, but then my dad talked me into getting the automatic. Less things to worry about if I became distracted."

"Distracted? I'm not following."

"Girls trying to make out while I'm driving. Shit like that."

"Oh." She pauses for a moment then says, "Whoa. Your dad said that?"

I laugh. "Yeah. He's always full of genius advice when it comes to when-I-was-your-age stories. Sometimes I'm embarrassed for him." We pull out of the parking lot and I take us over to Moe's. I hope her sister is still there.

"Why did you really leave the Pizzeria?" she asks.

I shrug as I shift gears. "Pretty sure a few people would kill me if I let you drive off all upset and get hurt. Plus, Selena was giving me a headache."

"I thought you two were dating."

I swerve a bit and then shoot her an incredulous look. "Why would you think that?"

"She is always around you lately. You didn't seem to brush off her advances. Call me crazy, but those are signs of being an item."

"Shit!"

If Juliet thinks this then Layla probably thinks the same thing.

"You like my sister, don't you?" Juliet blurts out.

"Yeah. So?"

I catch her smirk. "No reason. I think you'd be good for her. A lot better than Adam. He was a dick."

"Why do you say that?"

"Well, you know how I got upset with Mark for making fun of the waitress?" She sighs. "Adam used to do that same crap all the time. Layla would always laugh it off and be a good sport about it but he was jerk."

He made fun of her? What a toolbag.

I pull into the diner. "Thanks for driving," Juliet says.

"Anytime. You coming in to get some food?"

"Sure."

We walk into the diner and I immediately spot Layla sitting in a booth. Jared is next to her and Rachel is sitting across from them. My blood is bubbling again. My fists tighten as I march over ready to beat the hell out of him.

He looks up at me right before I reach the table, stands,

and starts glowering at me. "Dude, what are you doing?" he asks as he steps out of the booth.

"I could ask you the same thing. Juliet and I weren't really feeling pizza so we bounced. Mind if we join?"

Rachel scoots over with a smile. "Sure, hop on in."

Juliet sits beside her sister and Jared slouches down beside her. I kick him under the table and nudge my head a smidge. He glares at me for a second then he says, "Not in the mood for pizza then?"

"It wasn't exactly the pizza. More like the company. Tyler needed to get away from a clinger," Juliet amends.

"She was upset and I didn't think it was safe for her to be driving. But yes, I was getting away from a suction cup," I admit.

Layla snorts. "Selena wouldn't happen to be the supposed—what did you call her? —suction cup, would she?"

Rachel giggles. "That will be her next cheer."

I shake my head. "You two are vicious."

Jared asks Juliet, "Why were you upset? Did Mark do something?" There is an edge to his tone. I catch it quickly but I'm pretty sure the girls haven't picked up on it at all.

"Kind of. He was acting like a jerk, that's all. I just needed some space. Can someone pass me a menu please?" Juliet responds.

Jared leans over Juliet and snatches up a menu for her and me. He slaps mine on the table but hands Juliet hers as if it was made of glass. "Here you go."

"Thanks."

I notice Layla glancing over at them and then back at me.

Then she pulls out her phone and starts texting.

Rachel growls, "Layla. You need to chill with the texting over there. He's going to start thinking you've got issues."

"He is not," she argues.

"Oh Layla, please tell me you aren't texting the mystery guy again. We've been over this. He could be a psycho trying to lure you into the woods and kill you," Juliet says.

I laugh and everyone stares at me except for Jared. Pretty sure it's because he knows they're talking about me. Being described as a creepy serial killer is kind of funny. My phone buzzes against my leg.

I pull out my cell and push the ringer completely off. I look over at Rachel and she arches a brow. "Is the clinger texting you?" she asks.

"Nope. I'm not an idiot."

Layla shoots me a scowl. "What's that supposed to mean?"

"I don't give out my number to everyone. So why do you call that person a mystery guy?" I ask.

"He's not a mystery per se. His name is R."

"What?" I ask, laughing. "What kind of a name is R?"

Layla's face scrunches up and her skin turns pink. "He's sweet, unlike someone I know. He doesn't sit there and be nice to me one day and blow me off the next without a reason."

"Oh, I'm sorry, are you referring to me? You're the one who told me to stop coming over and we should just pretend not to be friends. So, don't turn this around on me and call me an asshole!" I stand up. "You know what, screw this. I'm not going to sit here on trial for something I didn't do. I was just following a request."

There is only so much time left before we have to get the

fieldhouse. I'm carless, pissed off, and starving. Rachel and Layla seem to have a silent conversation going on between them. Juliet is chewing on her lower lip and Jared is staring at the table.

"Where are you going?" Layla finally asks.

"Who cares? We're not friends, remember?"

Layla gets out of the booth just as I'm turning to leave. She stomps over to me and smacks my arm. "You don't get to do this!"

"I don't get to do what, Layla? I don't get to walk away after being called an asshole for following your request?"

"You know why I did that!"

I take a step back. "No, I don't. I'm not a mind reader!"

"You were making out with Selena in the hallway. I saw you."

"Really? Were you really watching? Because if you'd seen the whole thing you would know Selena attacked me in the hall. I wasn't reciprocating."

She makes a face and laughs. "Right. Like I'm going to believe that you turned down making out with a pretty girl throwing herself at you."

"Believe whatever the hell you want to. You already made up your mind." I pull out my phone to request a cab and head for the door. She yanks on my arm and my phone falls to the ground.

"What?" I ask.

"Why are you acting so mean? I thought you'd want the distance. I saw you making out with her and I'm sorry if I was wrong. But if the tables were turned and you saw me making out with some guy what would you have done? Would you continue coming to my house?"

I shake my head. "I'm not going to tell you what I would have done. It doesn't matter." I bend down to pick up my phone at the same time she does and her phone drops to the ground too. It's hard to tell which is which because she doesn't have bedazzled shit all over the case like most girls. I need to get away from her before I say something I'll really regret. I quickly snatch up both phones and hand over the one that is closest to her. "I gotta go."

She doesn't argue anymore and lets me go.

# Chapter Thirty-Nine

*Layla*

I stare dumbfound at the door he exited. Maybe I was wrong. I couldn't have been though. I saw him kissing her. I saw their lips locked together.

Another thing bothering me is why he wouldn't answer my question about if the roles were reversed. Why couldn't he tell me what he would have done? Is it possible that he likes me too?

No. That can't be. He's with Selena. Isn't he?

I'm so confused.

I glare at the cell in my hand and realize quickly it's not my phone at all. I am about to run out and tell him he mixed up our phones but I stop myself. If he's not with Selena his cell will surely prove it.

I slide my finger across the screen and laugh. Who doesn't passcode their electronics anymore? Either he's too trusting or just doesn't give a crap.

I scan his messages. There are two unanswered ones

waiting in his message box. Bingo. I click on the icon and almost drop the phone right then and there. It's my message. MY MESSAGE. Oh, my God! R is Tyler!

My face instantly heats and I scream.

"Lays, you okay?" Rachel asks.

I whip around to the table and point at Jared. "Did you know?"

"Did I know what?" he asks.

I show him the phone. "Did you know that he was R? Huh?" I feel so stupid right now. The things I told him. Did Tyler know that I was me before I told him? Did he come here to make fun of me?

The humiliation is endless.

"I knew for a while," Jared admits.

My sister glances between Jared and me then says, "Hold on. So, mystery serial killer is Tyler?" She shrugs as if pondering this. "That makes a lot of sense now. He looked like he was about to murder someone at the Pizzeria before we left."

I glare at her. "You're not helping, Juliet! He made me feel like a fool and, oh God, I fell for him like an idiot. Twice. I can't go to the game."

Jared looks up at me. "I'm not supposed to say this but he likes you too, you know."

"No. He made fun of me. How long has he really known it was me? Be honest."

Jared sighs. "I don't know, a few weeks."

Weeks? Weeks!

I slump down in the booth next to Rachel. "I want to get out of here. I'm not in the mood for burgers and shakes."

Juliet frowns. "Why are you upset? You two like each other, just go talk to him."

I slam my hand on the table. "He made me think I was talking to a stranger. He knew it was me the whole time. He knew and didn't say shit! How long was he going to drag it out? Was he having a good laugh about it behind my back?"

Jared doesn't say anything. Juliet rolls her eyes at me. "You're being ridiculous. He obviously likes you back," she says.

"You don't know that." I get back out of the booth slap some money down on the table and say, "I'm out. Rach?"

"Yeah, let's go. Jared, you staying or going?" Rachel asks.

"Staying. Juliet, do you mind giving me a lift to the field?"

"Sure," she says.

He smiles and moves over to our now empty side of the table and sits down.

"Box up our things and bring it to the field, will you Jared?" Rachel asks.

"No problem," he answers without taking his eyes off my sister.

I storm out of the diner and get into Rachel's car. She looks over at me like she's scared to say something. I hope she doesn't say anything.

"Music? No music?" she asks.

I glower at her. "I don't care."

"Okay. Look, I hate to agree with Juliet about anything, but I think she's right. You two like each other. This shouldn't be a big deal."

"Does he really like me or has he been making fun of me this entire time? He asked me to a dance. Did he do it as a joke or was he being serious? How can I possibly know how he really feels if he's led me on this whole time?"

"This is exactly what I mean. Talk to him. You'll get answers."

"No! I'll get another Adam. I'm not doing it."

Rachel stops hard at a red light and looks over at me. "You can't be serious. You're comparing Tyler to that asshat? Tyler isn't Adam. He knows about your dyslexia; did he laugh in your face like Adam? Because I'll kick him in his package if he did."

"No." I sigh. "I know he didn't lose his phone. He was ignoring me this morning. He was probably weighing his options with Selena. Doesn't that make him the same as Adam?"

The light turns green. Rachel turns her attention back to the road and continues to drive us to the field in silence.

I glance out the passenger window. Maybe I'm being silly. I doubt it.

# Chapter Forty

*Tyler*

My cell buzzes as I stalk over to my Jeep ready to put it in the glove. I look down at it and curse. This isn't mine.

"Hey!" Layla yells.

I turn and face her. If looks could kill I'd be dead. She shoves my phone into my chest and then slaps me. My jawline stings from the contact and I growl. "What the hell was that for?"

"You lied to me! You pretended this whole time to be some guy named R and it was you."

"Whoa! I didn't lie! My last name is Richardson. People call me R or T, or sometimes they call me Ty or Richardson. Excuse me for not elaborating. Still doesn't make me a liar. And what about you?"

Tears spring from her eyes and she sticks out her hand. "Just give me my phone back. I wish I never accidentally texted you."

"You and me both, sweetheart." I drop her phone into her hand.

I don't watch her walk away. I can hear her sobs but refuse to go to her. I turn to my Jeep and slip my cell into the glove compartment. After I lock it up I make my way to the locker room.

As I approach the brick building Adam pushes himself from the wall and comes toward me. "Are you into her?"

"Am I into who?"

"Don't play games, man. How long have you been into Layla?"

I shove him away from me. "Get the hell out of my face Adam, before I knock you out. I'm not in the mood."

"Did she turn you down? I told you she's nothing but a tease."

I don't know why, but his words set me off. I lift him up and shove him against the wall. I press my forearm against his collarbone and snarl, "Shut the hell up. Don't talk about her like that. You hear me?"

"You think she's into you? She isn't. She hates you. Any time I said I was going to your house she would say what a jackass you are and she didn't know why I would hang out with you. Face facts: Layla can't stand you."

I loosen my grip and walk away. The dumbass is probably right. The sad part is, I feel like a moron thinking I had a chance with Layla. She probably concocted those tears because that's what girls like her do when they don't get their way. She's probably trying to bait me into that little game of hers.

I storm into the locker room and dress into my gear.

Jared opens his locker right as I'm about to close mine. He looks over at me. "You okay?"

"I just want to get this game over with so I can drink

myself stupid tonight."

"So, are you in game mode or not?"

I slam my hand against my locker and yell, "I'm ready!"

Jared nods and continues dressing in his gear. I notice a bag of food containers next to him. "What's that?"

He glances at the bag and then up at me. "Layla and Rachel's dinner. And before you even ask, you should know you and Layla somehow mixed up phones. So now she knows it was you that she's been texting. She started having a meltdown. Then she basically bit my head off, thinking I knew about this the whole time and you were making a big joke about it. I tried telling her you weren't but she didn't listen."

"I know."

"You do?"

"Yeah. She stomped her princess self-up to my Jeep, slapped my face, and yelled at me. I'm done. Screw her."

"So, she didn't talk to you?"

"No man, she yelled at me. Called me a liar. Basically, I'm a jerkface. Whatever. I didn't text her first. She texted me. Yet, I'm the dick in this situation."

He shakes his head. "Dude. You both are stubborn idiots. I told you from the beginning it was a terrible idea. The whole texting and not knowing each other thing was going to blow up in your face. I told her to talk to you. Neither of you listen."

"Thanks. Like I need a reminder."

He shuts his locker, helmet in hand, and says, "Whatever. Our focus is on the game not this crap. I gotta take this food to the girls."

I snatch up my helmet and walk out of the locker room and onto the field. The cheerleaders are already lined up in the end zone. Some are standing around, some are doing flips, others are practicing cheers. No matter how much I want to ignore her I can't. My eyes zero in on her perfect body, up her toned legs to her sexy ass.

I shake my head and focus on the field. Some of the guys on the receiving team are already out there running routes. I head over to them and go about the usual warm-up routine. Run straight down the field and dart left, catch a ball. We do this five times then change to slants, then run plays.

Blackhawk takes the field at the opposite end. The one guy I have a major beef with is Vince Fario. He seems to spot me, takes off his helmet, and gives me the universal sign for "You're dead." Yeah, right. I flip him off then turn my back on him. He's still ticked off I screwed his sister last year.

A hand slams down on my shoulder and I glance over at Jared. "Ready?"

"For?"

"The usual drills."

I nod. "Yep."

He calls us all into a huddle and says, "All right, right cross eight. Break," and slaps his hands together.

# Chapter Forty-One

*Layla*

I can't think. Our coach is spouting off cheers to perform and even though my body is going through the motions like a programmed robot, my mind is definitely elsewhere.

Rachel stares at me. "Hey, Jared brought our food. Want some?"

I shake my head. The only thing I want is a bed or a rock. Something to hide under for a few days, possibly forever.

"Okay, no food for you then." Rachel puts the box back by our bags. When she returns, she says, "We're going to a party tonight. No ifs, ands, or buts. You need it. Even if you don't hook up with someone, alcohol will help you forget. I'll keep an eye on you. In fact, I solemnly swear to watch you the entire time so no creeps will hang on you."

"I don't know, Rach. That sounds like a terrible idea."

"Well, it's not. You'll have hours of blissful unawareness. Sure, you'll wake up with a bitch of a hangover, but at least you won't think about him for a while."

When she puts it like that, I'll gladly take that headache in the morning. "I'm in."

"Awesome! I'll drive us there, and once you're good and liquored up I'll take us back to my house. This way you won't get grounded by your mom for drinking and stuff. Cool?"

I could do this. The more she talked about forgetting, the more I wanted it. Tyler who? Yes. I want to forget every damn thing about him. I want to erase every feeling and every word I wasted on him.

With a plan in hand, I was ready for the rest of this night.

♥

Okay, I lied. I'm not ready for this night. People will not be in the mood for partying or drinking if we lose to freaking Blackhawk tonight. This is our year to kick butt.

The girls and I go through all our cheers a few times as we watch our guys try to drive the ball down the field. Rachel squeals as Jared drops back into a shotgun formation and scans the field, but number fifty-six on Blackhawk breaks through the line.

Jared dodges the first attempt at a sack. He releases the ball just before another guy tackles him. The ball sails almost impossibly high, too high for any of the receivers to catch, but somehow Tyler leaps in the air and wraps his fingers around it. He catches the ball as if that pass were designed just for him and then he takes off.

He stiff-arms one guy attempting to tackle him. Tyler hops over another who dives for his legs. He pumps his arms and makes his way from the forty-yard line, to the thirty, he's almost at the twenty, there is one guy chasing him. My heart speeds up and suddenly I'm yelling, "Go Tyler! Go! Go! Go!"

Selena shouts, "That's it, baby! Go! Whooooa!"

I glare at her. "He's not her baby," I grumble to Rachel.

Rachel groans. "He's not yours either, so don't act like that."

She's right. I can't keep acting like this, otherwise I'm no better than Adam.

Tyler runs in for a touchdown and our fans go wild, our whole cheering squad goes nuts, except me. I just stare like an idiot at him as he high-fives his teammates and then looks back at the cheerleaders.

I feel like our eyes lock for a moment but it could be trickery of the lighting or something.

Chase kicks the field goal and then screaming fans storm the field. While the cheering crowd pushes towards the players, I snatch up my bag and make my way to the parking lot.

I'm halfway to Rachel's car when she finally catches up. "Wow, you really need a drink. We beat Blackhawk. That hasn't happened in five years. Surely that should bring you some kind of joy."

"Can we hit that party?" I ask, because the last thing I want to talk about is the game.

"Okay. Keep your pants on."

We whip out of the parking lot and I watch the scenery change from street lamps and city life to big houses, thick woods, and darkness punctuated by occasional lampposts.

"Where are we?" I ask as she pulls up to a mansion that is very familiar to me.

"Don't get pissed. It's the only party happening tonight."

I turn my full attention to Rachel and snap, "You've got to be kidding me! I'm trying to forget about the idiot, not party it up with him."

"It'll be cool. His house is so huge, we can grab you some bottles of whatever you want to get smashed on and we'll go hang out at the opposite end." She nudges me. "Come on. I'll be by your side the whole time."

This is a really bad idea. I'm already here, though, and cars are filling up the drive. It's too late to back out at this point. Rachel promises she'll have my back the whole night. Maybe it won't be so terrible after all.

♥

Whoever decided that getting drunk was a great way to get over people is flat-out the stupidest person ever. In fact, that person needs to be kicked in the face.

I'm trying to avoid Tyler at his own house party, that's problem number one. Problem number two is, he's literally everywhere. Baby Tyler, toddler Tyler, and Pop Warner football Tyler. I have to stop myself from melting. He's so freaking cute. Why didn't I realize how cute he was even as a kid?

I stumble along the hallway feeling queasy. Oh yeah, I'm going to puke. Where the hell is Rachel? She's supposed to make sure this doesn't happen. Lies. All lies. I knew better too. This was such a bad, very, very bad idea. I find the first open door and groan. It's a bedroom. Why for once couldn't I get lucky and find the bathroom on the first try?

The room is dark, but there is glimmer of light streaming the window that guides me to the light switch. Maybe there is a trashcan around here, because I'm not going to make it to the bathroom.

My fingers fumble along the wall and I press on a button. The room brightens, and I set the bottle of vodka in my hand on a desk then hurl. It's safe to say I didn't make it to a trashcan either. Nope. I puked all over Tyler's hardwood floor.

I know it's Tyler's room because his uniform is on top of the hamper. Crap! I can't even throw up without thinking of him. That right there is a sign I'm cursed.

Peering around the room, I notice there are way too many doors. I walk over to one and open it.

"HA HA HA HA, oh, of course, you would have your own bathroom." I pray there are cleaning supplies of some sort in here.

The only things I find are some sort of bleach spray and towels. Not paper towels, but nice, plushy, you-could-make-a-fluffy-bed-out-of-them towels. Well, that's just going to have to do. I snatch two white hand cloths and get to cleaning.

While I'm on my hands and knees, wiping up my mess, I hear a throat clear from behind me. "Layla?"

"Go away Tyler," I snap as I spray the area and rub the floor. "I'm cleaning it up."

"Cleaning what up? Why the hell are you in my room and using leather cleaner on my floor?"

"What?" I glare at the bottle in my hand and try to make out the words. Oh, being dyslexic and drunk is not a good combination at all.

"Right. Okay, I appreciate you cleaning ... Why are you cleaning?"

"I threw up on your floor," I admit, completely embarrassed.

He pulls me to a stand and looks me over. "Are you okay or do you feel dizzy?"

"I feel off my axis but that could be just from being around you."

He smiles. "Okay, let me get you over to the bed."

"That doesn't mean I'm going to screw you, you moron!" I shout.

He laughs. "Calm down, Princess! I'm not into screwing girls who don't want me sober." He guides me to the bed and commands, "Sit! Please."

I obey like a silly dog. He grabs a trashcan and places it in front of my feet. He walks over to the door and locks it. At least I think he locks it. I'm not sure at this point. My head is spinning.

Tyler walks into the bathroom and comes out a few seconds later with a bucket filled with soapy water. "I looked," I declare.

"I'm sure you did. It's okay. I really meant it when you said you were cleaning up your mess."

"Do people just leave messes for you?"

He shrugs. "More than I care to talk about. I'm going to get you a bottle of water. Do not let anyone in this room."

"How are you going to get in?" I ask annoyed.

He pulls out a key. "I usually lock my door."

"Right, 'cause you wouldn't want anyone walking in on you going at it with Selena." Then I bend over and projectile my insides in the trash can. Why do I have to be in a room with him while I'm sick? Stupid Rachel! This is all her doing.

I feel my hair being tugged back. His fingers draw circles on my back as I hang my head between my legs. My stomach churns, my heart speeds up, and my palms sweat. I pull back and Tyler leads me into the bathroom.

"You need to take a shower."

"I'm not getting naked in front of you."

He narrows his eyes. "As much as I want to see that, you have vomit all over your shirt. It's kind of a turnoff." He flips on the shower and I can see the steam billowing out.

"I'm going to be outside the door." Tyler leaves and I stand there staring at the shower.

I look down at my shirt and cringe. Yeah, there is a big streak of my current mess. That's so great. I peel out of my clothes and step into the hot spray. It beats my skin and a moan escapes my lips.

"Oh God, this feels so good," I say.

"Soap is on the back wall. I'm going to put your clothes in the wash," Tyler shouts from the other side of the curtain.

"Um ... okay." Wait what am I agreeing to? He can't have my clothes. What am I supposed to do, sit in this shower until they're clean? As lovely as this water is against my aching muscles there is no way in the world I'm going to stay in this bathroom that long.

"Uh, you know what? It's cool. I just want to go home anyway, so ... Tyler?"

There is no answer. Whatever. I glance at the back wall and try to figure out what bottles are what. It's easier in my own shower because everything is in its own place.

I pick up a peach-colored bottle and pop the lid. Taking a deep whiff, the scent of oranges hits me. I squirt a small amount into my hand. The gel is almost clear, with just a hint of color. I put the bottle down and rub the mystery orange along my wet palms. As it suds up I pick up the bottle again and put more in my hand.

I'm not sure if it's shampoo or body wash and at this point I don't really care. I use it all over, head to toe. Once I'm lathered up and rinsed off, I step out of the shower and find a fluffy stack of towels on the sink.

I use one to dry myself off then wrap my hair with it. The other I wrap tightly around my body then I ease my way out of the bathroom.

Tyler is sitting on his bed with his head dropped into his hands, like he's frustrated or something.

"I didn't know how to shut it off."

He looks up at me then his eyes drift down my body and back up.

"Are you okay?" I ask.

He clears his throat. "Fine. Are you feeling better?"

"Not exactly. I'm naked. Have no clothes to change into. And I threw up in front of you. A shower doesn't cure humiliation. And, oh my God. I said all of this aloud. I'm never drinking again."

He grins as he makes his way toward me. "I have some clothes for you. The sweatpants are my sister's and the shirt is mine." He hands me the stack of clothes sitting on his desk and says, "I'll be in the bathroom. Go ahead and change. My closet is a walk-in if you prefer more privacy. Oh, and there is a bottle of water on the desk. Please drink it."

"Thanks."

"You're welcome."

# Chapter Forty-Two

*Tyler*

While I'm in the bathroom all I can think about is she's naked under that towel. She's about to slip into my clothes. Well, the pants are my sister's but that doesn't matter. I need to get ahold of myself.

I don't know how the hell I've controlled myself this long, truth be told. Do I want to touch her? Hell yeah! Do I want to hold her and beg her forgiveness? Absolutely. Can I do any of this right now? Definitely not. Even though she seems lucid and slightly less drunk, she still got sick less than thirty minutes ago in my room. Plus, I meant what I said to her: I will not do anything with anyone who isn't sober.

When or if I ever am with her, I want her to remember every detail as clear as a bell. I'm not that big of a jackass.

I shut off the shower and pace my bathroom. The girl I want is one hundred percent naked in my room. I run my hands through my hair. She's going to be the death of me. Plain and simple.

*Keep it together. Watch over her. Do not be an asshole!*

I knock on the bathroom door and open it a slit, "Hey, are you dressed?"

"Yeah."

I open the door and am greeted with a quick flash of her bare back as my shirt drops down and covers it. I groan as my pants instantly become the most uncomfortable thing I've ever worn in my life.

"Um ... hold on a second." I enter the bathroom again and grab two ibuprofens from my cabinet then return to her. She looks down at the pills in my hands and grumbles. "I shouldn't say this, but I am not taking what's in your hand."

"Why not?"

"Because they could be something other than aspirin or whatever."

I laugh. She basically said to my face that she thinks I would drug her, and I find that hilarious. Complete freaking goner for this silly girl. "What's so funny?" she asks.

"You. Come on." I guide her to the bathroom and throw out the pills in my hand. She watches me grab a plastic cup, rinse it out twice before filling it up, and hand it to her. Then I reach in the cabinet and grab the bottle of ibuprofen.

"If you don't believe this is simple over-the-counter pain reliever, grab your phone and text a picture to someone you trust," I say.

"Okay." She takes her glass and leaves the bathroom. She returns with her phone and snaps a picture of the pill bottle. Then she sends off a text.

A few seconds later someone replies and she sticks out her hand. I place two pills in her palm. Once she takes the pills I take the cup from her. I fill it with mouthwash and watch her use it. I toss the cup and lead her back to my bed.

Layla takes a seat and I ask, "Who did you text?"

"Juliet. There are only a handful of people I'd trust my life with and she's one. She never drinks. She's the perfect poster child, you know? Smart, pretty, fun, doesn't care what anyone thinks about her. Sometimes I wish we were identical in more ways than just looks."

I take her hand in mine and squeeze it. "I'm glad you aren't."

"Why?"

"Because, Layla, I like you. Just the way you are. You're beautiful, smart, and outgoing. You have faults and they challenge you, but that's what makes you awesome. I'm sorry we never really talked before."

She blinks at me. "Why are you telling me this?"

"I don't know. Probably because you won't remember a lick of this conversation in the morning, so it's easier to get it all out there. I didn't tell you I was R because you didn't like me. You liked R but not all of him. Not all of me. I'm not sorry for that. I'm not sorry for letting you like all of me Layla."

She swipes her hand under her eyes. "I keep screwing up. This isn't normal for me."

"What isn't?"

"Us. Our whole relationship. Most people usually get a couple of dates in before all the massive bombshells drop. The deal breakers, if you will. Like, ew, does he actually clean out his ears with his fingers and wipes it on his pants?"

I scrunch up my nose. "Uh, no. Why, do you?"

"No. That's gross. But this is what I'm talking about. You know all these flaws about me and I barely know any about you. This is so messed up. Do you know when I told Adam I was dyslexic? I waited three months before I told him."

"So what? I don't exactly open up to people either. I told you I don't care that you're dyslexic, it's not a deal breaker for me. How people like Adam treat it is bullshit! For you to think it's a flaw or something completely wrong with you is messed up."

She lies down on my pillow and sighs. "You're not listening to me."

"I am listening. You're just not comprehending that I love you as you are." Shit! I said something I didn't want to tell her just yet. Now it's out there and she remains silent.

"Layla?"

She sits up. "I should probably call my sister."

"Yeah. Okay." Perfect. Real freaking great.

I get off the bed and go directly to my closet. I pull down a sweatshirt and toss it to her. "I don't know where your coat is but I assume it's in someone's car."

"Rachel has it."

"Rachel Little drove you here?"

"Yes."

I shake my head. "You know she left with Austin two hours ago?"

She frowns. "Figures."

"The party is dying down. I can take you home. I didn't drink."

"That's okay. I'll call Juliet. She's still up."

I take her phone from her. "It's one in the morning. Will

you please let me do this tiny thing? I won't say another word to you the rest of the night. Just please let me do this."

"Is that what you want?"

I nod. I want to be the one to take care of her and get her home. I have a feeling she means something else though.

"Okay. If that's what you want." She stands and walks over to my door.

I snatch up the sweatshirt and approach her. Layla looks at it and I pull it over her head. She tugs the bottom. She looks damn good in my shirts. Before my mind gets carried away, I give her phone back to her. "Come on," I say and grab her free hand. She doesn't try to break away from my grasp, but she's not holding onto very tight either. It shouldn't bother me but it does.

I guide us downstairs and into the kitchen. I drop her hand for a second. "Help me, please." I gather four almost empty liquor bottles in my arms and she does the same, and then follows me out into the den. There are a few couples in there, making out on the couches or talking. "Get out," I tell them.

One couple shrug and leave the room. The other, in a heavy make-out session, is apparently deaf. I set the bottles down and smack the back of some guy's head. He startles and glares at me. "What the hell, man?"

"Get the hell out of my house!"

"Psh. Yeah, whatever man."

He tries to go back to kissing the girl he's with but I snatch the back of his collar and yank it. "Get out before I really get pissed off."

"Such a buzz kill." He finally gets the hint and leaves with the girl.

I turn back to Layla and she's just staring at me with three bottles in her hands.

"Set those over there, please." I point to the mahogany chest behind her.

"You were really tense," she notes.

"I need people to leave so I can lock this all back up. The two quickest ways to shut down a party: get rid of the alcohol and shout that the cops are coming." I frown. "I don't want drunk people thinking they should get behind a wheel of a car so I never shout that the cops are coming. I get rid of the drinks, and then I call cabs for people or let them crash here, if I can stand them. That guy is definitely getting a freaking cab."

She doesn't say a word. She places the bottles where I ask. I do the same with the ones I carried in here. We proceed to do this a second time and I lock up everything.

We return to the kitchen right as Jared stumbles in and sways a bit toward the island. "Hey. Where did all the beer go?"

"Dude, how much have you had?"

He shrugs. "Don't remember. I started chugging as soon as she started kissing Mark. I can't stand it. I love you, damn it. How can you not see that?" He is glowering at Layla. Layla has the most confused expression on her face. "Say something. Please say something."

"Jare, that's not Juliet, man. Come on, let's go find you a room."

He squints and then growls, "Son of a bitch. Don't tell anyone I said that. I'm begging you."

I glance back at Layla and pat Jared's back. "Pretty sure

she'll forget this conversation in the morning. Let's go. Layla, I'll be back in a second. Don't leave. Okay?"

"Okay," she says. "And Jared, I won't say anything."

I take him to the spare room next to mine. As soon as he's settled I rush back down to Layla. She is still in the kitchen, cleaning. Throwing away empty cups and wiping up messes. I'm in awe of her. Why is she helping? No one else bothers to do that.

I'm grateful and annoyed. I'm trying not to fall for her any more than I have but then she does crap like this. She's making it impossible for me. "You don't have to do that."

She turns. "I know. You don't have to take me home either, but you are. So, I want to help clean up."

"I don't want you to help though." I practically growl at her.

She lowers the trash bag in her hand. "Why not?"

"Damn it Layla. Just stop."

"That's not a reason."

I walk over and try prying the bag from her. She's a strong little thing though, and she jerks it back every time I tug. Any more pulling from either us, and the bag is going to rip. I finally let go and snap, "You're really making it impossible for me. I want to hate you, damn it! I want to be pissed at you. I can't. Not when you're looking sexy as hell in my sweatshirt. Not when you're helping me clean up without being asked. I told you I love you and you haven't said a word about it. I shouldn't want to be anywhere near you after you put my feelings in a blender and ground them up."

"You think I don't have feelings? Sure, I have feelings. Tyler, I was trying to forget about you. I drank myself stupid.

I threw up on your floor. I'm wearing your shirts and they smell like you. And God help me, I just want to melt with every stupid sniff. But I saw you with Selena and I hate that she kissed you. Then R stopped texting me and I felt so confused. How could I possibly miss two different people so much that it hurts? But I find out it was you the whole time and I'm relieved, but I'm also so mad at you. I feel cheated. Which one of those guys is the real you? Was this all a joke?"

I step toward her and brush away the tears. "No. It was never a joke. You got all of me. Only very few people get this. You're one of them. I don't have a thing for Selena. Did I see the jealous flare in your eyes whenever she was around? Yeah, I noticed. And maybe I'm the world's biggest jerk because I wanted you to be jealous. I wanted you to pick me."

"I did pick you."

She tries to bring my lips to hers but I pull back. A frown appears and then she shoves me. "I thought you wanted me?"

"I do. Not like this."

"Like what? I practically threw myself at you." She shakes her head. "I'm such an idiot."

"It's not like that. Knock it off. I told you before, if you aren't sober, this isn't going to happen."

She flips me off. "There won't be a second chance. I'll find my own ride." She drops the trash bag and storms toward the living room.

There are people all around and the music is still going. No one seems to notice I'm pissed off or that Layla is angry. They don't even seem to notice when she whips around and smacks me in the face.

I rub my jaw and she snarls, "Stop following me!"

"No. If you don't want me driving you home, fine. I'm calling you a cab and I'll wait with you to make sure you get in the damn thing."

"Don't bother. You can quit pretending you care."

"It's not pretending. I do actually give a shit."

I follow her out the door, call her cab, and wait outside in the freezing cold with no coat on. I'd go in to fetch my jacket but I don't trust her to stay put.

"I'll call my sister," she suggests.

"I called you a cab it should be here in less than ten minutes. Stop being difficult."

"I am not being anything."

I am not going to argue with her anymore. She's not listening, and there is no point in explaining myself.

I don't know how the night went from winning a game to confessing my feelings to Layla, to watching her getting into a back of a cab and loathing me for probably all eternity. But it did. It downright sucks too.

# Chapter Forty-Three

*Layla*

At school Tyler doesn't acknowledge me. It's fine. I don't want to talk to him either.

I can't believe I made a fool of myself in front of him. Oh, and every time I see Jared he looks away. I haven't told Juliet what he told me. In fact, I haven't told anyone that I remembered anything from that party.

Playoffs are this week and then it's the winter formal. I still don't have a date and I don't care. My sister wants me to go dress shopping with her this weekend. Normally I would love nothing more, because Juliet really hates dressing up and it would be fun to watch. I told her I'd think about it but honestly, I'm not in the mood.

The last bell sounds and people rush out of the room like the building is on fire. I take my time. There is nothing to hurry off to anymore. The boy I want basically pushed me away because I wasn't sober. Okay. Why though, if he really likes me has he been ignoring me all day? There isn't a lick of alcohol running through my veins. Now what the heck is stopping him?

I pass by Selena and she giggles loudly to her group of silly sophomores. "Tyler and I are going to the winter formal together. Eeeeeeek!"

My heart drops into my stomach. He asked *her*? Her!

*I will not cry.*

I hurry to my locker, grab my things and then make my way to my car. Adam is leaning against the door. "What?" I snap.

"I just wanted to let you know I'm sorry. I messed up." He actually looks remorseful.

I shake my head. "Okay, fine. I have to get to practice."

"I know." He backs away from the door and smiles. "You won't ever take me back, will you?"

"No."

"I figured."

I open the door and slide in. As soon as the door closes I feel like a chapter of my life has finally ended. I just wish another chapter of my life didn't feel like it ended as well. I've got to let it go though, and accept that Tyler and I were not meant to be.

♥

It's been weeks and I'm miserable. There, I said it. I finally broke down and admitted it. I'm absolutely, one hundred percent miserable. It's been weeks and Tyler and I are still not speaking. I miss him. I miss his voice, his laugh, but most of all I just miss him.

I lie back on my bed and sigh.

My door springs open, and Juliet enters wearing a really pretty, long, flowing, blue gown. I smile at my sister.

"Can you help me with my hair?"

"Sure."

She takes a seat at my vanity and I roll off my bed. "Does my makeup look okay?" she asks.

"It's fine."

"Stop it Layla. Really look at me, please. I need my sister right now, not this weird zombie that's been pretending to be her for weeks."

I stare at her. "Fine. I'll fix that too."

"Why don't you talk to him?" she prods.

I roll my eyes and run the brush through her hair. If I start working on her hair maybe she'll forget I didn't answer her. She knows why I can't talk to him. I embarrassed myself in front of him at that party. There is no coming back from that. No chance at all.

She holds up a folded piece of paper. "If you don't answer me I'm not giving this note to you. I don't care if he told me it was a matter of life and death that you get it."

I go to grab it and she drops her hand and smiles. "Nope. Answer me. Why won't you talk to him?"

"I did talk to him. I told him I wanted him and he said he didn't want me when I was drunk."

Juliet sighs. "Why is that a bad thing?"

It's not. I just didn't want to be rejected then ignored. She hands me the note and I place it on my nightstand. "You're going to read it, aren't you?" she asks.

"No. Now shut up so I can fix your hair."

Juliet scowls at me. "Dang it. Layla, he wrote you a letter. Most boys don't do that. Not even through email, text, nothing. They barely tell you to your face. You need to read it."

"Did you read it already? How do you know what's in it, nosey pants?"

She shrugs. "That was the deal I struck with Tyler. I read the letter to decide if I should give it to you or not. He was all red in the face but he agreed. I needed to be sure whatever was in the letter wasn't going to upset you more. Sue me for caring."

"I think I might." I smirk. "What does it say exactly?"

Juliet starts to shake her head but I hold her down by her shoulders. "Don't, you'll get the brush stuck in your hair and you don't want to go to the dance looking like that. It's not exactly an in-style look."

"Fine. But I'm not telling you what's in the letter. You need to read it."

I groan. "That could take all night and you know it."

"Well, I can read it to you while you do my hair. Deal?"

Shady. Can't believe she's striking deals with me. "Ugh. Fine. You're impossible sometimes."

I drop the brush and reach for the note. She takes it from me and smiles wickedly. "I'll read this on two conditions."

"What?"

"One, you've got to talk to him after I read this. Two, you have to go to the dance with me."

"Have you lost your marbles? I don't have a dress, or a date."

She continues to smile. "There is a dress in my room that I was told to buy, with matching shoes. And if we stop wasting time you'll have enough of it to get everything done and still have a date and a ride to the dance. In or out?"

I scowl at her. "Fine. I'm in."

She opens the note and starts to read while I heat up the curling iron and pull out my big box of bobby pins. "'Layla, you drive me nuts. Your scent is embedded in my car. Your laugh is in my head. Your face invades my dreams. There are so many times I want to go up to you and apologize. At this point though, I'm not sure what I should apologize for.'"

"This letter sounds awful!" I glare at my sister.

"It's getting there. Hold on." She clears her throat and continues. "'Should I apologize for how I've acted recently? Should I apologize for the years I've spent misjudging you? Should I apologize for falling in love with you twice? Should I apologize for not having the balls to tell you to your face how I feel when you can actually remember the words I'm saying?'"

"Wait, what did he say?"

"You want me to read it again or do you just want me to repeat the last question?"

"The last question. Are you making that up?"

"Layla, he loves you."

I smile for the first time in weeks. "What's the rest of it say?"

"I'm getting to it." I continue working on her hair while she reads. "'You texted me out of the blue as a wrong number.

At first, I thought you were some drunk. After a few more texts I became hooked. I don't even like texting or talking on the phone. But there I was, drawn to you, Layla Faye. I needed to know more about you. When I figured out who you were I was already head over heels.'"

"He was?"

"Quit interrupting me," She snaps. "Where was I. Oh okay. 'I was already head over heels. Putting a face to the texts made it better. I thought if I could get you to feel the same way about me, either as R or myself, then at least I'd have a chance. But after you told me we should stop hanging out and then rejected my offer to take you to the dance I felt like maybe you didn't like me the way I liked you. So, I backed off. This didn't make how I felt any better. I don't like us not talking, Layla.'"

I start to sniffle.

"Please don't burn my hair," Juliet warns.

"I'm not going to mess up your hair," I say. "Is that the whole letter?"

"No. There is a little bit left." She smiles. "'I miss you and hope you miss me too.'"

I blink back a few unshed tears. "I do miss him."

"You need to call him."

But I heard Selena, isn't he taking her to the dance?

I finish curling and pinning my sister's hair and then start to fix her makeup. Juliet keeps shooting me looks every so often. "What?"

"You're going to call him, right?"

I chew on the inside of my cheek. "I thought he already had a date?"

Juliet arches a brow. "Um. No. He wouldn't have written this letter and paid for your dress and shoes if he had another date Layla. Call him."

"I heard her telling everyone that."

She scowls at me. "That thot? He didn't ask her out. She's been begging him to take her and he never gave her an answer. She spread that rumor, probably to force him to take her. He doesn't want her, though. He wants you. Remember the day I came to Moe's?"

I shrug. "Sure. What about it?"

"He left the Pizzeria not just because he was worried about me, but because he was upset that people were making fun of our waitress, who obviously had a learning disorder. He wasn't laughing, he was ticked off."

I drop the eyeshadow brush. "Layla!" Juliet swipes at her dress and I pick it swiftly.

"Sorry."

"Am I done?" she asks. I nod. "Good. Call him."

She stands and goes toward the door. "Then come get your dress, okay?"

I agree and she leaves.

# Chapter Forty-Four

*Tyler*

What the hell was I thinking, telling Juliet to buy Layla a dress and shoes? What if she decides not to come to the dance? I stare at myself dressed in my tux and shake my head. I should have never given Juliet that note. Make that the second stupidest thing I've ever done.

I leave my room and head downstairs in a very empty house. Taking a seat on the couch, I channel surf while I wait for her call like a loser on a Saturday night.

My phone rings and I glance over at the caller ID.

"What's up, man?" I ask Jared.

"Hey, what are you doing right now?"

"Trying to find something to watch on TV." I'm not about to tell him I'm waiting for Layla to call me.

He grumbles and says, "So you aren't going to the dance?"

"I'm heading over there in a bit. Why?"

He sighs. "Good. I can't believe I agreed to take Kelly. I'm not going to be able to sit there the whole night with her."

"Well, at least you have a date. I'm not sure mine's coming."

He laughs. "I wouldn't call her a 'date.' More like a platonic friend. Whatever. If you're there at least I will be able to keep myself in check and not take off Mark's head."

I flick through the cable guide and say, "Austin will be there too."

"He has an attention span of a small child."

I set the controller down and laugh. "Good thing I'm going. I'll meet you at the school. You gotta do me a solid, though."

"Name it."

"Keep Selena the hell away from me."

"Got it." He hangs up and I groan.

My phone rings again and I answer right away. "I said I'd be there. Geez."

"Um. Okay. Hi," Layla says.

"Layla? Shit. Uh. I didn't know it was you."

"Oh. Did I catch you at a bad time?"

"No." My palms are sweating. Why are my palms sweating? I rub them against my pants and make my way up to my room. "It's fine. What's up?"

"You're going somewhere. I caught you at a bad time. I can tell. I'm sorry."

"Layla, calm down. You didn't catch me at a bad time."

"Okay." I hear her sigh. "I got your letter. And the dress."

"Oh. Yeah. It's cool if you don't feel the same."

"No. I, um … I want to do this in person. Not over the phone. So, I assume you're my date for the dance?"

"Only if you want me to be. It's cool if you don't. I'm still going because Jared kind of needs my help with something."

"He likes my sister, doesn't he?"

283

"Shit, did he tell you?"

"No. But I could tell. The way his nostrils flare when Mark touches her. The way he looks at her when he thinks no one is paying attention. It's really obvious unless you are my sister, then you'd be completely blind to all the signs."

"Yeah, well, he's into her. He's just not making his move because he's friends with Mark and he wants to see your sister happy. Even if it's hard for him to watch."

"I get that. But yes, I want to be your date. Unless you were trying to tell me in a roundabout way that Jared's your date."

"Uh, no. We don't roll like that. He's going with Kelly, so I'm all yours if you want?"

"I wouldn't want to go with anyone else. It's getting late; I'll meet you there, is that okay?"

I smile at the image of her in a pretty dress. I didn't see what I bought her. Juliet refused to snap a picture of it. "Perfect. I'll meet you there."

"Okay. See you soon."

"Cool. I'll see you in a little bit." Before I end the call, I say, "Layla?"

"Yeah?"

"I'm glad you called. I really missed you."

"I missed you a lot too."

We hang up and I fist pump the air.

I'm jittery at the dance. Like a nervous, I'm-going-to-pee-my-pants-any-second wreck. Jared is just as bad. We don't say anything to one another, but I know we're both staring at the door waiting for the Valentine twins to arrive.

Austin takes a seat next to me. "What are you doing?"

"Looking for someone." I answer.

"Oh yeah, who? Pretty sure all the hot single ladies are already here."

"Um. No."

He glares at me. "Who's missing, then?" Then he looks past me at Jared. "Are you waiting for someone too? Cause I could have sworn I saw your date on the dance floor, bro."

"She probably is," Jared growls. "Just don't worry about what I'm doing. I didn't want to come here to begin with."

I shrug.

"Don't let Kelly hear that; she might cry."

"She looks like she'd be fine with it to me. She's grinding herself against Adam's junk," Jared says.

Austin follows his stare for a second and shakes his head. "Wow. Are you just going to let him take your date like that?"

"She's not really my date, just a friend dude." Jared doesn't look like he truly cares if Adam and Kelly end up together or not. In fact, the only thing he really cares about is Juliet, but I'm not telling Austin that.

"Where's your date?" I ask.

Austin smiles. "What date? I'm riding the single boat. All these fools are trying to get into relationships, I'm just happy to fly solo."

"Right," I say, and turn my attention back to the door.

Austin laughs. "I'll tell you one thing I won't be doing,

is turning into a whipped puppy like Mark. Don't get me wrong, Juliet is cool as hell. I never actually met a girl who can whoop me in Dungeon Wars before. But Mark acts like he's too good for us or something. Like all the sudden he wants to read books or whatever. Oh, and don't get me started on his ass trying to correct my grammar. Him of all people, trying to correct me. I'm about two seconds from losing it on him."

I finally stop looking at the door and stare at Austin for a second. "So, what you're saying is Mark is trying to be something he's not in order to keep Juliet?"

"That's exactly what I'm saying. He's so fake now I just want to punch him in the mouth."

I laugh and glance back at the door. Jared gasps next to me. I almost do the same. A few yards from us emerge Layla in a long red dress, her hair pulled to the side and draped in curls, and Juliet in a long blue dress with her hair pinned up. They both look great but my attention is all on Layla. Both girls head toward our table. I'm not sure where Mark is, but I'm pretty certain Jared doesn't give a damn.

He actually stands and pulls out a chair next to him and guides Juliet to sit. I'd do that too, but freaking Austin is next to me. Instead, I get up and take Layla's hand in mine. "Would you like to dance?"

"I'd love to."

I lead us out to the dance floor. I should probably warn her I can't dance worth a damn to anything that has a beat. I'm that guy who stands there bobbing his head to a song while the girl does all the work. I can waltz and slow dance, so hopefully the music flowing through the speakers of the gym switches to a softer tempo.

That doesn't happen. Layla sways her hips to the left and right and I keep my hands there as some sort of guide. She finally stops dancing and pulls back so I drop my hands from her waist. "You have no idea what to do, do you?"

"Not a clue."

She smiles. "Looks like I get to teach you something then. Ready?"

I swallow hard. "I guess."

She places my hands on her hips and says, "When I move, you move in the same direction."

"I can manage that."

As we start dancing I realize I need to say something to her right now. I pull her close to me and whisper, "Layla, I can't go another second without telling you something."

She blinks up at me. "What is it?" Worry lines ebb her beautiful face.

I dip my head and press my lips against hers. "I love you."

She smiles. "I love you too." Then her lips caress mine again.

And I'd like to say we danced all night but it's not ... in fact, that's another story. For now, this is our ending.

# Epilogue

*Juliet*

Everything is almost perfect. I say almost because Mark is swaying me left and right, but I have to pee. Really bad.

"I have to go to the ladies' room," I say.

"Okay," Mark replies.

He walks us back to our table and I immediately dash off to the restroom. After I finish my business, I make my way to the sink and wash my hands. The person in the mirror is a familiar reflection but not really my own. Honestly, it's more Layla than me because there is makeup on my face, something my sister never leaves the house without and I always do.

My stomach knots instantly. I have a sick sense something horrible is about to happen. I got it when our father died a few years ago. I got it when my sister started dating Adam. I ignored it those times but I won't ignore it now.

I quickly dry my hands and bolt from the bathroom. I stumble a bit because hello, I'm not my sister and I'm not used to walking, let alone running, in heels. In fact, I should probably stop so I don't fall and break my leg.

I slow from a run to a speed walk as I enter the gym. Going directly to the table where we were sitting, I notice it's basically empty. Only Jared is sitting there. "Hey, have you seen where Mark went?" He should know. They're best friends, plus Mark was just at the table with him two minutes ago. I know I didn't take longer than that to pee.

Jared's stare cuts me raw. "I'm not his babysitter, Juliet!"

What the heck? Jared's usually sweet and never takes a horrible tone with me. What did I do to tick him off? Whatever, that's his problem.

I break my attention from his stony expression and scan the rest of the gym. Couples are swaying left and right, and at the center of the room I spot Mark. Arms are locked around his neck. A couple obscures my view of Mark and whomever he's dancing with.

My feet carry me closer. A sharp pain stabs my stomach and works its way to my chest. "Oh God, no. Please, no," I whisper.

I watch the display unfold before me. Mark laughs, a girl with blond hair giggles, and then she pulls his head down to hers. His lips touch hers and a scream launches from my throat.

Time seems to stand still as my heart shatters. Can everyone in the room hear it? They all stop dancing and it feels like all eyes are on me. I feel something grip my left arm and tug me backwards. I look and it's Layla.

My arms launch around her and I burst into tears. "How could he? Why?"

"Shhhh. Don't. Okay. It hurts. I know it hurts. Just keep walking with me."

"I want an answer."

"Not here. Trust me. Juliet, you have to trust me on this."

I stiffly nod and let her lead me out of the gym. Before we reach the doors, I hear Tyler say, "Whoa, buddy. You can't. Not here, man."

"Let me go, Ty! I'm going to rip his face off," Jared growls.

I peek over at them. Tyler is holding Jared back and says something to him that I can't hear. Jared narrows his eyes at Tyler but his bunched shoulders sag. Layla is about to guide me through the threshold of the gym doors when I see Mark barreling his way toward me.

Tyler steps in front of Mark and Jared and I'm pulled away from the scene. "You don't need to see him or hear his bullshit right now."

"But what if … " I start.

"No! He's not sorry. He shouldn't have been out there in the first place."

She's right. I knew someone like him couldn't really fall for me. "I'm never dating a football player ever again."

# Acknowledgments

Each day I am grateful and blessed to have such support from all of you wonderful readers. Thank you for being a part of this amazing journey with me. Every one of you holds a special place in my heart for I know without any of you none of this would ever be possible. Thank you!

To my awesome family, and my two incredibly awesome children, you inspire me to be the very best version of myself I can be. You push me to do better, make me laugh, and are always there encouraging me each and every day. I love you so much.

To my kick-ass Agent Brittany Booker, you are fantastic! Your advice makes my writing better so thank you so much for your insight!

To my most awesome publisher, Georgia McBride, thank you so much for believing in my book! Without you this wouldn't be possible so thank you so much for all you do. I'm truly thankful to be here and a part of this wonderful imprint!

My friends, fellow writers, and CPs, without you I don't think I could have gotten through some days. You're always in my corner listening to my frustrations or helping me make my work shine even more. Thank you for being my eyes and ears you all are truly the best!

Of course, I can't forget my wonderful and super amazing staff at Swoon Romance. You all rock! Keep doing what you are doing. Total love for all of you!

Special thanks to: Jason, Ethan, and Leeah. Brittany Booker, Josie Glauser, Tracey Chapman, Tiffanie Marks, Ricky Allen, Clarissa Grimes, Angie Ball, Georgia McBride, Sheri Larsen, Kelly Mooney, and Michelle Aker.

## Natalie Decker

**Natalie Decker** is the author of the bestselling YA Rival Love Series, YA/NA Scandalous Boys Series and Offsides series. She loves oceans, sunsets, sand between her toes, and carefree days. Her imagination is always going, which some find odd. But she believes in seeing the world in a different light at all times. Avid reader of everything. She's a huge Denver Broncos fan, loves football, and fuzzy blankets. She's a mean cook in the kitchen, loves her family and friends and misses her awesome dog infinity times infinity. If she's not writing, reading, traveling, hanging out with her family and friends, then she's off having an adventure. Because Natalie believes in a saying: Your life is your own journey, so make it amazing!

# OTHER SWOON ROMANCE TITLES YOU MIGHT LIKE

RIVAL LOVE
RIVAL HEARTS
RIVAL DREAMS
FRENCH FRIES WITH A SIDE OF GUYS
THE D.B. LIST

Find more books like this at http://www.myswoonromance.com/

Connect with Swoon Romance online:
Facebook: www.Facebook.com/swoonromance
Twitter: https://twitter.com/SwoonRomance
Instagram: https://instagram.com/swoonromance/

NATALIE DECKER

# Rival Love

No Rules. Game On.

*Bestselling Teen Romance Author of Rival Love*

# NATALIE DECKER

# Rival Hearts

*New Rules. Game On.*

Bestselling Teen Romance Author of Rival Love and Rival Hearts
# NATALIE DECKER

# Rival Dreams

*Their Rules. Game On.*

# FRENCH FRIES WITH A SIDE OF GUYS

## REBEKAH L. PURDY

THE ONLY THING WORSE THAN ADDING TO IT IS BEING ON IT!

# The D.U.F.F. List

## REBEKAH L. PURDY